# THE AGING

## JACK HUNT

DIRECT RESPONSE PUBLISHING

*For my Family*

### A Powerless World series

Escape the Breakdown

Survive the Lawless

Defend the Homestead

Outlive the Darkness

### Outlaws of the Midwest series

Chaos Erupts

Panic Ensues

Havoc Endures

### The Cyber Apocalypse series

As Our World Ends

As Our World Falls

As Our World Burns

### The Agora Virus series

Phobia

Anxiety

Strain

**The War Buds series**

War Buds 1

War Buds 2

War Buds 3

**Camp Zero series**

State of Panic

State of Shock

State of Decay

**Renegades series**

The Renegades

The Renegades Book 2: Aftermath

The Renegades Book 3: Fortress

The Renegades Book 4: Colony

The Renegades Book 5: United

**The Wild Ones Duology**

The Wild Ones Book 1

The Wild Ones Book 2

**The EMP Survival series**

Days of Panic

Days of Chaos

Days of Danger

Days of Terror

**Against All Odds Duology**

The Last Magician

The Lookout

Class of 1989

Out of the Wild

As We Fall

As We Break

**The Amygdala Syndrome Duology**

Unstable

Unhinged

**Survival Rules series**

Rules of Survival

Rules of Conflict

Rules of Darkness

Rules of Engagement

**Lone Survivor series**

All That Remains

All That Survives

All That Escapes

All That Rises

**Mavericks series**

Mavericks: Hunters Moon

**Time Agents series**

Killing Time

**Single Novels**

Blackout

Defiant

Darkest Hour

Final Impact

The Year Without Summer

The Last Storm

It went against the natural order of life.

He walked out of the room, down a dimly lit hallway. The walls were adorned with family photos. In the kitchen, the sink had piles of dirty dishes. Trash overflowed from the garbage can. The air smelled musty from not opening the windows in days. He turned on the faucet and splashed a few handfuls of water over his face and dark hair. It was humid. July. The height of summer in Texas. Even with the air conditioning on, it was sweltering. In the middle of the room on a round table was an army green molle backpack full of essentials for the journey. The destination wasn't far.

He stared at it for longer than he should.

In his minds eye, he heard laughter. An uncommon sound. The smell of a home-cooked meal. Big colorful balloons celebrating Lily's tenth birthday. A cake. It wasn't always bad. He wasn't always a problem. It had once been a home full of love. A typical life for an ordinary family making their way in the world. Now it was just an empty shell, four walls, and a murky reminder of the past, the pain, and division.

"Please."

He clenched his hand. "Okay. Just give me a minute."

Josh checked the items in the pack against a list on his phone, the list she'd sent. Medication, Lily's inhaler, blankets, matches, and food were among the items including a state map just in case the power grid shut down. All he could think about was the worst, only what could go wrong. That had been his existence for the last three years.

He considered reasoning with her again. They could

wait a few more days and see if the situation improved. These kinds of matters took time, didn't they? Besides, it was safer here. He could continue to go into town and bring back supplies. They could hold out here until it was over.

*Over? What a joke. It would never be over.*

Even as he thought this, he heard her reasons again.

*You're too young, you need to take care of her, they will eventually come here, it's safer at this new location.* He looked at the message she'd texted him. He knew the area but didn't recognize the address. Why wouldn't she tell him who was there? Why not give him a phone number to talk to the person? Why was it safe there? And what if they arrived and no one was there?

Even worse, what if the wrong person was there?

No, it was safer here, he told himself.

Josh's eyes welled up again. He was making excuses, putting off the inevitable. A tear streaked his cheek. He wanted to smash the house to pieces. Unleash his anger. He wanted to lash out at the world. He wanted answers, a solution. This was too much for him to carry. No one his age should have to deal with this.

He looked back down the hallway to the bedroom, trying to summon the courage to go through with it. How could he explain it to her? As much as he had tried to talk his way out of it, he knew the alternative. Josh knew he'd only be doing it for him. A wave of regret hit him. All the times he'd been problematic — acted out. It weighed heavy. What he would give for another chance, more time. More time with her. He needed her. He couldn't make this trip without her.

Ah, who was he fooling? He couldn't stop it.

Josh set the gun down on the table and fought back more tears.

Anger rose.

His father should have been the one dealing with this. Not him. Not her.

"Please, Josh." Her voice persisted.

"There has to be another way."

"There isn't."

He sniffed hard and smeared tears against his cheek.

"I can't. I can't go through with it."

Silence.

More silence.

Josh knew he couldn't change her mind. No amount of pleading or denying would change the outcome. It was a matter of what was right, she'd say. Right for who? None of this was right. Less than thirty days, he thought. That's all he got. That's all she had.

How could they be sure? The news always got things wrong. They didn't know how this worked anymore than they did the common flu. Every person was different.

He wanted to see her but she wouldn't let him.

Stuck inside that room. Day after day.

Even if he went through with it, what life would he or Lily have?

Josh thought about the future and the responsibility. Could he keep her safe? What if it happened to Lily? To him? Who would take care of her? He looked at the address again.

"Why won't you tell me?" he asked from the kitchen.

"It's best this way."

"We deserve to know."

"Do you trust me?"

He closed his eyes and gripped the table tight. Frustration rising. A myriad of arguments from the past flooded back in. Yelling, slamming doors, unable to express what he wanted to say. Trust was a contentious word. It was loaded. A point of multiple disputes and now she was asking him to trust her?

How could she ask that?

"If not for me, do it for her."

Twisting the knife with her words. She knew how to push his buttons.

Josh wiped his eyes and pulled away, leaving the kitchen. He quickly made his way down the hall to the bedroom before he changed his mind. He tightened his grip on the gun. Entering the room again, he strode up to the bed and shook the mound.

"Lily," he said. "Wake up."

He went over to the window and tugged the board away to let warm sunlight bathe her face. She groaned and lifted an arm to block the glare.

"I'm tired."

"Get up and get dressed," he said.

Josh collected his MP3 player and large headphones from the living room and returned a moment later as Lily slid her arms into a red top. He helped her when she got stuck as one of the arms was turned inside out. Once she was dressed, he led her over to the closet and opened it, then had her sit down below a rack full of clothes. The closet also held football gear, an old school bag, and old video games that he'd been meaning to give away. "Listen to me carefully. Put these on, and don't take them off. Don't come out of this closet until I return. Do you understand?"

"But Josh."

"Do you understand?"

She nodded.

"Repeat it back," he said.

"I..." she muttered.

"Lily!" he barked.

"I'm not to take these off and not to come out."

"Good. Until when?"

"Until you get back," she said.

"Okay." He set the headphones over her small head. They were too big. They pressed down her blonde bob cut. He adjusted them and then turned on the music, making sure to increase the volume so that it was loud enough that she wouldn't hear but low enough that it wouldn't hurt her ears. Josh mouthed the words, "Is that okay?"

Lily gave a nod. He kissed her forehead and stepped back. Josh closed the closet doors.

Reaching around into the back of his jeans, he pulled the Glock and walked out of the room before he fell back into hesitation. He hurried down the hallway, took a left turn, and approached the door. He set it down and knocked. "It's outside."

As he walked away, she said, "Josh."

He stopped but never looked back. He knew the door was still locked.

"I love you," she said. "Always remember that."

His body trembled as he muttered an inaudible reply before running into the kitchen, away from the room, away from her, away from what he'd done. Did she hear his reply? What if she never heard? The anguish was already setting in, eating away at the back of his mind. *This is for her. This is not for you.* He slumped down into a chair, staring at the backpack.

Seconds passed.

More time, maybe a minute.

Only the sound of a ticking clock.

Then a sudden noise. Unmistakable.

*Crack.*

It echoed so loud. His body shuddered, his muscles froze then his shoulders went limp.

It was a sound he wouldn't ever forget.

Josh lifted his eyes to the window, to the perilous world beyond, through a curtain of tears. Wiping his face, he sat there for a moment longer, reining in his emotions before collecting the bag from the table, shrugging it over his left shoulder, and returning for Lily, hoping she didn't hear, hoping she wouldn't see he'd been crying.

He had to be strong for her.

For the two of them.

In the bedroom, Josh opened the closet door to find her still there, head bobbing to the music, blissfully unaware. A strained smile tugged at the corner of his lip then vanished fast. Had she heard it? Did she know? He extended a hand and she took it, following him out of the room toward the back of the house.

"Put this on," he said, taking her small denim jacket off the rack and handing it to her.

"What about mom?"

"I told you."

He'd gone over it multiple times.

"I'm not leaving without mom."

"We have to go."

"But I…"

Lily tried to pull away but he held her tight.

She was forcing him to tell her. He didn't want to tell her but he did. It came out.

"Stop it. Stop it. She's gone, Lily! She's gone. She's never coming back. You hear me?" He paused. "It's just you and me now."

Somewhere behind those teary eyes, she understood, at least he hoped so.

"We're taking the motorcycle, you'll need to hold on tight. Can you do that? If you don't, you will fall off and hurt yourself. Do you understand?"

She nodded, taking a hit of her inhaler, trying to calm her nerves. "Okay," she said, her tone full of false confidence.

"Let's go then." He kissed her on the forehead and led her to the front of the house. A warm breeze brushed up against his skin as they exited. He looked around nervously, knowing that at any moment health officials could show up and take them away. They wouldn't believe them, his mother had said.

They would have taken the two of them.

Fifty feet away was the carport. A rusty shack that covered the SUV. A black tarp was draped over his white Suzuki DR-Z400. It had been a gift from his uncle Harley, a man who shared his love of bikes. Weeks of no use had left a thin layer of dust on top of the SUV. He led her over there and removed the tarp and pushed the bike out. He leaned it up against a shed before telling Lily to wait there while he removed a ten-gallon canister of gasoline.

"Don't move."

He trudged back to the house and entered, shaking out the contents, a steady trickle unfurling over the floor and furniture. He went into every room except hers. She was adamant that he wasn't to go in there. She didn't want him to see her that way. Not like that. The smell of gasoline made him cough as he retraced his steps. Outside he took out a Zippo lighter.

Josh looked over his shoulder at Lily who was watching, mesmerized and confused.

With a clack of metal, a flame burst to life. He tossed it into the house, then hurried away. At the bike, he took a smaller helmet and pushed it over Lily's head, and then put his own on. He mounted the bike first. Josh kick-started it to life. It rumbled loudly. All the while behind them, flames chewed through the house, sending thick black smoke out. He flipped up the visor and helped Lily onto the back of the bike. "Hold on to me tight," he said, his voice muffled behind the helmet. Lily wrapped her arms around his waist. Flipping down his visor, Josh looked back at the house one more time. The weight of the moment felt heavy on his shoulders. There was no going back now.

Suddenly, an explosion rocked the house, shattering windows and sending shards of glass out like jagged knives. Josh felt Lily grip hard. She pressed against his back. He gave her hand a reassuring squeeze before the bike lurched forward.

The engine rattled between his legs. Josh squeezed the clutch, shifting into second, leaving behind the home. Clutch, throttle, and a good amount of gas, and they surged up the driveway. Josh glanced in his mirror at the flames.

The world they knew was now gone in the blink of an eye.

# CHAPTER TWO

21 days earlier
June 14

*M*innie Rogers Juvenile Justice Center was sandwiched between the cities of Beaumont and Port Arthur. The drab government institution was set back from U.S. 69.

Out of sight, out of mind.

It was, however, within spitting distance of the Jefferson County Correctional Facility to the north. Elizabeth wondered if it was purposely placed there to make the youth mindful of what the outcome would be if they continued down the path of crime.

She veered into the parking lot in front of the one-story building and noticed tall fencing that encircled the rear yard. It contained delinquents. The ages varied from ten to seventeen. For many, the institution was a chance at rehabilitation, a place of education, and care. For her son, it was misery, a place he'd been warned about only two years earlier.

Elizabeth felt a heavy weight on her chest at the thought of collecting him after the 90 days inside for property damage. Like most juvenile courts, the local ones would often bend over backward to avoid sending kids here. Time in custody was seen as the first step toward institutionalization and unless the offense was violent, residential placement was preferred. The juvenile court had shown a great deal of leniency toward Josh, far more than she'd expected under the circumstances.

Especially since this wasn't his first offense.

He'd already been through a diversion program and done a stint in a residential treatment facility for petty theft back when he was fourteen. Two years later, and he was arrested for property damage.

Contrary to what some might have said, he wasn't a bad kid. Many of the youth who found their way into the juvenile justice system were products of their environment. Elizabeth would have been lying to think that her separation from his father ten years earlier hadn't been a factor, that and the long hours she was putting in at the hospital. As a single mom without support from her parents who were in Florida, the struggle to raise him and Lily only made life more challenging. It also didn't help that he'd fallen in with the wrong crowd.

Elizabeth parked her silver SUV in the lot. She turned to Lily in the back. Lily was ten now, blonde, with short straight hair tucked behind her ears. She was listening to music and swiping at a tablet screen. "Hey," Elizabeth said, clicking her fingers to get her attention. Lily removed her headphones.

"Yeah?"

"Remember what I said."

"Be nice. Don't ask how it was. I got it, Mom."

She smiled. Like many kids of divorce, she'd had to grow up fast. "All right. Good. I just don't want to make him feel any worse. He probably won't be in the best mood." As she was saying that, her phone rang. The caller ID displayed a friend of hers from the hospital. She tapped accept while flipping down the visor to adjust one of her contact lenses. Elizabeth had green eyes, pale skin from spending the majority of the time working inside, and an oval face with shoulder-length dark hair much like her own mother. Now she was closing in on forty-one, a few gray strands were peeking through. "Jenna. Everything okay?"

"You home already?" Jenna asked.

"No, I'm picking up Josh."

"Oh, right, I forgot. How's that going?"

"I'll let you know. He hasn't come out yet." She sighed and looked out the window toward the main doors, feeling a twinge of anxiety. "He blames me."

"Isn't that always the case with teens?"

"Yeah, but..."

"It wasn't you who destroyed the property."

"No, but maybe I should have listened more. You know, been there..."

"Hey, you've done the best you could. Don't beat yourself up. Look, I don't mean to change the subject but can you come in tonight?"

"I've already worked a shift."

"I know but Carol just called in sick."

"Another one?" There had been an increase in staff taking sick leave. "Must be one hell of a bug going around."

"It's more than a bug, it's all they're talking about right now."

"Who is?"

"Turn on your radio. It's on multiple stations. Something big is happening."

"And by big you mean?"

Over the phone, she heard someone call Jenna. "Look, I got to dash. Can you fill the shift?"

"Jenna, you know I would help in a heartbeat but it's Josh's first night out. Can't you find someone else?"

Jenna released a tired sigh. In their profession, it was rare to feel anything but tired.

"All right. I'll see what I can do. If you change your mind, call me."

She hung up abruptly. Elizabeth was about to turn on the radio to hear what all the drama was about when Josh came out of the main doors. "Okay, he's here. Remember what I said."

Lily told her to relax as she got out. Elizabeth crossed the lot, a smile forming as Josh and a detention center officer approached. With each year he was beginning to look more like his father when she first met him. Loose dark hair, five foot ten, a smile that when he let it show could put anyone at ease, and a swagger that exuded confidence. He was wearing a black V-neck T-shirt, blue jeans, and military ankle boots.

"Ms. Davenport."

She gave a nod.

"You good from here?" He asked.

Elizabeth waved him off. "Sure. Thank you."

"Let's hope we don't see you again, Josh."

Josh grunted.

"Hey, darlin'."

She placed a hand on his shoulder and he shrugged it off. There was no malice in his stare, more a need for space, to be alone.

As the officer walked back to the building, they made their way to the vehicle. "So. How was it?" The words flew out without even thinking. It was instinct. A normal question any parent would ask, yet the very thing she'd told Lily not to say.

"Peachy. You know, like summer camp without the fun," he said, walking on.

She sidled up beside him as they got closer to the SUV. "I figured we could order in pizza this evening. Your favorite."

"I'm going out tonight."

Her eyes widened. "But you just got back."

"Uh-huh," he said, without a smile, as he made his way around the vehicle.

Elizabeth had told herself before going to collect him that she wouldn't lose her cool. She'd expected resentment or at least for him to be distant. Most days he was difficult to gauge. His mood changed like the weather. The once bubbly kid had become withdrawn over the past few years. It had worried her, especially with so many teen suicides. If she pressed too hard he might think she was smothering him, if she gave him too much space, she'd regret it if something bad happened. "Lily's in the back so jump in the front."

"Yes, ma'am."

The ma'am bit at the end caught her off guard. She wasn't sure if he was being sarcastic or if his time inside had helped. She figured it would have added some structure to his life, respect even. God knows, he needed some guidance without his father in the mix. Inside the car, Lily was her usual happy-go-lucky self. She looked up to her big brother. Idolized him. The thought of him dragging her into trouble was another thing that worried Elizabeth.

"Josh, look at the tablet mom got me."

She leaned forward, jabbing it out so he could see as Elizabeth started the engine. "That's cool, Bean," he said, buckling into his seat and taking out his phone, eager to get back to texting his friends. Bean was a nickname he'd given Lily. He used it from time to time. When he was six, he'd gone with Elizabeth to an ultrasound and had said she looked like a bean. He'd wanted her to be called that but they'd named her Lily instead. Still, it didn't stop him from calling her that. The nickname stuck.

Josh was quick to pull out his phone and power it up.

"Do you think that can wait until later?" Elizabeth said.

"Why?"

She shifted the gear into reverse and backed out of the space. "Uh, because, I want us to talk. We haven't chatted in a while."

"About what?"

She smirked. "Anything."

He kept navel-gazing as he tapped out a message to a friend.

"Josh."

"Yeah, one minute."

She reached over and took the phone out of his hand and tossed it into the back seat. He lifted his hands with an expression of utter disbelief. "What the...?"

"Listen, I don't want to go back to how things were before you went in. There's a reason why you went there. So there are going to be some changes made around here. That starts with when I want to talk to you, you listen, okay?"

He exhaled hard, making it clear he was annoyed. "I might as well be back inside."

Elizabeth wanted to slam the brakes on and get into it with him but instead, she held her tongue and continued. "All right. If you don't want to talk. Fine." Conversations only led to disagreements and the first day out, that was the last thing she wanted. For the past three months, the house had been peaceful. No outbursts. No arguments. No trying to track him down or deal with unruly behavior. As much as she wanted to shake some sense into him, she knew it wouldn't do any good. She could only hope he'd learned from his time in the facility.

Elizabeth switched on the radio, and within a few presses of the scan button, she heard the reports Jenna was talking about. She caught the tail end of one. "Homeland Security and the Centers for Disease Control are still unsure of what they are dealing with, while some are calling it some kind of terrorist attack. As the death toll rises and cases surge in hospitals, it has led to speculation that eastern U.S. cities may have been the target of a biological attack. We will continue to update you as we learn more."

Elizabeth flipped through a few more stations, hoping to catch some more, anything that might offer clarity, but it was just the same, vague, general details, still early. Either that or they were being tight-lipped about what was happening in the hopes of reeling it in before the situation got out of hand.

"Glad to see the world is still as messed up as ever," Josh muttered.

"Mom!" Lily bellowed. She glanced in her rearview mirror to see Lily looking over her shoulder. "You just went by it," Lily said. She'd promised to get her ice cream from Baskin-Robbins on the way back.

"All right, hold on," she said, pulling over and making a quick U-turn.

Home was Vidor, Texas, a small town east of Beaumont with a population of just over ten thousand. She'd been there for the past twenty years, commuting to Beaumont to work at the hospital as an RN. She could have raised them in the larger city as it would have made her commute a lot shorter, but it was only fifteen minutes away, and she preferred small towns.

Lily was out the door before she could even put the SUV in park.

"Lily!"

Josh remained in the vehicle.

"You coming?" Elizabeth asked.

He shook his head.

"Can I get you anything then?"

"Nah, I'm good."

She could feel the familiar weight of having him home. Lily was already standing by the store door as she made it across the lot. Elizabeth looked back and saw Josh on his phone again.

After getting ice cream, Elizabeth and Lily were making their way back to the vehicle when she noticed an elderly woman at the edge of the road, just staring absently as the traffic rolled by. It might not have caught her attention if it wasn't for the youthful attire. It was the kind of clothing a teenager might have worn.

At that moment it felt like the world slowed as she saw her take two steps into the traffic at the exact moment a delivery van was approaching.

It happened so fast.

One second she was on grass, the next soaring through the air. Her body slammed into the road hard, with a sickening thud. Brakes screeched, vehicles swerved, as one after the other they collided.

Elizabeth dropped the ice cream in her hand and yelled for Lily to get into the SUV as she dashed to the trunk of her vehicle where she kept additional medical supplies.

She scooped up the bag and hurried over to the chaotic scene.

Now, the van driver was out and staring at the woman, shock set in. "I didn't see her. I didn't..." Elizabeth dropped down beside the woman. There was blood coming from the back of her head and her entire body was rigid.

"Call an ambulance," she yelled, taking charge of the situation.

Other pedestrians and drivers gathered.

"Lady, do you know what you're doing?" someone behind her asked.

"I'm a nurse," she replied.

Elizabeth checked vitals. She was still alive but if they didn't get her to a hospital fast, she wouldn't make it. There was a chance she wouldn't survive anyway. The damage was severe. While the van driver had managed to swerve and only clipped her, it still could have been enough to cause major internal damage.

As she began performing CPR and someone called 911, Josh jogged over.

She immediately raised a hand at him.

"Josh, I need you to stay in the vehicle with Lily."

He stared at the woman as if he recognized her, his head tilting to the side.

"Hey! Do you hear me?" She clicked her fingers. She didn't want this image in his head. He turned, glancing back as he returned to the vehicle where Lily was out, watching.

The woman began coughing.

"Stay with me." She wasn't even close to being out of the woods. "You got a name, honey?" Elizabeth asked.

There was no reply.

It didn't take long for police and EMTs to arrive. Within minutes there was a flurry of activity on the street as officers took control. One erected cones while another got the traffic flowing. Two more cruisers arrived and officers kept back curious onlookers to allow the medics to do their job.

"She just stepped out in front of my vehicle," the van

driver said. "There was nothing I could do. You saw it. Isn't that right?"

A cop turned to Elizabeth. "Did you see it?"

She nodded, still looking at the woman.

Crouched beside the medics as they worked, she listened as they went through their usual routine, trying to communicate while applying the necessary life-saving equipment.

"Hey hon, can you hear me?" a medic asked, shining a light in her eyes while peppering her with questions. "Are you on any medication? Do you have a name?"

A cop strolled across to a leather handbag nearby. Its contents were strewn all over the asphalt. He collected some and then rifled through to find an ID. Elizabeth rose to her feet and looked at him as he gave this confused expression. His gaze darted to the woman and then back to the ID.

The medic asked, "Officer, you got a name?"

"Yeah, it's…uh…" He paused. "This bag can't be hers." He shook his head as he made his way over and flashed the driver's license. The photo didn't match the woman. "This is for a Carla Harris."

The name rang a bell. The daughter of a local restaurant owner.

"You saw the accident, ma'am?" the cop asked.

"Yeah."

"Do you remember her carrying this bag?"

Elizabeth looked at it again. "I think so."

"Maybe she stole it," the medic said.

"Did you say the name is Carla Harris?" Elizabeth asked.

"Yeah, you know her?"

Elizabeth nodded and looked at the ID again and then gazed down at the elderly woman with an incredulous look. She squinted, tilted her head, and then looked at the ID one more time. She was older, but the resemblance was uncanny. It couldn't be. It was impossible. Carla was twenty-four, but this woman had to be in her eighties.

# CHAPTER THREE

July 5

The black Suzuki DR-Z400 crapped out roughly ten miles from their destination of Jasper, Texas. It had only managed to get around fifty miles on the tank of gas. They'd been coasting on fumes for the last mile.

Josh veered off the highway onto a country road somewhere past Kirbyville. They were in the middle of nowhere. No gas station, no small town to speak of, just a rural area of farmhouses spread apart over the landscape.

"Why are we stopping?" Lily asked.

"Out of gas. Hop off," he said before rolling the bike into the tree line of a nearby forest. Besides the chirping of birds, it was quiet. The journey north had been harder than he'd expected. Twenty-one days inside his home, he'd only seen the world through video footage across online media outlets. The reality was far worse. Several times, he'd had to adjust the course when he found a road blocked, or when vehicles had been purposely lit on fire to create a wall of smoke in an attempt to get drivers to slow down so they could be ambushed.

The attacks on people were brutal.

Had it not been for a couple in a car ahead of him gesturing out their window to turn off, he might have driven right into a trap.

"I miss mom," Lily said as she walked beside him.

"Me too. But it's just you and me now, okay?" he said. He took some loose foliage, branches, and undergrowth and covered the bike up. After that, he crouched down beside Lily and held her gently with both hands. He surveyed the area. There were few options. Take her with him or leave her here — both were equally terrifying. "Listen, Bean, I need to go over to that farmhouse and find some gas. I want you to stay here with the bike. You are not to move."

"Can I come with you?"

"No."

"Why?"

"Because you'll slow me down."

"I can run fast."

"I know you can but it's not fast enough."

Lily looked around her, disconcerted. "I don't want to stay here."

"I won't be long. Look, I'll be right over there," he said, pointing across the road to an old, white clapboard farmhouse with a large barn. "Now I'll cover you up with some branches. No one will see you. I'll be back before you know it."

"How long?"

"I don't know. Five, maybe ten minutes."

"Ten minutes?"

It might as well have been an hour to her.

Tears welled in her big brown eyes. Her breathing sped up to the point that it was bringing on an asthma attack. Josh rooted through her pocket and gave her the inhaler. She took a few hard hits on it.

"Lily. Hey. Hey, look at me." Her lips quivered. "It'll be okay. I promise."

"You won't leave me, will you?"

"Of course not."

"That's what mom said."

His stomach sank and he sighed as he looked off toward the house. They were burning daylight. If they were to make it to Jasper before nightfall, they needed to get moving. "What are the rules?"

"If I see anyone, hide. Unless it's you, I say nothing. Trust no one."

"Good. Okay, now get beside the bike under the tree." She crouched, wrapping her small arms around her legs, pulling her knees to her chest. Josh collected some heavy branches with lots of leaves and started covering her up.

As he was about to lay the last one, Lily raised a hand. "Josh."

"Yeah?"

She looked as if she wanted to say something but then changed her mind. "Nothing."

He covered her up and stepped back and walked around the bushes and tree to make sure that both Lily and the bike couldn't be seen from any angle. It wasn't perfect but it would do for the moment.

Shrugging off his backpack, he took out the second Glock his mother owned. He made sure a magazine was loaded and then took off, hurrying across the road and climbing over a small wooden fence that wrapped the property. There were multiple structures. A two-story home, another one farther back, a weathered red barn off to the right, along with a two-car garage, and an old rusted 18-wheel unhitched trailer, and a metal shed nearby. Parked out front was a couple of old trucks and a beat-up Honda Accord. Josh scanned the windows and zigzagged across the yard. He couldn't be too careful. Even when things were good, Texas was known as a shoot first and ask questions later kind of state. The homeowner wouldn't take too kindly to a stranger trespassing, especially now.

There was no movement.

He headed straight for the garage, figuring there might be a fuel canister he could use. He'd siphon out whatever he could from the vehicles and then be on his way. He didn't need much. The dirt bike only needed 2.6 gallons. That would be more than enough to get them the rest of the way.

The side door on the garage was unlocked.

Carefully, Josh slipped inside and gazed around. He took one more glance behind him before exploring. Inside there was a classic Ford car covered by a cream-colored tarp. The whole place smelled of oil and grease except it wasn't dirty, there was order to it. Every tool had a place. All of them hanging from a rack. It didn't take long to find an empty red gasoline container beside a lawn mower. Josh snatched it up and figured he'd try to siphon gas from the Ford. All the while he kept looking nervously at the side door while he opened the gas cap and took some old tubing from underneath a wooden bench and sliced it to the right size.

He stuck it in the car and began to suck on the other end. Almost immediately liquid came up and his mouth was full. He spat it out and gagged. It tasted foul. He took the end and stuck it into the canister.

*Okay. Good.* A sense of relief washed over him.

It didn't last.

As it was filling, he heard someone approach.

Fear spiked. A shot of panic went through him and he pulled the tubing out of the canister and closed the gas cap on the car. Josh shuffled to the rear of the Ford where he took cover behind a collection of Rubbermaid boxes.

The door opened and he heard someone step inside.

There was a moment of silence, then a gruff voice said, "Come on out. I know you're in here."

Josh remained still.

"I'm not going to harm you."

Other than the main garage door, that side entrance was the only way in and out. There was a chance the stranger would eventually make his way to the back and find him. Keeping a firm grip on the pistol, he peered out to get a look at who it was. The guy was in his late fifties wearing a white, dirty T-shirt beneath blue dungarees. Gray hair shot out the sides of his green John Deere baseball cap.

He was wielding a shotgun.

Josh weighed the odds. There was a fifty-fifty chance he

was trigger happy and would shoot, but right now he had the car between him and the threat.

Josh slowly rose.

"Ah, there you are."

"Sorry. I just needed some gas."

"And you figured you could take what we have without asking?"

"Looked as if no one was home."

"Still don't make it right. Come on out from there. Let me get a good look at you."

Hesitantly, Josh shuffled a little but remained at the back of the car. He kept his finger hovering over the trigger of the Glock. If the guy lifted that shotgun, Josh wouldn't think twice. He didn't want to kill, let alone shoot anyone, but Lily was depending on him returning. "Where you from?"

"Vidor," Josh replied.

"Huh." The man squinted. "How is it down there?"

"Bad."

Nervously he swallowed.

"Where are you heading?"

"North."

"Anyone else with you?"

He didn't hesitate for a second. "No. Just me. Look, mister, I don't want any trouble. I'll be going now." He moved around the side of the car to make his way to the main garage door, hoping he would open it.

The old guy looked out again then closed the side door behind him and locked it.

The clunk sounded final.

The man took the key and placed it in his upper pocket.

"No. No, you won't. I'm sorry, kid, but I've got a boy inside who is sick. So if you want that gas, it's going to cost you." Josh knew what he meant. It wasn't money he wanted.

The reports on the news had to be true.

Josh shifted ever so slightly. The old-timer hadn't seen the Glock he was holding beside his leg. In an instant, Josh lifted his arm and pointed it at him before he had a chance to aim the shotgun. Hand trembling, he gestured to his right. "Mister, open the garage door. Now!"

"Can't do that."

"Look, I don't want any trouble."

"You already said that. But waltzing in here tells me different."

He had to have a death wish.

Josh shuffled forward. "Listen, this can go one of two ways. Open the garage door and I go on my way and you live to see your son again, or... Don't make me do it. Please." Josh pleaded with him but whether he thought Josh was bluffing or he was desperate to change his son's grim situation, he made the wrong choice.

In a sudden move of stupidity, the man raised the shotgun. Before he managed to get it above his waist, Josh squeezed the trigger. The Glock let out a crack and the old-timer hit the ground, disappearing behind the car. Josh skirted around the Ford and found the guy holding his shoulder, the shotgun nearby. Not wasting a second, he dashed past him, kicked the shotgun out of the way, bounded up three small wooden steps, and stabbed the button to open the garage door.

It groaned as it rose.

Josh looked down at the man.

He'd live.

"I'm sorry. I never wanted this to happen," he said as he darted out, taking the gas with him. His heart pounded in his chest as he made it back to the tree line. Even before he uncovered her, he was yelling. "Lily, let's go," he said looking over his shoulder, expecting any minute to see other members of the man's family following.

Josh tore away the foliage covering the bike only to find her gone.

"No. No, no."

A lump caught in his throat. He turned 360 degrees. "Lily!"

No response.

"Lily!"

He called out to her multiple times before she appeared. "I'm here."

He turned toward her, angry as hell. "I told you not to move."

"I saw a rabbit. I just wanted to…"

He grabbed hold of her, frustration boiling over, the impact of what had just happened getting the better of him. "If you don't do what I say, you will die like mom. Do you understand?" The words rushed out before he could remember that he hadn't told her the truth of what had happened to their mother.

Tears welled in Lily's eyes.

She pulled away and took a few steps back.

"Lily. I… I meant to…"

"You lied to me."

"No. I just…"

Before he could find the words, Lily turned tail and ran

into the forest, crying. Josh took off after her, weaving in and out of the trees, calling her name until he was able to tackle her to the ground. Both of them hit the forest floor hard. She writhed in his arms like a wildcat. "Get off me. You lied. YOU LIED!"

Josh held her tight. "I'm sorry, Lily, I'm sorry. Please."

"You lied to me."

"I..." he sighed. "I was going to tell you. Just not this way. Not now."

"Then when?"

"At the right time."

"You still lied to me."

Slowly but surely she stopped fighting and sat up. "You're right. From here on out I promise I will always tell you the truth."

"Promise?"

"I swear."

He gripped her tightly, feeling the weight of their changing world.

~

*Why here?*

Josh looked down at the address on his phone again and then back at the rundown shack on the outskirts of Jasper, Texas. Had she given him the wrong location? He'd seen better doghouses than this. The home had fallen into disrepair or had taken one hell of a beating from the weather. White paint was peeling, the brown shingles were almost nonexistent and one side of the one-story abode looked as if someone had begun renovations but had abandoned the work mid-project.

Surely his mother couldn't expect them to stay here.

The yard, if it could even be called that, was overgrown with weeds and covered with rotting apples. The dirt path shrouded by cedar, elm, and live oak had huge ruts in the mud where a truck had worn it down. It all snaked up to a warped wooden porch.

Josh looked again at the metal box.

The name on the dented mailbox with an American flag sticker matched the initials RW. This was it. It had to be. After a few setbacks in the last leg of their journey, they had arrived by early evening.

The dirt bike rattled between his legs.

"Is this it?" Lily asked.

"I hope not," he muttered before squeezing the clutch, shifting gear, and giving the bike some gas to get up the short driveway.

There was no vehicle out front or a garage to speak of other than a cheap carport that had a tear in the side and a heavy amount of leaves and rainwater on top. There were oil stains on the driveway and a few broken bricks that were stacked as if they'd been used to support a vehicle for repair.

Josh killed the engine and Lily climbed off, removing her helmet.

He removed his and set it on the handlebars. They made their way over to the porch steps and both looked down at one of the planks which had a hole in it.

"Hello?" Josh asked.

There was no answer.

"Stay here," he said.

He went up the stairs and knocked on the storm door. No response. He made his way over to one of the two front windows and cupped his hand to see inside. When he turned, Lily was looking through the other one. "What did I tell you?"

"You're not the boss, Josh."

He shook his head.

"Looks like no one is home," she added.

"Well, then let's go." As he made his way down the steps he heard the storm door open and the handle on the door turn. Josh glanced over his shoulder to see Lily peering in.

"It's open," Lily said.

"Lily."

"What? You had no problems entering at the last place and this is the address mom gave."

He looked around for a second.

"We came all this way," she said. "Can't we stick around?"

"It's not safe."

"And going out there is?"

He groaned. "All right, just for a while, but we should just wait on the porch." He beckoned her away from the door and they took a seat on a porch rocker. They gazed out across the yard. The owner didn't give two hoots about gardening. There was a vinyl shed nearby that had collapsed, and a well without a bucket.

Lily picked at the porch rocker. "What happened back at the house?"

"What?" Josh replied his thoughts elsewhere.

"At the property. I heard a gunshot."

"Oh. That. It's nothing."

"Didn't sound like nothing."

She wasn't going to let it go so he said, "Look, let's go inside."

"But I thought you…"

"Lily."

She huffed as they entered.

Although the outside of the home had taken a beating, the interior was surprisingly clean. It wasn't modern by any means. The décor was dated, a decade or two old. The appliances looked vintage. Thick pine cabinets framed the kitchen.

Nearby was a glass table with three cushioned chairs tucked beneath. On top of that were a dirty bowl, a newspaper, and a coffee-stained cup. Josh glanced at the white fridge covered in magnets. He stepped inside and noticed the dark hardwood flooring was scuffed and buckled.

The small living room had a brown sofa, and a creme recliner positioned in front of a boxy TV. There was a single dinner tray with a few leftovers. Lasagna by the looks of it. Perched on the edge of the sofa was an empty ashtray with several brown apple cores and chewing gum in it. "Nasty," he muttered.

Josh turned. Lily wasn't there.

"Lily?"

He found her around the corner, peering into a bedroom. "Take a look at this," she said, holding up a kid's toy. "Maybe they have a kid."

"What makes you think it's a couple?"

"Well, mom wouldn't send us to live with someone who wasn't good with kids."

They poked around in the bedroom for a minute or two, picking up décor items off a dresser drawer that had a fine layer of dust on it. Josh ran his fingers through it and showed Lily. "I wouldn't get your hopes up. Doesn't look like anyone's been here in a while." They made their way out and glanced in the main bedroom. There were no photos on the walls. Nothing to indicate who the home-owner was, let alone if they had children. The bed was made. The curtains open. As much as Josh was intrigued by why their mother had sent them there, he was a little disturbed.

In the kitchen, Lily opened the fridge while he looked at a corkboard of notes, postcards, and mail.

"It's full," she said, sounding surprised.

He took a look. There were cans of soda pop, eggs, milk, ham, other food, pretty much all the essentials. "It looks fresh."

"You think they'd mind if I had some water?"

"Help yourself, Bean."

While she took out a glass from the cupboard and filled it, he looked again at the corkboard and pulled off several envelopes. Bills. They had a big red stamp on the outside with the word OVERDUE. He took one out because the address wasn't on the outside. As soon as he opened the letter, he noticed it was from years earlier.

That's when Josh saw a name at the top.

A different name to the one on the mailbox.

A familiar name.

His jaw dropped.

"Lily, let's go."

"What?" she asked, smacking her lips together.

He tossed the envelopes down and grabbed her by the wrist and led her out.

"Josh. Hold on. I wasn't finished."

"I'll get you a drink elsewhere."

"But…"

He pushed wide the storm door and was arguing with her as they stepped outside.

"Josh?" He glanced off toward his bike to see a middle-aged, bearded man, roughly six-foot, wearing a blue jean jacket, a checked shirt, and cream-colored khakis with boots. He was broad-shouldered and had a full head of short hair.

He was carrying a duffel bag. Behind him was an old black pickup truck parked a little farther down by the entrance. That's why he hadn't heard him.

Josh froze.

"Do you know him?" Lily asked.

The man must have heard. His eyes darted to Lily. "And who might you be?"

Lily looked up at Josh as if waiting for direction but neither of them answered.

Instead, he said, "Get on the bike, Lily."

Josh ushered her down the steps and across to the bike. The man watched quietly as Josh made his way over and climbed on, put his helmet on, and attempted to start the engine. It spluttered a few times but wouldn't catch. "Come on."

He looked at the man.

Again he tried.

Nothing. He slapped the handlebars.

"Start, you sonofabitch!"

All the while the man observed with curiosity. When the bike wouldn't start, the two of them climbed off with Josh intending to roll it out. He didn't get far.

"So that's it? You're just going to come all this way, break in, and leave?" the man said.

"I didn't break-in. The door was open," Josh said over his shoulder.

"But you entered. Are you in the habit of doing that?"

"No."

"Yeah, he is, he broke into a house earlier to get gas."

"Lily."

"Well, it's true."

That got a smile out of the man.

"So you're out of gas?"

"No, there's gas. But Josh says sometimes the figmajig gets clogged."

"Figmajig?"

"She means the fuel injector," Josh added, scowling.

"I can take a look at it."

"So can I," Josh said, continuing to push the bike forward.

"Listen, I was about to cook up some chicken and rice for supper." That got their attention. "Are you hungry?"

"Nope."

"I am," Lily said.

"It would be a shame to eat alone."

"Thanks but we're leaving."

"That's too bad," he replied.

Josh told Lily to hurry up. She sidled up beside him as he rolled the bike up to the gate. "I'm hungry. Can't we just stay for something to eat?"

Without looking at her he replied, "No."

"Why not?"

"Because…"

"Because what?"

"Because…" He stopped rolling the bike and looked at her then at the man who still hadn't moved and was watching them. Josh looked out toward the road.

"It'll be dark soon. You don't want to be out there after dark. It's not safe," the man said.

"We'll be fine," Josh replied.

He rolled the bike on but Lily had stopped walking. "Bean, let's go!"

"I want to stay."

"We can't."

"But mom sent us here."

"Your mom sent you here?" the man asked, taking a step forward. Josh squeezed his eyes tight. Oh no, that's all he needed. Now he'd want an explanation. The man looked back at the house then at them. "Look, why don't you stay for supper? If you want to leave after, you can. How's that sound?"

Lily's eyes widened. "Josh? Please."

He exhaled hard. Josh grit his teeth. He nodded and Lily let out a squeal. "But only until after supper."

Lily hurried back over to the man without any thought of whether he was dangerous or not.

"LILY!" Josh bellowed.

"It's okay," the man said, raising a hand. "I'm clean."

She looked back at her brother then at the man.

"I'm Lily by the way."

"That's a pretty name. Lily, I'm Ryan. Would you mind

taking this inside?" he asked, handing her a small bag of vegetables. She took them in while the man waited for Josh as he veered the dirt bike back around and rolled it in.

Josh scoffed. "Now it all makes sense. RW. So, should I call you Ryan or Andy?"

He'd changed his name.

"How about dad?"

Josh shook his head. "Yeah, right."

"How's your mom?"

Josh glanced at him, stopped the bike, put the kickstand down, and walked on into the shack without giving him an answer.

CHAPTER FOUR

17 days earlier
June 18

*J*osh carried a disposable plate of food and set it down outside her door.

He walked away and lingered at the corner of the hallway, waiting for the door to open. It didn't. She didn't want him to see her.

Four days. Four days had passed since the strange incident in the town and that's when things got really weird. His mother hadn't returned home with them on the evening of his release. Instead, she'd gone with the victim to the hospital and called a friend to pick them up outside the ice cream store. They were dropped home and given instructions not to leave the house until she returned.

A request he'd ignored after being locked up for the past 90 days.

"But mom told us not to leave," Lily said as he prepared to head out for the evening and go to an open-air party. There was to be a huge bonfire. Everyone he knew would be there. Alcohol. Weed. Good company. Time to catch up. It was just what he needed after what he'd been through.

"That was for you. Not me."

"Josh, you can't go out."

"Lily, you're always talking about not wanting to be treated like a little kid, here's your chance. You get full run of the house. Eat ice cream, watch whatever shows you like, blare the music loud. Keep the doors locked. I'll be home by midnight."

"But I'm ten."

"And in a year you'll be eleven. That's how getting old works."

Standing in front of the bathroom mirror, he dabbed cologne on. "Besides, I'm meant to see someone tonight."

"Callie Wright?" She asked, a grin forming.

He shot her a surprised look. "How do you know her name?"

Lily leaned against the doorway all proud of herself. "She came by while you were inside."

His brow furrowed. "What did you tell her?"

"Oh, nothing."

His eyebrows shot up. "Lily."

"Only that you kiss her photo every night and…"

She burst out laughing as he dug his hands into her sides and tickled her. "All right, all right, I'm lying."

He grinned as he returned to checking his jean shirt.

"So is it her?"

"Yeah," Josh replied.

"I could go with you."

"Oh no," he said, brushing past her and ruffling her blonde hair. "You're staying here."

"I'll stay out of the way."

He turned and crouched down in front of her. "I can't be taking you to a party. I'd never live that down. Babysitting my kid sister? C'mon, Bean, do you know how that would look? It would be social suicide. I know you don't understand but when you are old enough, you will."

"I'm already old enough. I'll be eleven soon. You said it yourself."

He laughed, slipping his feet into boots.

She refused to give up. "I'll tell mom."

"You wouldn't dare."

"Try me."

He narrowed his eyes, growled, and relented. He stabbed a finger at her. "You're too smart for your own good. All right. But you stay nearby. I don't want you drinking, smoking, or saying anything that would…"

"Embarrass you?" She gave a wry smile.

"Yes. Not that. And… you don't say anything to mom."

She ran two fingers across her lips and mimicked throwing away a key.

Lily held to that word. Strangely, everyone at the party was too preoccupied or intoxicated to care. And it turned out fine in the end. Callie actually thought it was kind of endearing that he brought her.

Right then, little did he know that would be the last night of normality he would experience.

~

In the early hours of the morning after the incident, Josh had awoken to a ding on his phone. The screen lit up, illuminating his dark room. He reached over and glanced at several text messages from his mother.

*I'm home.*

*Josh, I'm not feeling well.*

*Please don't enter my bedroom.*

*Leave food and liquids outside and I'll get it.*

*Tell Lily not to worry. I'll speak to you later. I need to sleep. Love you.*

It was vague and unlike her, especially since she'd been adamant about spending time together after his release from the facility. After her second day of not coming out, he thought it was some kind of protest, an odd way of getting back at him for the hell he'd put her through over the past year.

It wasn't. Not even close.

Over the next few days, his mother forwarded him articles and multiple videos about some aging syndrome that had gripped the USA. He flipped through news channels and listened to a few segments mentioning some mysterious illness that was rapidly spreading.

Someone else might have laughed, thinking his mother was exaggerating because of her profession, but that wasn't her, she was quite the opposite and he knew that. She was the firm anchor. Not swayed by public opinion or fake news. His mother's background in the medical field had made her the first person to dismiss conspiracy theories or fear-mongering. She questioned any news reports of small outbreaks, especially ones that listed unusual medical symptoms.

However, this was different.

It was serious enough that borders were immediately closed, airlines were grounded, and train and bus stations in all major cities were shut down. All of which had led to widespread speculating by conspiracy theorists, outrage by others, and panic purchasing. It didn't take too long to realize the government was trying to contain something that they'd never come across before.

Something was spreading faster than they could contain.

Pinpointing when it started was challenging with so many online media outlets picking up stories and running with them. But if reports online or the news on the radio were to be believed, the first details came in weeks before he got out.

Sitting in front of his phone and reading online reports was like going down a rabbit hole that seemed to have no end. The internet was full of conspiracy theories, people grasping at straws, and others speaking of government control. Josh eventually managed to find one of the earliest news articles that came out of Long Island, New York.

*Mysterious Aging Syndrome Baffles US Doctors*

*Four weeks after first reported, an unusual aging syndrome appears to have shaken Long Island and left doctors confused.*

*When 63 residents of Long Island were showing a puzzling mixture of symptoms related to aging including cataracts, skin problems, hip pain, wrinkles, weight loss, gray hair, and balding, it had all the makings of what doctors believed was an isolated form of Werner Syndrome, a rare disease that causes the body to age too fast for which there still is no cure. However, unlike Werner, these symptoms appear at an accelerated speed and can be transmitted to others. This has experts alarmed, and many are calling it a virus.*

*A team of epidemiologists from the Centers for Disease Control (CDC) were brought in to work around the clock to find answers after it was reported to be contagious.*

*Almost immediately, conspiracy theories have begun pointing the finger at biotech anti-aging companies, the World Health Organization, rogue government experiments, a targeted terror attack, and even vaccines. These are just some of the speculations swirling around a mystery that has baffled the US medical field. It's also what has added fuel to the fire of residents throughout the greater Long Island region as they search to unravel the clues.*

*So far in the last month, dozens have contracted and died from what now seems to have all the makings of an Ebola-style virus due to its ability to spread by direct contact. As the death toll rises, leading health authorities fear that it could be even more deadly than the Black Death.*

*Worried residents of Long Island are calling for answers. Could it be airborne? Is it environmental? Was it transferred through water or food? What is causing it? Can it be stopped?*

*US health officials are scrambling to understand the severity of this outbreak, which only came to light after a video was leaked to the local press by someone experiencing advanced stages of what they are now calling The Aging syndrome. With so many questions going unanswered and the confusion* surrounding this unusual and deadly illness, it has left scientific minds stumped and residents fearful.

Among the victims so far, Julia Garner, 44, was a student of the Juilliard School who went on to have a career as a dancer and then as a teacher. She was suddenly overcome by a rash and frequent nosebleeds, followed by the rapid symptoms of aging. Initially, it was suspected to be Werner Syndrome. However, a battery of tests soon ruled out Werner. What differentiates this new illness is the speed, how contagious it is, and a unique phenomenon that not even doctors can decipher.

No longer able to continue regular life, Julia was soon forced to close her dance school. At first, she was misdiagnosed and sent home from the emergency room after being told that it was probably the common cold. Further tests by her doctor resulted in her transfer to a hospital where specialists and an epidemiologist were brought in as her health quickly deteriorated and she began to age years in a matter of days. In less than thirty days she was dead.

Dr. Alice Munroe, an epidemiologist from the CDC in Atlanta, who is investigating the illness, said it's a true mystery and one that is horrifying to witness. "We are working hard to try and understand the cause but more specifically why the aging process slows in individuals after they transfer it to another person. What we know so far is that this is no longer an isolated incident. Our focus right now is on studying the ways it is transferred, how widespread this may already be, and what we can do to contain it while we search for a permanent cure."

~

"Contain it?" They were beyond that point. The article was dated one week ago with details of people with symptoms that went back a month earlier, which meant it had been in full swing for at least five weeks. And what was this talk about it slowing in individuals after transfer? That made no sense. Viruses didn't work that way. But was this a typical virus?

He flipped through channels on the TV to try and find some up-to-date info.

As he was doing that a notification came on his phone from Callie.

"Have you seen this?"

She sent him a video that was making the rounds across social media. He tapped it and a shaky camera revealed the face of a middle-aged man. Josh turned up the volume. "By the time you see this, I'll probably be dead or in a government lab. I know I look as if I'm fifty but I'm not. At least I wasn't 16 days ago." He lifted an ID and brought it up to the camera.

It was of a college freshman at the MIT campus in Cambridge, Massachusetts. He pointed a gnarled finger to his date of birth. "I was born in 2002. That's right. That makes me nineteen years old but clearly, I don't look like that anymore. And for those who would say I am making this up to get attention…" He set the ID down and lifted a university newspaper that had a snapshot of him and was dated sixteen days earlier. He tossed the paper to one side and pulled the skin on his face. "It's all real. I don't know how I contracted this or why this is happening. I am filming this to get the truth out. There's no hope for me, just as there hasn't been for those who have already died.

They've brushed this under the rug and tried to contain it but failed." The guy turned his face away from the camera at the sound of banging. "They're here. They're here for me." His voice rose as he hurried to get out what he knew. "I can't be sure, but by my estimate, I have to be aging several years a day. I figure if the average life of a human is eighty years, at this rate, I could be dead within thirty, maybe forty days." He reached forward, and the camera went dark.

*Several years a day?* Josh thought back to the night he got out. The incident in the downtown. He'd overheard what the cop said about the victim's ID. If this had reached Massachusetts, it had gone far beyond Long Island, New York. And now it was on his doorstep. What other states were affected?

Another text appeared from Callie.

*They are talking about preventing travel outside of major cities.*

He quickly typed back a message. *Any other states?*

He waited. Within seconds she came back with a link to an unapproved and unregulated website tracker that had been put up by someone in the medical community to keep track of reported cases in real-time. A map of the United States appeared, and all over it were blinking red dots indicating clusters of outbreaks. "Holy crap."

Panic gripped him. He got up and hurried down the hallway, and began banging on the door of his mother's room. "Mom!"

# CHAPTER FIVE

July 5

They devoured food like ravenous beasts.

All the while, Ryan studied them from across the table. It had been ten years since he'd last seen Josh. He was only six when the life he knew was upended in the worst way possible. He could hardly believe his eyes.

"Take a picture, it might last longer," Josh said, noticing him staring.

"Just noticing how much you've grown."

"Yeah, amazing what happens when you're not around."

Awkwardness followed.

"About that."

"Don't waste your breath."

That stung. He couldn't fault the kid. He was caught up in the middle of the separation, an innocent bystander who didn't get a say in how it went down, the drawn-out divorce, the public humiliation, and the court ruling. Lily's eyes darted between them, a smile tugging at her lips. Ryan could see Elizabeth in her. Those mousy brown eyes and tiny curved nose.

Shifting the topic, Lily asked, "So what do you do?"

"Do?"

"For a job?"

He smiled. It sounded like a grown-up question, one she'd overheard adults ask and was now mimicking. "I guess you could say I'm a handyman. I do a little of everything."

Josh snorted but didn't say anything.

"How old are you, Lily?"

"Ten but I'll be eleven next year. Then I'll be old enough to do more things."

He chuckled. "Is that right?"

"Yeah. That's what Josh says. Though I did get to go to this party a few weeks back. Josh took me there. Mom didn't know because…"

"Lily." Josh scowled at her.

She dipped her chin. "I wasn't supposed to say anything."

Ryan glanced at Josh who was hurrying to finish his food so he could get out of there. "So was your mom seeing anyone?"

"What kind of question is that?" Josh asked.

"Just curious."

"Does it matter?" He replied.

"I guess not. Just wanted to ask."

"Yeah. Well, maybe if you'd picked up the phone once in a while you wouldn't need to ask."

And the hits just kept coming.

Ryan nodded. "Right. So your mom. She sent you this way?"

"Apparently so," Josh said with a mouth full of food. "Had I known I wouldn't have come. I was wondering why she never told me. Should have figured."

Ryan shifted in his seat. "Look, Josh. I know—"

"Let me just stop you there," he said, setting his cutlery down. "This," he pointed at Ryan and then back at himself and Lily. "This isn't a family reunion. You don't need to make small talk or explain anything. We'll be leaving soon and you can go back to whatever the hell you were doing before this. Okay? You don't owe me anything. I've done perfectly fine without you."

Lily nearly choked on her food. Ryan got her a glass of water.

"I guess what I'm asking, Josh, is did your mother say anything? Did she give you a message for me?"

Still chewing, he reached for his bag and opened it. That's when Ryan caught a glimpse of a handgun. He didn't say anything. The streets outside had become dangerous. Josh handed him a flash drive. "She sent a file to me, I put it on this."

"What is it?"

"I don't know. I never looked."

Ryan took it and backed out of the kitchen.

"She said you would know the password. Something about the location of your honeymoon? Obviously didn't trust me." He was angry. It was to be expected. So many years with no father figure, it couldn't have been easy.

made concerning you and me, the custody of Josh, and visitation rights. I'm sorry about the way it went down."

She released a nervous laugh. "Crazy, isn't it. I'm apologizing when I didn't do anything wrong." She looked away from the camera and this time touched the tissue beneath her eyes. Ryan had always wondered what she would look like in her old age. They'd had dreams of growing old together. She'd wanted a home with a wraparound porch and two Adirondack chairs. She'd talk about looking forward to having grandchildren. So many dreams. All of them shattered. "Listen. For all the mistakes made, one thing I know is that you were a good father in the few years we were together. I couldn't think of anyone else to send Josh to who I trust. I have been in contact with my parents over the past few days and they've told me that there are groups of people who are riding out this event on an island in the Gulf of Mexico. At least until things improve. I want you to take Josh and Lily to my parents. Get them on a boat. I want them safe and while I can't be sure if they will even make it to you, if they do, I would ask you do this for me, for Josh, and Lily." She reached for a glass of water and took a few sips, almost choking in the process. She disappeared for a second. All he could hear was coughing then she returned. "Ryan. I should have told you sooner, but... Lily is your daughter. I never remarried, I didn't date anyone after you. I couldn't bring myself to do it. I know I should have told you but I figured with everything that happened it would have only made things worse and those kids needed stability. I needed stability. I couldn't deal with another argument, or lawyers, so I just kept it to myself."

He remembered all the conversations with her in those final days were done via phone. Never in person. All communication went through lawyers and even the day in court when they gave the ruling regarding custody and denial of visitation rights due to his alcohol use, he never saw her. Years passed and without seeing Josh, he had no reason to think that she was pregnant with another child.

"I'm sorry, Ryan. I can't change the past but I can give you time with them now. Be patient with Josh. He's been through a lot. He's a really good kid, just a little lost and damaged. Like both of us." She took a deep breath. "By now you will have seen how this event is playing out. I'm not sure what it is exactly but I'm going to die because of it. I just want to get things in place before the end. I haven't told Josh that I'm sending him to you because he wouldn't go. He's so bent out of shape over this. I need you to look after him. Lily as well. Do what I can't do. Be there for them." She drew a long breath. "You remember the cottage in Franklin County…" She reeled its location off just in case he'd forgotten. He hadn't. How could he? He didn't need to scribble it down, it was responsible for some of his best memories. "You'll need to get there before July 10 because that's when the boats will be leaving for the island. If you miss that slot, they won't be back for a month." She sighed and looked down. Ryan glanced at his watch. It was the fifth. He had five days. Elizabeth continued. "This wasn't how I intended things to end. I plan to go out on my terms. I don't want to suffer. I won't do that. Look after them, Ryan. I'm trusting you. Please forgive me. Thank you."

And that was it. She switched off the camera.

Ryan sat there chewing over what she'd said and thinking about the past and the first time he'd met Elizabeth in college. He was studying to be a teacher, and she was taking nursing. He'd seen her on the way to his classes and had approached her on a day she was stressed out from all the studying. They began dating and within a few years, they were engaged and then married. Their firstborn, Josh, arrived four years later. Ryan adored that kid. Life seemed almost too good to be true. They were both in professions they enjoyed, making good money, living in a nice neighborhood, and making their way in the world as parents.

Then it happened.

The incident that changed it all.

In many ways, his life ended back then, ten years ago.

It destroyed his marriage, his career, his reputation and sent him spiraling down into depression and heavy drinking as a means to cope.

Those were dark days. He'd eventually pulled himself out from the abyss with the help of AA meetings, medication, and moving away to where he could start afresh. He'd even gone as far as to change his name. His second job wasn't even close to what he had done before but it paid the bills.

Ryan took out the flash drive and pocketed it. He would watch that video another three times just so he could see her. He'd never stopped loving Elizabeth. He knew every decision she made was done out of pain, out of a need to shield Josh. For that, he didn't blame her. He went back into the kitchen and glanced at his kids. They were done eating. Lily was drinking a glass of water, blissfully unaware of the life-changing event that was unraveling around her.

"Josh says we have to leave soon."

Josh never met his gaze. It was like he was uncomfortable even looking at him. What had he learned about his past? What conclusion had he come to about his father? Did he know the truth? "Well... it's dark out," Ryan said, looking out the window.

"Doesn't matter," Josh replied, rising and placing his plate in the sink.

"Where will you go?"

"That's not your problem. It's mine."

"No, it's mine now. Your mom wants me to take you to your grandparents."

"We don't need a babysitter."

He had no filter when it came to saying how he felt.

"No you don't but it's what she wanted."

"Yeah, well, maybe she should have asked me what I wanted. Seems you and her have a habit of deciding what you want."

He knew he wasn't just referring to now.

"You were six, Josh."

"Now I'm sixteen. Funny how quickly time flies," he said, collecting his bag and slipping his arm through it, and adjusting it on his shoulder. "Lily, get your coat on."

"Thank you for the food, Ryan," Lily said in a small voice.

"Josh. Listen. Wait. Think about Lily here."

"I am."

He took hold of her hand and led her toward the door.

"Josh, I've got plenty of room for both of you here. Now

it's dark out and this area is not where a ten-year-old should be right now."

"How would you know what a ten-year-old needs?"

"Look, you can be as angry as you want at me. You have every right but I'm still your father."

Josh chuckled. "You stopped being that ten years ago. Now the agreement was to stay for a meal. I didn't want to do that but for Lily's sake, I did. But now it's time for us to leave."

"Yeah, well that was before I listened to what your mother wanted."

Josh fired back. "Our mother is dead! Okay? What she wants now means very little."

He knew he didn't mean it. He was speaking out of his pain.

"I would beg to differ."

Josh narrowed his eyes. "Lily, go wait outside."

"Why?"

"Just do it," he said loudly. Lily looked at Ryan and he nodded. Lily stepped out onto the lit-up porch and took a seat. Josh closed the door. As soon as he knew she couldn't hear them, he opened up on Ryan. "I don't know why my mother sent us to you. I never wanted to come here. I wouldn't have come here if I knew where she was sending us. Now if she wants us to go to our grandparents, fine, we'll go but not with you. Lily is my sister and I've always watched out for her."

"And she's my daughter."

"Like I said. If that really mattered to you, you would have visited us. Where were you, man? Huh? Where were you when I needed you? When we needed you? That's right. Nowhere. From what I heard you were too busy."

"That's not the truth."

He shifted from one foot to the next. "Oh no, that's right, you were dealing with sexual assault charges of a minor. A student of yours, right?"

It was like someone had opened the wound again.

Ryan blew out his cheeks. "So she told you?"

"She didn't need to, man. I found the articles online. It's all out there."

"I guess you never read the one where I was cleared of all charges a few years after the allegations."

"Whatever, man. We don't need you. I don't want you around me. And I sure as hell don't want you around Lily." He turned to head out and Ryan placed his hand against the door to stop him for just a second.

"Really? You're going to hold us captive now? Is that it?"

"You don't know the whole truth, Josh."

"And I don't care to know. If it mattered so much, you would have shown up a long time ago and told me. So just move out of the way."

Ryan hesitated to lift his hand. He had every right to play the father card, especially after hearing what Elizabeth wanted, but where would that have gotten him? Josh would just leave the first chance he got when he wasn't looking. He removed his hand from the door and Josh exited.

"Are we staying?" Lily asked.

"No. Let's go."

"But…"

"Lily." He urged her down the porch steps. She looked back

at Ryan and gave a small wave. He stood on the porch in the dim lighting and watched as they went over to his dirt bike and tried to start it. A few failed attempts, a quick check of the engine and it fired up, a growl almost as angry as the look Josh was giving him. Josh glared at him as he flipped down his visor and tore out of there, into the darkness, into the unknown.

# CHAPTER SIX

15 days earlier
June 20

*J*t was fifteen days before they would leave home for good. Josh had been inside the house for six days watching the unexplainable event unfold before his eyes. His mother still hadn't come out of her room. All communication was done through the door or by way of texting but by now he knew what was afflicting her and how she'd gotten it. The frequency of reported deaths was increasing by the day. State officials had instructed people to stay in their homes and only come out for necessities. The National Guard in every state had been deployed to all the affected areas to keep law and order while the CDC dispatched Epidemic Intelligence Service (EIS) officers to handle the infected. They were told they were there to stem the outbreak by responding to the emerging pathogen, nothing more.

People weren't buying it.

The online tracker continued to reveal more cases from the west of California through to the tip of Cape Cod. Callie sent him links to videos released on social media of people going out of their way to spread it to others. Spitting purposely, or touching people like it was nothing more than a game of tag. The worst video was of a man bursting into the home of a single woman and killing her just so he could spread it to her child. What did he have to gain?

At first, the reports were confusing.

That's when he began to learn more about why the government was having a hard time containing it.

Callie's text said, "They're saying it stops in those who spread it."

If that was true, it certainly made it clear why people were acting desperate.

With so much misinformation being shared online, he wasn't sure what was real or just a hoax. It was hard to know what to believe. And quite frankly, he didn't want to believe it.

The stories online changed from day to day.

Josh kept Lily busy with video games and Netflix but eventually he'd have to tell her the truth. She was already asking questions about mom. He didn't want to scare her any more than his mother did so they'd agreed to hold off and say that she'd caught a bad cold and didn't want either of them to catch it.

Before the conversation turned to leaving, his mother

had told him the best course of action was to stay home. Venturing out would only place them in harm's way and that made no sense. Still, that didn't stop people from fleeing the large cities and heading for small towns.

Towns like his.

That's why he'd taken precautions. Josh had locked all the doors. He barricaded all entry points and slept less. It was beginning to catch up with him. "You need to sleep," his mother said through the door as he rested his head against the door frame. He struggled to keep his eyes open and his emotions in check. "Lily needs you."

They argued about the future, about her not wanting to get help, about the syndrome.

"If they come for me, Josh, you know as well as I do they will take you and Lily. I don't want that for either of you. I don't know how they are handling this."

"You make it sound like they're going to execute us."

She went silent.

"Look, Mom, they're probably coming anyway if you're right about contact tracing."

"That's why I need you to act now, son. Collect what you need for the journey."

"Journey? To where?"

"I've sent a file to your phone, and provided you with an address. When you get there, give the person the file. They'll help."

"Who is it?"

"A friend."

"Does this friend have a name?"

"Josh, that's not important."

"Maybe not for you."

His phone dinged with a text message of a place to download a video file, and then another followed with an address, and a list of items she wanted him to get.

His mother told him he would have to be strong. This whole thing was over his head. He couldn't deal with it. But it didn't matter what he said. Josh realized fast that his mother couldn't help.

"Listen, we're almost out of food."

"Right. Well..." she replied.

There was a long stretch of silence. He knew what he had to do. He'd have to venture into town but that was like putting a single bullet in a revolver, spinning it, putting it to his head, and pulling the trigger. There was a high chance he wouldn't survive. He'd seen the videos online. People being tackled to the ground. Residents being robbed. The looting. The chaos. He'd spent hours poring over articles. Regardless of martial law or curfews, it was out of control.

"You'll have to go," she said.

"And Lily?"

"She can stay here. I'll talk to her."

"She's asking more questions, Mom."

"I know. You'll tell her when it's the right time but I want to spare her the pain."

He nodded. Everything inside him wanted to lash out for so many reasons. "Mom, I was thinking. Perhaps there is an alternative to reporting your infection. Callie sent me another video. People are saying this can be given away. I mean, that it stops the aging process in the carrier once they come in contact with someone else who doesn't have it."

"That's nonsense."

"Not if it's nanotechnology. Nanobots. That's what some are saying. That it's not a typical virus."

"Josh."

"Think about it, Mom. Is it any more ridiculous than what we are already seeing? People shouldn't be aging several years in twenty-four hours."

"I hear what you're saying, Josh, but…"

"No, listen to me. I've been reading up on this. They have been testing nanotechnology for years and have been talking about human trials in cancer patients. This could be some kind of variant of the Werner Syndrome. That's very real, Mom."

"I know, Josh. I've read about it. It makes people grow old too fast but Werner Syndrome occurs over years, not days. And that also wouldn't explain how it could stop the aging process in you if you transmitted it to someone else."

"It could if we understood more about nanobots and how they're being used in medicine."

"Where did you hear about this?"

"Online."

She sighed. "Josh. You can't believe everything online."

"Where else are we meant to find out?" he shot back. "Look, they're saying that if someone gives it to you, you can spread it to someone who doesn't have it and it will slow the aging process back to normal in you. Think about that, Mom. Wouldn't that be something worth exploring? You could live. We could stop this."

"Josh."

He continued, desperate for her to understand. "No. You're not listening. I saw it. I witnessed it with my own eyes. There was this guy online that said he hasn't aged in over a week since he transmitted it to someone else. The rash, the nosebleeds, and the aging slowed to its normal rate. That's got to be good, right?"

"Sure, if it's true, which, c'mon, Josh, it's probably not. But think about it. Even if it was true. It might be okay for the person who gave it away. But what about the one who receives it?"

"They give it away to someone else."

He heard her sigh. "That goes against—"

"Everything you and the medical field has taught," he said, cutting her off. "I get it. Self-isolation. Wait it out. Don't be selfish. Stay clear. I understand, Mom. But that doesn't look as if it's working for you."

Josh thought about the man in the video breaking into a house and attacking that woman just so he could infect someone else. Or a live video of people swarming innocent bystanders so they could touch them. "If you could give it to someone else to save yourself, would you?" Josh asked.

"No," his mother said without hesitation. "It's not right. Besides, it's probably just a lie. Every virus that comes along, someone claims there is a cure but there isn't. If there isn't a cure for Werner Syndrome, there most definitely isn't a cure for this."

He lifted his eyes to the ceiling. "It seems ironic, doesn't it. No one wants to grow old and yet we all are. And now it's happening even faster."

"It's one of humanity's greatest fears," she said. "They've created a billion-dollar anti-aging industry from that fear. Serums, pills, diets, injections, anything and everything to turn back the hands of time and then this happens." She snorted. "Just like us to screw it up."

There was quiet as he contemplated what she said. Had they screwed up?

"Mom, how old are you now? I mean, how old do you look?"

Six days had passed since he'd last seen her.

"You know you shouldn't ask a woman that." She laughed a little but it faded fast. "I don't want you to remember me like this, Josh."

"I would have eventually seen it."

"Yes, over time. Not this way."

"Please."

Josh heard her sigh.

"Please. I have to know."

"If I send you this, you delete it immediately. You hear me?"

"You have my word."

He heard the sound of her camera snapping. Then a few seconds later a photo message came through and he opened it and felt his eyes begin to well with tears. She looked as if she'd aged more than ten years. It was like time itself was moving too fast, robbing her of the life she was meant to have. It was taking away his mother before she had a chance to see them become who they were meant to be.

"Josh?"

"Yeah."

"Delete it. I don't want Lily seeing it."

He nodded and hit delete. He let out a lungful of air and

shook his head, unable to believe this was happening. But it was.

He slammed a fist against the door. "It's not fair."

"Oh, son… life's not fair. Some people lose a parent when they're young. Others don't even know theirs."

There was silence before he got up.

"Where are you going?" she asked.

"To get supplies."

"Take the Glock. And Josh. Cover yourself up. Don't go near anyone. Keep your distance."

"Don't worry, I'm good at that," he said, thinking of how for years he'd kept people at arm's length, never allowing anyone to get too close, close enough that they could cause him pain. It was easier to live that way.

Over the next five minutes, he made a list of essentials. Non-perishables. Food that would last, along with medical supplies. Using the motorcycle, he wouldn't be able to carry much.

Josh changed into a long-sleeved, black polo top that covered his neck. He slipped into his thick leather coat, donned gloves, then used some masking tape around his wrists and ankles. He collected an N95 mask from his mother's medical bag just in case he had to take off his helmet. He grabbed two backpacks that could be used for carrying groceries and checked that he had a full magazine before collecting his motorcycle helmet. He made his way down to the room where Lily was watching TV. She was laid back on a bean bag eating chips while watching a movie. He tapped the door. "I'm going into town, I'll be back in half an hour."

She twisted in his direction. "Can I come?"

"No. I need you to stay here just in case mom wants anything."

"Why are you going out?"

"To get food."

She sighed. "I haven't been out in days. I want to go out."

"You can't. Okay?"

"But you can?"

"I'm older than you."

She tossed her pack of chips to one side and folded her arms and looked at the TV. "I wish I was older," she said, saying what he and many his age had muttered at one time or another. Somehow there was a perceived belief that freedom was attached to being older as if it afforded them the ability to do whatever they wanted. It did to some extent. Well nature had just flipped the coin. Now freedom was staying young or you died. "I want you to lock the door behind me. And Lily, don't answer that door unless it's me. You don't even make a sound. You understand?"

"I got it," she said, scowling.

"We can't trust anyone."

He headed for the front of the house and moved a heavy piece of furniture jammed behind the door out of the way. Lily wouldn't have the strength to shift it back into place but she could lock it and stay hidden. The road they lived on was far enough out of town and away from the main suburbs that he didn't expect trouble. His nearest neighbor was half a mile down the road. The home was off Route 12, at the far northeastern corner of the boundary line, and nestled among pines. If it wasn't for the mailbox at the end of their driveway, it could have easily been missed.

Josh added fuel to his dirt bike and fired it up, then veered out onto Route 12 heading southwest. There were only a few options. He figured Walmart was his best shot. He could head up North Tram Road then dart east over to it and that way avoid the heart of town.

In and out. He wouldn't linger.

He already had a list.

His mind began thinking of the worst.

But how bad could it be out here? He'd always considered Vidor, Texas, to be in the middle of nowhere. If there was trouble to be had, it would be in Beaumont which was a lot bigger. However, after witnessing what he had on the day of his release, he wasn't taking any chances.

On the way in, the roads looked clear.

He shot past several pedestrians, folks on bicycles, other vehicles doing the rounds. Life was for the most part continuing as usual though now people weren't taking chances. As Josh got closer to Walmart, he saw a large line of people outside, separated by at least ten feet. All right. That was good. There was order. At least among those who weren't affected.

He parked the dirt bike a good distance away from the main entrance and kept his helmet on, observing and treating every person as a potential death threat.

Josh joined the line, glancing over his shoulder as others fell in behind him. He turned and stood at an angle so he could see those in front and those that were behind him as well as anyone else approaching from the lot full of cars. He noticed the same degree of vigilance being taken by others. The smart ones weren't showing any skin and their faces were covered in balaclavas. The rest were taking a chance.

What was clear was the infection, if it could be called that, was meant to spread person-to-person via touch, saliva, blood, sex, or a scratch. Unlike the incubation period of three to five days for other viruses, this was aggressive, fast-acting and within twenty-four hours those who had contracted it would show symptoms. The challenge was identifying those who had it before those symptoms showed up. Besides frequent nosebleeds and a rash, the only other way to know was if the person told you or you knew them and had seen them age. Otherwise, anyone could have it.

Young, middle-aged, elderly, everyone around him was aging naturally, the challenge was discerning who was aging abnormally. That's what made it so dangerous. Someone infected could hide a nosebleed, they could cover up a rash, and they certainly could say they were a certain age.

And IDs? Well, teens had been creating fake IDs for decades. How would this be any different? There was no fever, no red eyes, no sneezing that would indicate someone had it. It wasn't sending people out of control.

Attacks were purposeful, and at times planned.

One thing they did know was that it wasn't airborne as there were still many that didn't have it. Unlike other viruses that required people to self-isolate and play the waiting game, this didn't work that way, not unless you wanted to die alone.

The aging didn't go away with time. Time was the enemy.

The only known way to slow it, or some said stop it, was for the virus to attach itself to a new host. Someone who didn't have it. Why it worked that way was anyone's guess. Right now, he had to wonder how many locals knew about that.

The unusual manner in which the virus transferred was like pouring a glass of water from one cup into another, leaving the first one dry. It had led to conspiracy theories that this had been manufactured in a lab — that it was some kind of medical nanobot, a collection of microscopic machines that could travel through the body, repair damaged cells and organs, wipe out disease, cure cancer, restore memory and even slow aging.

What if the testing for slowing aging had gone wrong?

Maybe that's why they'd tried to keep this under wraps for the first few weeks.

How many others knew about this unusual method of transfer?

He figured he wasn't the only one staying abreast of online reports.

No words were exchanged by anyone. It was quiet. People kept their distance. The grim reality hung heavy like a fog. Infection was a death sentence, plain and simple.

Josh made it to the front of the line, showed his ID and face, and was waved inside by a security guard who was outfitted in as much protective gear as he was. They only allowed in a small number of people at a time. As soon as he was in, he hurried down the aisles, filling the cart with food. In a matter of a week, the shelves were almost bare.

Fear had driven many to overbuy, leading to limitations. Big signs informed people of how many items they could take. Gone were the days of taking whatever you liked. Every item was accounted for. Now the only trucks allowed in and out of the city were delivery and supply trucks. He didn't expect that to last.

Once Josh had what he needed, he was directed to roll his cart over to the checkout. As they filled a couple of bags, some of the staff watched on an overhead TV the chaos unfold in Lexington. It was the same stories on repeat.

Was there any hope that it would end? He wanted to believe it but the news footage told a very different story, one of the downfall, people purposely passing on what they had to avoid death.

"Thanks," he said, giving a nod to the checkout lady as he strolled out with two bags. He hadn't made it but a few feet outside when two vehicles, seemingly going at a normal speed, sped up and plowed into the line of people.

One SUV crashed into the glass window, shattering it and pinning multiple adults under the wheels. The driver and several occupants got out and began touching and coughing blood over people they'd downed.

That was another symptom. It was called hemoptysis.

That was the medical term. At least that's what his mother said. It was blood that came from the lungs as well as internal hemorrhaging of the capillaries. Bright red, and frothy. The result of prolonged infection. It was the body's reaction to aging too fast.

Josh's eyes darted.

It was pure pandemonium.

Some were screaming at the sight of downed people while others fled in every direction to escape those looking to spread the pathogen.

Fear spiked. Josh bolted.

Juggling bags of groceries, he fled across the parking lot, almost losing his footing as he looked over his shoulder at the unraveling chaos. It felt surreal watching young and old choosing to spread the pathogen. He understood, they were desperate to survive, but as his mother said, that didn't make it right. It was selfish but then that had been the history of the human race. Survival of the fittest.

Josh made it to his bike and was filling one of the backpacks he'd taken with him when he heard heavy footfalls approaching fast.

He didn't even think twice, he grabbed the Glock and swung around.

"Whoa!" a guy cried out, lifting his hands in the air. "I'm not infected."

"Stay back!" Josh shouted from behind his visor. His voice came out muffled but his actions were clear.

The ginger-headed guy was middle-aged. "I just need a ride."

"I can't help you."

"C'mon man," he said, looking back at the crowd.

Josh fired a round at his feet. "I won't tell you again."

The sound caught the attention of others in the lot. Some fled, others headed in his direction. Were they infected? He wasn't sticking around to find out. The ginger guy darted east and weaved around cars as Josh stuffed the last bag into the second backpack. He zipped it up and put one on his back and his arms through the other so that it was resting against his chest. He climbed onto the bike and kick-started it to life.

All the while he could see people heading his way.

Some were young, others old. It wasn't like they were dealing with only old people. Newly infected had more than enough time to infect others. And a hell of a lot more energy. He spun the bike around, burning rubber as he buzzed away, glancing in his mirror.

Behind his visor, his breathing was heavy.

His chest rising and falling fast.

The image of people spreading the pathogen blazed in his mind.

# CHAPTER SEVEN

July 5

The door of the barn started shaking. It was made from flimsy wood that had weathered over the years, so it wouldn't take much to break it if someone wanted to attack in the middle of the night. The shaking was loud enough to get her mind racing.

"Josh, Josh," Lily said, shaking him.

They'd bedded down for the night in an old barn a few miles from his father's house. He figured it would keep them out of the wind, and there was enough hay to provide a soft bed. While he wasn't asleep, he was beginning to drift into that state between sleep and being awake, seeing images form in his mind of places less dangerous than the world they were now in.

"What is it?"

"Did you hear that?"

He lifted his head and listened.

"It's just the wind. Go back to sleep."

He adjusted the handful of hay that he was using as a pillow for the night. He'd covered it in his leather jacket and created a barrier of haystacks around them just in case someone came up to the second tier. The dirt bike was in one of the horse stalls down below, covered with hay.

"Josh."

He groaned. "What?" he said, revealing his frustration.

"Ryan is your dad, yes?"

"Biologically. I guess you could say that."

A moment later. "Is he mine?"

He opened his eyes and stared at her. There was very little light filtering through the slats of wood. He could just make out the features of her small face. "Does it matter?"

"Well, it's just that mom never told me anything about him."

"Trust me, Bean, you're not missing out."

He closed his eyes.

"Well, how do you know?"

He opened them again. "I just do. Now go to sleep."

Josh was almost anticipating her asking another question. He knew her well enough that once she latched on to something, she didn't stop talking about it until she understood.

"He seemed nice."

"Appearances can be deceiving," he said without opening his eyes.

"What do you mean?"

"Ugh." He wiped a hand across his face and looked at her, pulling himself up onto his side. "Take for instance this event. People could look like they're eighteen, thirty, or fifty, but they could be younger. I mean if they have the pathogen. You might meet someone who seems friendly enough and they look my age, for instance, but they could be your age in reality."

"So we can't trust anyone?"

"No."

"But you trusted him."

"Because I know what he looks like."

"But you said you haven't seen him in ten years?"

"I haven't. In person. But… well…"

"You looked him up on social media, didn't you?"

"Yeah, something like that."

Josh laid back down and folded his arms behind his head and looked up at the barn roof, thinking about the period in his life when he was curious about his father. Where he'd gone. Why he'd gone. All he could remember was he was there one day and gone the next. His mother had told him that he had to move out. That they were separating for a while. He never questioned it. He was too young. After several years he kind of figured it was permanent. Curious, as anyone would be, he asked his mother if he could call him but she always gave some excuse. He was working. He was out of town. She lost his number. Eventually, he found out the truth for himself when he checked his mother's computer history. There were articles, lots of them about his father, about charges involving an alleged sexual assault of one of his students. He couldn't believe it. His father? Why would he do that? Josh pitied his mother. How humiliated she must have felt being dragged through it. Having those she knew question her husband's integrity.

Right then and there he dismissed his father. Anyone that would do that, didn't deserve his time. His mother, on the other hand, he placed on a pedestal, at least until he became a teenager and his hormones went out of whack. It was a different story then.

"So Ryan doesn't have the aging?"

"Oh, he's old. He's just not getting old fast enough," he replied, chuckling to himself.

"But is he my dad?"

There it was, the big question. She'd never brought it up before and Josh had never thought to ask his mother. He just assumed it was Ryan and that she'd told her. Now he wondered if she'd withheld it to protect her from the same disappointment that he felt. Still, she deserved to know. There was always the potential that his mother had a one-night stand as some kind of rebound but if she did, he never saw any guys come home with her.

"I don't know, Bean."

Lily plumped her jacket pillow and curled up in a ball trying to go to sleep. Josh lifted his head and took his jacket and wrapped it around her. It was hard enough for him to come to terms with who his father was but she was still in the dark. He remained awake for an unknown amount of time listening to the cacophony of night sounds. Mostly cicadas chirping.

~

How many minutes or hours passed he wasn't sure.

In the dead of night, the sound of a branch breaking was akin to a crash. But it wasn't a branch, it was someone trying to break into the barn. Josh bolted upright, his heart hammering against his chest. There was another shake, this time louder, distinct from the kind created by the wind. It was followed by another crash. Then silence.

"Josh?" Lily asked.

"Shh," he replied.

He quietly shifted one of the bales of hay that surrounded them to the side and crawled over to the edge of the second floor. Without light, it was hard to see but as his eyes adjusted, he saw two strapping individuals step into the barn. Were they the owners? Had they seen them enter earlier? Was it cops? Quickly, Josh crawled back over, bringing a finger up to his lips. Lily looked as if she was about to cry. There was only one ladder up and down. The other exit would have been to go through the upper barn door but that was a good ten-foot drop. He could lower her but she still might injure her legs.

Fearful, Josh knew he couldn't get her out of the barn but he could hide her. She was small and there were enough haystacks that she could stay out of sight. "Get into here," he said, pointing to a gap between the stacks. She followed his directions like her life depended on it. "I'll be back."

"Josh, don't leave me."

"I won't."

Tears fell from her cheeks.

"Bean. I'm not going anywhere," he whispered.

She scurried backward into her hole and tucked her body into a fetal position while Josh quietly stacked a few more hay bales on top, in front and around her. Satisfied, he withdrew the Glock from his bag and made his way back to the edge. The two strangers didn't say a word but moved down either side of the barn, opening the horse stalls and looking inside. One disappeared into a stall only to emerge and let out a low whistle. His partner joined him and looked inside. They'd found the bike. Josh kept a firm grip on the gun. He considered opening fire but if there was a chance they could make it out of this without killing anyone, he would take that option. He hadn't killed anyone so far. At least not that he knew of. The old man he'd shot was still alive when he left. Still, if it came down to Lily or these strangers, he wouldn't hesitate.

He heard them talking in a low voice.

It was a male and a female.

They exited the stall and he pulled back from the edge.

Had they seen him?

His throat was dry. His pulse beating fast.

He listened intently as they did the rounds through the rest of the stalls. The hinges on the doors alerted him to where they were without him looking.

Then he heard what he hoped he wouldn't — boots on the rungs of the ladder, making their way up. Laying on his belly, he brought the sight up and waited until he saw a head. Instead of shooting whoever it was in cold blood, he fired a warning shot, just slightly off to the side. It worked. The guy dropped from that ladder so fast. He swore he must have broken a leg. "The next one goes in your head."

He waited for a reply but didn't get one. It wasn't the owners. They would have been shouting bloody murder and cursing up a storm and telling him to get the hell off their property. Not these two. They were silent. Determined. He wanted to look over. Get a bead on where they were, but he figured they were armed and might not extend the courtesy he gave.

The sound of fast footfalls followed.

A moment later he heard the door close on the barn.

Then silence fell.

Josh waited to be sure there was no one there before he crawled over to the edge and took a look. Nothing. No movement. But that didn't mean they were gone. He wasn't stupid. If they had the pathogen, they were desperate and would wait him out even if it meant staying there until morning, or until they fell asleep, whatever came first.

Damn it.

They now knew where he was.

Was one of them in a stall below while the other was outside? He couldn't risk checking. If anything happened to him, Lily wouldn't be able to survive. He was beginning to think that maybe Ryan was right. Perhaps he should have stayed the night. It was a long way to St. George Island, at least seven hundred miles. They'd barely made it a couple of miles.

He was about to check on Lily when he heard a splash, then another. As he tilted his head to make out what it was, he wondered if the strangers had continued through the brush as there was a stream nearby.

Josh had taken a few steps toward the edge when he heard a familiar crackling sound, then a whoosh. It was the amber light that gave it away. "Shit! Lily." They'd set the side of the barn on fire. If they couldn't get them down, they'd smoke them out or let them die trying to escape. An old dry barn like this would go up in no time.

He moved fast, hauling bales of hay out of the way to

get at her. Clasping her hand, and grabbing his bag, he raced over to the ladder only to see the fire blocking the second exit.

Those bastards. They were herding them toward one exit.

Was one of them down below? Just waiting for them to hit the ground and then they would spread the pathogen to them? Moving fast to the upper doors, where hay bales were inserted, Josh pushed them wide only to be driven back by a gunshot.

"Sonofabitch!"

By now the fire was raging, licking up to the top of the eastern side of the barn.

They were screwed if they went out and damned to hellfire if they didn't.

He'd rather take his chances with a pathogen that could be passed on to others than burn to death. Lily was holding his hand tight, tears streaming down her face. "Listen to me, Lily. When we get outside, I want you to run into the woods. You hear me?"

"What about you?"

"You don't worry about me. Do you understand? You get far away from here. Head that way." He pointed. "Toward Jasper. Do you think you can find your way back to Ryan?"

She shook her head. "No."

He clenched his eyes tight and began coughing hard. The air inside was turning black. If they didn't leave now, they would die of smoke inhalation. One half of the barn was an inferno. They hurried to the ladder and he went down first, gun at the ready, expecting one of the strangers to lunge out at him. They never did.

"All right. Hurry up," he said, scanning the barn as he beckoned her down.

That's when two rounds erupted. They were shooting at him. Josh dropped. Staying low, he guided Lily along the far stalls toward the doorway on the western side, preparing to burst out and open fire on the first person he saw while Lily fled.

Instead, the door at the far end opened. "Josh. Lily!"

"Ryan?"

A face emerged, a rifle in hand. "C'mon. Let's go!"

He urged them out as they raced toward him. Then Josh remembered.

"My motorcycle."

"There's no time."

The intensity of the fire and smoke was overwhelming. He wasn't leaving his motorcycle there. That was their ticket out of here. Josh turned and ran back just as a large section of the barn collapsed in on itself, covering the area where his bike was. A huge gust of black smoke billowed toward him. He coughed hard, arm raised as the heat intensified.

Ryan grabbed him by the collar and hauled him out of there, dragging him away from the barn. As he did, they passed by the strangers now lying on the ground, dead.

# CHAPTER EIGHT

"*A*re you trying to get yourself killed?" Ryan bellowed before scanning the trees for more threats. He loomed over him, a figure larger than life, facing him at an angle, rifle in hand. His dark silhouette sliced into the orange blaze behind him. Josh could feel the heat coming off the roaring inferno as it chewed its way through what remained. The second half of the barn collapsed inward, sending a plume of smoke high into the starry sky. It hissed, crackled, and popped. The glow of the fire arced over the forest. Birds broke away from the trees, flying in the opposite direction.

"The bike was a gift from my mother."

"Yeah, and had I not pulled you back, you would have joined her."

He turned away from Josh to check on Lily. "You okay, sweetheart?"

She was coughing but nodded. "Here, drink this," he said, taking out a bottle of water from a backpack nearby.

Leaning back on the ground, also coughing, Josh asked, "Were you stalking us?"

"I told you it was dangerous out here," Ryan replied, stabbing a finger at the ground.

"That doesn't answer the question."

"But it proves my point, right?"

"Whatever, man."

He got up and brushed himself off.

"Look, I was making sure you and Lily were safe. Okay?"

"What, by following us?"

"If that's what it takes."

"Well, you can stop. I told you. I don't need you."

"You might not, but she does. And I'm her father."

Lily stared at them both, speechless.

"So grab your bag and let's go."

"We're not going with you."

"No? What are you going to do, Josh? Walk to Florida?"

"If that's what it takes."

"Don't be stupid."

Josh grabbed his bag and slung it over his shoulder. He reached into his pocket, took out a pack of cigarettes, and tapped one out, staring back at Ryan as if he couldn't do a damn thing. He lit the end and blew smoke his way. "Thanks for the save, man, but as I said, we can take care of ourselves." He jerked a thumb over his shoulder. "Let's go, Lily."

Ryan snatched the cigarette out of Josh's mouth and stomped on it. "Nice try, bud, but you're not taking her. You had your chance. You screwed up. She's going with me and if you want to walk so be it, but we're heading back to the truck."

Ryan strolled past him.

"What the hell is your problem, man?"

"I was about to ask you the same thing. Come on, Lily," Ryan said, extending his hand. She clasped it but Josh didn't let go of her other hand.

"My problem is you, man. You. If you think you can waltz on in here after ten years and tell us what to do, you are out of your mind. We don't even know you."

"Well, you will by the time we make it to Florida."

"We're not going with you!" He tugged on Lily but Ryan didn't let go.

"Yeah, you are."

"Lily, tell him. Tell him you're not going with him. Remember what I said about people."

"We can't trust them," she said.

"That's right."

She looked up at Ryan. He still had his steely gaze fixed on Josh. "You done bellyaching?"

"Lily." Josh pleaded with her.

"I… Um.."

"Josh. Don't do this. Don't make her choose a side, that's not your place."

"Of course it is. I've earned that right unlike you."

Ryan was beginning to lose his cool. "You are not putting her life in danger again. Now you can hate me all you want, you can tell Lily to hate me but—"

"I don't hate you," Lily interjected.

Josh looked at her as Ryan narrowed his eyes. "But you are not going to drag her down with you. Lily is going with me to Florida just as your mother requested. She's my daughter. And that's final."

"Screw you, man. Screw you!"

Josh released his grip on Lily, picked up his bag, and went to walk past him when Ryan grabbed him. He tried to pull away but Ryan held tight. "Look. I know you and I don't see eye to eye right now and that's perfectly fine. But for the sake of Lily and until we reach Florida, I would appreciate it if you show me some damn respect. I'm still your father after all. That means no swearing at me. No smoking. And no pills. Yeah, I saw them in your bag. Now you may still hate me by the time we reach Florida but it's what your mother wanted and I am going to do what she asked come hell or high water. So shelve the attitude and go get in the truck."

Josh sneered. "I hate you."

"Welcome to the club. I hated my father too."

In the truck with the window down, Josh slapped a mosquito on his neck. It was humid and hot and the night was alive with them. Brooding, he stared off into the distance, not looking once at him. The journey back to his house was tense. When they arrived, Lily was the first in the door. She looked pleased to be somewhere safe, anywhere was better than that old barn. He hated to admit to it, but for her sake he was glad. But he wasn't telling Ryan that. Once inside, Ryan set his rifle down and motioned to the back room. "You can sleep in here tonight, Lily," he said, turning on the light.

Josh stood at the door as Ryan collected some bedding from the closet and Lily looked around at some of the toys. They were for a kid younger than her, a boy. The wallpaper was old. Dated. There was a small TV, a radio and a computer. It was tidy. The whole room looked like it was frozen in time. "Whose room is this?" she asked as Ryan made the bed.

"It was meant for Josh but he never got to see it."

Ryan looked at him for a second and Josh looked away. He walked off into the living room, chewing over what he'd said. He paced for a moment and then stopped in front of a fireplace mantel and noticed several photos. He hadn't seen them. Josh picked one up. They were from when he was five or six. A couple of him and Ryan together. He was all smiles. There was one of them together by a beach. The memories were there, vague but buried far back in his mind.

Beside those were a few others of his father dressed in army gear. Holding a rifle alongside some other military guys.

Josh took a seat in a recliner chair and kicked off his boots and felt himself sink. It felt good to be out of that godforsaken barn. Lily came out and put her arms around Josh's neck, still coughing a little. "Night, Josh."

"Night, Bean. Sleep well."

"I'm glad we came back." She paused. "Are you?"

She only ever wanted to please him.

His lip curled. "If you are. That's enough for me."

She beamed.

It was happiness he hadn't seen since leaving.

She wasn't a kid to wallow in self-pity or hold a grudge like him. He could hear her talking with Ryan as he tucked her into bed. "Will it be safe on the boat?"

"You ever been on one?"

"Only a small one. Josh took me fishing a few times."

"Let me guess, you caught a fish this big."

She laughed. "No. Not that big. Maybe this size."

"Ah, like a tadpole."

She laughed again. There was more conversation, then he asked about the butterflies on her T-shirt. Lily had always loved butterflies.

"So do I call you dad now?"

Josh waited for a response. There was a pause. A little hesitation.

Ryan replied. "You can call me whatever is comfortable for you."

"Um. Uh, I guess, Ryan for now?"

"That's good too."

"Night, Ryan."

"Night, Lily."

The door closed and Ryan joined Josh in the living room. "You want a drink?"

"I'll take a beer or whiskey if you have one."

Ryan's eyebrows raised. "How's water sound?"

Josh shrugged. "Sure."

A moment later he returned with a bottle and handed it to him. He unscrewed the cap and chugged it like he was putting out a fire. The smoke had gotten into his throat and given him a dry cough. "You can use my room if you like."

"The couch is fine," Josh replied before taking another sip. "I've slept in worse places." He felt uncomfortable. Awkward even after what he'd said. Ryan sat down across from him. The memories of his father were so few that he just felt like a stranger. Josh closed his eyes.

Ryan leaned forward, hands clasped together.

"Your mother meant a lot to me. I don't expect you to understand or accept my version of the events, but I hope you'll give me a chance to explain over the coming days."

"If we live that long."

"Right." Ryan chuckled. "Who taught you to fire a gun?"

"I taught myself."

He nodded. "Is it yours?"

"No. It was mom's."

The tension in the room was thick.

"Look, I know Lily means a lot to you, Josh. And I can appreciate you wanting to do right by her and under any normal conditions I might have been inclined to let you take her but what's happening out there right now is something far greater than what is happening here, between you and me. She needs more than you. If you had died out there tonight. What would she have done? Or better question, if she'd died, what would you have done?"

He let him ponder.

"We can't always do everything on our own, Josh. Sometimes we need a little help."

"Who taught you that, the AA meetings?"

"A little. Mostly I taught myself," he said, throwing his own words back at him.

Josh allowed a smile to form.

Ryan took a deep breath.

"Well, I should turn in. It's been one hell of a day. I'll get you a blanket and pillow."

"I'm fine."

"Just in case."

He came back with the bedding and set it on the couch.

"In the morning we'll head out after breakfast. It's a long journey."

Josh nodded, not looking at him. As Ryan went to walk away, Josh asked, "About the room. Why didn't I get to see it?"

He let out a breath. "It's complicated. I needed to prove to the court that I didn't have a drinking problem. I was eager to see you. I did everything I could to see you. But in Texas, they always work in the best interest of the child when it comes to custody and access. I wanted you here, Josh, I did, but I wasn't ready. I just wasn't ready."

"The problem with drinking, did it start before or after the sexual assault?"

"You mean the allegation?" He paused to make it clear that was all it was. "After," Ryan said. His father crossed the room and dug into a wood armoire and fished out a blue folder. He handed it to Josh but he didn't take it. "Everything you need to know about the case, the allegations and charges that I was eventually cleared of years later, can be found in there. Read it, or not. I don't care, anymore." He tossed it beside him and walked out of the room. "Sleep well."

Josh heard his bedroom door close, and Josh sat in the silence, staring at the folder.

He'd only ever seen the allegations, the early stages of the charges brought against him. He never revisited or looked up his father except to see if he was on social media when he was fifteen. Josh got up and went to the window and looked out. It was pitch black outside. He returned to the sofa and laid on top of the cover. For a moment he thought about all that had occurred that evening. How close they had come to dying.

The thought of what other dangers they would encounter lingered in his mind as he picked up the folder, flipped it open, turned on a small lamp, and began reading.

# CHAPTER NINE

July 6

ewton, Texas, felt more like a town than a city.
A speck on the map with just over two thousand people, it existed roughly twenty minutes south-east of Jasper. It had been a long time since Ryan had been welcome there. Thanksgiving. Golden leaves. Turkey. Laughter. Warm hugs. Gratitude. A real sense of family. That had always been his experience. But not the last time.

The last time was cold, distant, full of accusing eyes. The warm yearly event that at one time drew together a close-knit family was destroyed after he was thrown under the bus by a student. That was the thing about accusations. It didn't matter if someone was innocent or not. Once the rumor mill was in motion, any attempt at explaining only fell on deaf ears. He recalled the way his brother looked at him. It was different after that day.

There were words of support, and what might even be considered empathy, but the eyes didn't lie. Somewhere in the back of their minds, they were all asking the same question.

Did he really do it?

He saw that same look in Josh's eyes. It was unmistakable.

How times had changed.

But that was the fall season. They were now in the height of summer when the temperature rarely dipped below the 80-degree mark. His brother ran a motel and RV park on the outskirts of town set back from Highway 190. He couldn't leave without letting him know about the option of safety in the south.

Few words were exchanged the next day. Ryan saw the folder lying open on the floor next to the sofa. They'd packed up the truck early that morning with supplies, enough to last a few days. Ryan drove. Lily slept. Josh stared absently out the passenger window.

It was a short drive and made easy by the lack of traffic on the road. Homes they passed were quiet. Many boarded up. Some spray-painted with the word INFECTED. The few people on the street moved with purpose, not lingering. Strip malls were empty. Storefronts had boarded-up windows. With the pathogen in full swing, few ventured out, the brave ones that did carried a rifle or a handgun. Fortunately, he hadn't run into any trouble until the previous night. He'd seen the two strangers from afar and watched them enter the barn. Witnessed them trying to harm his kids. Whether they were infected or simply looking to take advantage of a teenager and a young girl traveling alone, he'd had no other choice than to put them down.

He hadn't slept much that night. His mind kept going back to that split-second decision to shoot them. They never saw it coming. It wasn't guilt he felt, as they gave him no other choice. It was something else. Disappointment? His humanity, perhaps? His mind was reeling from an act that wasn't an everyday occurrence. They were the first lives he'd taken. It would stay with him for some time. He couldn't shake the feeling that came with their death.

"Why are we stopping here?" Josh asked.

"To see your Uncle Tommy. You probably don't remember him."

They passed several vehicles that looked as if they'd been in a head-on collision. The doors were open. Attacks on strangers were becoming more frequent by the day as desperation set in among the afflicted to spread and stop the aging. They would do whatever it took to rid themselves of the pathogen. Kill anyone who got in the way. Josh touched the radio's scanner button, searching for updates on the situation, potentially hazardous areas to avoid.

In the first week, people were calling into radio stations and keeping them abreast of the situation but that had slowed to a crawl. Hospitals were turned into quarantine zones and funeral parlors were no longer offering service. They couldn't. Fear of contracting the unknown pathogen was warranted.

Static came out of the speakers this time.

"It's getting worse," he said, turning it off.

"Uncle Tommy. Does he have kids?" Josh asked.

"Many, they just don't live with him."

"Was he busted too?"

"No, Josh. He's just had several failed relationships."

"Sounds like it runs in the family," Josh added, looking out the window. Ryan wasn't sure how to respond. Navigating the teenage years was something parents gradually eased into, like moving out of the shallow into the deep end of a pool. By the time you got there, you might have felt like you were kicking water more than before, but you learned to adapt.

This, on the other hand, was akin to being dropped headfirst into a wild ocean.

Birds wheeled overhead, some diving down to search for roadkill.

Thick green trees and brush framed the sides of the highway like impenetrable walls before opening up to wide-open farmland until he saw the familiar blue sign: Willow Springs Motel and RV Park.

Ryan turned left into the lot, pulling up outside the office. To the right were newer suites. Farther down from the office were the main lodgings. All the rooms of the motel were ground level, with a log cabin exterior and green metal roofing. There were several RVs parked nearby. Like most of the landscape since the event, plants, bushes, and lawns had overgrown. Weeds dominated.

"You tight with him?" Josh asked.

"We were."

"Seems like a big risk we're taking."

"He's family. We look out for each other."

"I wouldn't know anything about that," he replied, looking out the window.

"Yes you would," Ryan added, glancing at Lily.

There was silence.

"And what if he has the aging?"

"That's why you're going to stay in the vehicle. If anything happens, you get the hell out."

He let the truck idle in front of the office and got out, taking his rifle with him. The building looked like an old Western saloon with a wood porch and tall posts holding up the extended roofing. It had wood paneling and a black metal roof. A rugged metal star set between two large lights was the central point. A few white Adirondack chairs were out front. A blue and white sign read: POOL For use by residents & guests only. Below that was a red mailbox where guests could drop off their keys. A small wind chime jangled. A garbage can nearby looked as if it hadn't been emptied in weeks. Wasps were buzzing around it. He scanned the area. It was deserted. There was a white pickup out front that belonged to Tommy. Ryan went to the window of the office, cupped a hand, and peered in. It was dark. The door was locked.

He rapped his knuckles against the pane of glass. "Tommy? It's Ryan."

He listened and watched for movement. Nothing. His stomach dropped at the thought of what might have happened. He rarely left the property.

He glanced back at Josh who shrugged.

Ryan tried again then skirted around the side of the building, knocking on a few more windows.

"Ryan!" Josh called out, getting out of the truck. His son pointed away from the office. Ryan made his way back to find Tommy standing by one of the RVs. A sense of relief washed over him. He still looked the same. Trimmed black hair. A goatee. Built like a bull. No noticeable difference in age. Not a day over forty-five. Like him he was armed, shotgun in hand. He wore a decal gray T-shirt, tight black jeans, and boots.

There was a second or two while he registered who he was staring at before he called out to him while cupping a hand over his eyes to block the glare of the sun. "That you, Ryan?"

"In the flesh."

"What are you doing here?"

"Is that any way to welcome your brother?"

"Depends. You infected?"

"Do you honestly think I would come here if I was?"

"Actually yes. Yes, I do."

"That's in the past, Tommy."

"Who's that with you?"

He glanced to Josh who had his door open and was standing on the edge of the truck's side step, observing over the top of the truck. "Oh, you remember Josh. My son."

Tommy squinted. "I'll be damned. Is he clean?"

"Of course he is."

"Can't be too careful." He scanned the property before beckoning them over.

Lily was still asleep but Josh gave her a shake to wake her up.

"We're here," Josh said.

"Where?"

"You'll see," Ryan said, helping her out. She held on to his hand. His dwarfed hers. At the RV Tommy kept his distance but had them step inside. He closed the door behind him and locked it. Inside it smelled musty. There was an ashtray on the table with a cigarette burning. Several open bottles of beer. A radio tuned into some station that was playing low in the background.

"You're his brother?" Josh asked.

"That's right."

"But you're black?" he added, his eyes darting between them. "Not that there's anything wrong with that but..."

Tommy went over to a mirror on the wall and glanced at himself. "Well isn't that something. All this time I thought I was white." He burst out laughing and Ryan chuckled. "Didn't you tell them you were adopted, Ryan?"

Ryan glanced at Josh.

"They only arrived yesterday."

"Is that right," he said, taking a seat. "Been a long time since I have seen you, kid. And who is this beautiful butterfly?"

"My daughter. Lily."

Tommy looked up from Lily to Ryan. "You are just full of surprises, aren't you, brother? Why didn't you tell me about her?"

"Because I only found out yesterday."

Ryan went to the window and looked out.

Tommy nodded and stared at the two of them. "Shoot. Where are my manners? Can I get you guys a drink? Coke? Sprite?" he said, walking to the back of the RV and opening the fridge. He held out their options and Lily took one.

"What do you say, Lily?" Josh said.

"Thank you."

"Ah, you are more than welcome, sweetheart." He grabbed two beers and offered one to Ryan.

"I don't do that anymore."

"Huh," Tommy replied. "Things must be better if you're turning down a beer." He turned to Josh. "If the young one wants to watch TV. You can. The remote is over there." He pointed then gestured to Ryan. "Pull up a chair." Tommy sank behind the table.

"You talked to mom?"

Tommy swallowed a mouthful of beer and set the bottle down. He picked up a burning cigarette and took a hit. "She called me eight days ago. Told me not to come out."

Ryan brought a hand over his face. "Shit."

His father had passed several years ago. He was pleased he didn't have to witness this.

"You alone here?"

"No, there are some guests. They're too scared to leave the lodgings."

"Had any trouble yet?" Ryan asked.

"Not to speak of but then we aren't in town, right? What's it like out there?"

"Every bit as bad as they are saying on the news. Listen, I came by to let you know that there is a safe place down in Florida. Boats are taking people to an island. I'm heading there. Taking the kids."

"Elizabeth?"

Ryan shook his head. Tommy looked over to Josh and Lily. "Poor bastards. First you. Then this."

"Hey. I thought you weren't going to bring that up."

"Hard to forget. I'm just saying it can't be easy. How's it been with them?"

"Every bit what I expected and more."

"That good?"

Ryan chuckled and downed his beer in one gulp, quenching his thirst. "Come with us."

"And leave all this behind?"

"Tommy, this is spreading faster than they can contain. You know what the government might eventually do to stop it. Do you want to be here for that? There are already curfews in effect. Martial law and widespread attacks. It might not have found its way to your doorstep today but you can be sure it will soon. And realistically, how long can you last here?"

Tommy looked tired. No doubt he wasn't getting sleep. No one was. He tapped ash into an ashtray and got up and crossed the RV to look outside. "These boats. Who's running the show?"

Ryan shrugged. "I don't know exactly. Elizabeth told me about them."

"And you believed her?" He laughed. "I thought she was dead?" Tommy glanced at Josh.

"She is. Look, it's what she wanted. Her parents are in Florida. At least on the water, we stand a chance while they chase their tail and find a cure."

"I figured I would wait it out," Tommy said, returning to his seat. "I mean, realistically how long are we looking at before the infected die out? Seems like this pathogen or whatever it is has a shelf life."

"If the infected self-isolated. Sure. But that's not what's happening."

In the background they could hear a news channel playing, reminding them of the uncontained situation.

Widespread panic had gripped large cities. It was no longer confined to the USA. It had gone international. Italy. Germany. Spain. France. The UK. Australia. The clock was ticking on people's lives. As people aged rapidly, reportedly two years per day, for some that meant death would come sooner than others. Either way, if infected even a newborn would be sixty within thirty days. "Change the channel, Josh," Tommy said.

"No, leave it on," Ryan said, making his way over and observing it with interest. "You can't wait this out, Tommy. Look."

"I don't want to."

"Look!" He turned the screen, realizing his brother had been downplaying the gravity of the situation. Josh placed his hand over his sister's eyes. "This is why this won't fizzle out. People are spreading it so they can survive."

"Then the next ones will die out."

It was Josh that spoke up this time. "That's not how it appears to work. Unlike other viruses where the immune response from past infection reduces the risk of catching it again within x number of months. The CDC has confirmed reports of reinfection occurring within weeks of transmitting it to someone else. I saw a video too. So you get it, you give it away, you might be good for a week or two but then capable of being a host again."

"And so the cycle continues," Ryan added. "That's why you can't just hole up here."

Tommy sank back into his seat. The weight of it sinking in. He wasn't alone in this mindset of waiting it out. Typically that's how the average approach to tackling a virus worked, but this was no ordinary pathogen.

"So you're saying this is here permanently?"

"Until they find a cure. It's death or pass it on to someone else and hope you don't get reinfected. And the older you are, the fewer days and less strength you'll have to give it away."

He could see his brother coming to terms with it. No one wanted to believe that others would go out of their way to spread this but it was that or die. "You are saying once it spreads, the aging stops in the person who transmitted it? How can that be?"

Josh piped up. "The World Health Organization hasn't released an official statement. Online, people are saying it's because it's a nanotech virus. They use nanobots in medicine. Tiny machines were designed to prevent, treat, and repair damaged cells and organs, and wipe out diseases as well as slow aging. Except we assume something went wrong."

"No shit!' Tommy got up and collected another beer. "As things always do when humanity gets involved. God. We're essentially guinea pigs. Human trials."

"Whether this was released intentionally or not, I don't know about that," Ryan said. "But what I do know is if we stick around, eventually they'll stop delivering food and supplies and will take drastic measures. You know what that means. They won't ask who's infected and who isn't."

"Are you talking about mass genocide?"

"I'm talking about the needs of the many outweighing the needs of the few."

CHAPTER TEN

10 days earlier
June 26

*I*t was called the AGING Alert mobile app. Touted as a way for individuals and the community to stay safe. It was rolled out before the internet became intermittent. With contact tracing being almost impossible to police, the CDC and the World Health Organization turned to neighbors, family members, the entire country. They expected everyone to report those who had been exposed to the Aging Syndrome to the public health authorities. Every day the app would check a list of random codes from those who had informed the app that they'd been exposed to the pathogen. This in turn would notify others to avoid certain areas.

It was good in theory.

Hotlines were provided and with curfews in full effect

and the National Guard units responding to volatile areas, it showed a determination unlike anything seen before.

But the app only worked to the extent that people knew about it or wanted to use it.

Fortunately, they had a plan for that too.

The announcement about reporting others was pushed to all phones, radio, and TVs, using the Emergency Alert System.

It was meant to be the first step toward containment.

If people didn't have cell phones they could use a tablet, computer, or one of the local alert stations being set up in communities. The problem was getting people to use it when no cure had been announced. It made people wary — concerned that big brother was looking to swoop in and handle matters as they pleased.

Initially, they were reassured that their privacy was protected and that GPS was not being used to track a user's location, or for any other reason but to track the outbreak.

*There is no way for us to know anything beyond what a person choses to share.*

They lied.

A flurry of posts on social media soon made the rounds, warning people to not use it. Videos were posted of EIS officers dispatched by the CDC along with soldiers wearing BSL 4 suits arriving at homes and dragging people out. Where they were taking them was anyone's guess. Death camps are what some suggested.

Conveniently enough, those warning posts vanished as quickly as they appeared.

With fewer people choosing to use the app, that's when the internet went black for a short time.

Many believed it was done by the country itself — a nationwide form of censorship to muzzle the outspoken and silence conspiracy theorists. All commenting on articles was turned off. It was reported on TV that it was a situation facing the entire country and it had nothing to do with censorship, but no one was buying it. Some were even saying keywords were flagged to avoid any opposing content appearing online. It was hard to know what to believe but it was getting more difficult to hear the truth.

After surviving the run for food at the grocery store in town, Josh never told his mother what happened. She would have only worried. Instead, he remained tight-lipped. Besides, there was no doubt that she was watching the chaos unfold from inside her room.

With every passing day, she was getting older.

Tired. Weak.

The nosebleeds were becoming more frequent. She said it was the body's response. Unable to handle the speed at which it was aging. It was breaking down.

"We need to talk about where you'll go."

"We have. You sent me the address. I got it."

"No, I mean if no one is there. There's a chance that it might not go to plan in which case I want you to head to Florida. To mama and pops." That's what he called them when he was younger. He hadn't seen them in several years. At one time they traveled down a few times a year or his grandparents came this way, but as age caught up with them it was getting more difficult to endure the trip.

"Why don't we just go directly to them? It would be faster."

"Because you must go to this address first."

"Why?"

"I can't tell you right now. You need to trust me." A pause followed. "Josh, I know I've made mistakes as a mother but I've always tried to do my best by you two."

"Don't talk like that."

"Like what?"

"Like you're not going to be around."

There was silence. "Listen, there will come a time when you'll need to leave me."

"I'm not leaving."

More silence.

"You need to do something for me, son. You won't want to. You will question it. You may even hate me for it but I need you to do it. I don't expect you to understand but one day you will."

"If you are suggesting what I think you are. Nope. There has to be another way."

"I'm not spreading this to survive, Josh."

"Why not?! Everyone else is," he yelled back.

There was silence.

"I don't care what everyone else does."

"What about us? Huh? What about Lily?"

"I'm thinking about both of you."

"Are you?" he said loudly through the door. "Because if you were, you would be looking at every avenue to survive, not die. It's not your time!"

He heard her chuckle. "Don't you think that's what everyone says when their number comes up?"

"No. Some people have already lived a long life and are ready."

"Yeah? What about those with cancer? Those murdered? Those who end up in an accident? Don't you think that they wish they could live longer, Josh? Listen, when it's my time—"

"Don't you say that. Don't you dare say that! This is not how you were meant to go out."

"How do you know?"

"I just do."

"You're only sixteen, honey."

He paced the hallway and banged a hand against the door. "Why do you always do that? Act as if I don't know anything."

"That's not what I meant, Josh, and you know it. You have your whole life ahead of you. When I was sixteen, there were things that I thought I knew but then later realized were false."

"You're not making any sense."

She sighed. Silence followed.

A few minutes later, she said, "Listen to me. Go look in the backyard."

He clenched his eyes shut and groaned. "Why?"

"Just do it. I want to show you something."

He grumbled and relented. He made his way down the hallway and she called him on the phone so she didn't have to shout. "Do you remember mowing the lawn last summer and telling me about how some of the grass was overly thick and lush in areas and was causing the mower to stop, and in other parts of the yard it was thinner, patchy, and even non-existent?"

"And?"

"That's like life, Josh. Some people get to live a lush, long life, others half of that, and some barely make it out of the ground. Just like grass. There's no rhyme or reason. You can say it's unfair but it is what it is. We're born, we live and we die. That's it. And the cycle repeats."

"What has any of that got to do with you or us?"

"Josh, we don't decide how many years we get with someone but we can decide how we spend that short time with them. You might not understand this now, hon, but you will later."

Josh groaned. He was about to say something when Lily called out. "I'm hungry. Anything to eat?"

"Lily, you have two feet. I'm not your servant. Get up and get it yourself."

"Look after her, Josh. She's going to need you."

"I need you! We need you."

He hung up on his mother, clenching the phone tight. He understood that she didn't want to turn herself in, as the health officials would return and collect them too, but if they didn't have the pathogen, they couldn't be held. Could they? He was beginning to realize why people were going out of their way to transmit the pathogen to others even if they could get reinfected weeks later. It meant more years, more time and when all was said and done, that was all humanity really had in this life. Time. No amount of riches could give you additional years. No station in life afforded you more of the most valuable commodity.

Lily walked out of the kitchen with bread in her hand. "Josh!"

His mind was lost in the future. What he would do and how he would raise Lily.

"What is it?"

"There's a vehicle coming up the driveway."

His stomach tensed. "Go to where I told you to hide."

"Why? Who is it?'

"Just go!"

She scurried away.

His mother had told Josh that someone from the hospital might show up. Contact tracing and all. When the incident occurred in town, most weren't aware of what was causing it, how it transferred or how quickly the pathogen was spreading across the country. That's why she figured no one had shown up, that or disorganization. The event was spiraling out of control faster than they could deal with it.

Josh ran down the hallway to the gun cabinet and took out a hunting rifle. His mother had learned how to shoot from her father when she was young. While she didn't have the time to do it, she still kept guns in the house because of living alone. As he was loading the bolt-action rifle, he heard the crunch of gravel under tires outside. As he passed his mother's bedroom she said, "Josh, don't do anything hasty."

"I'll do whatever is necessary."

"Josh!"

A knock at the front door followed.

All entry points were locked and protected by additional furniture.

He checked in on his sister to make sure she was where he'd told her to go before he made his way back to the front door. There was no way to see him on the other side. He expected anyone who approached the home to have a good reason as they were out of the way. They weren't part of a suburb, a small neighborhood, or sandwiched between neighbors who were within earshot. He slowed his pace as more heavy knocks ensued. "Who is it?" he called out.

"Josh. It's Mrs. Banks. Danny's mother. Your neighbor?"

He remembered her. Danny was another kid that went to his high school. He'd often see him at the bus stop in the mornings. His parents were overly protective. The kind of folks that would have escorted him to his first date if they had their way.

"What do you want?"

"I saw you down at the grocery store the other day. Everything okay with you?"

"Fine."

"And your mother?"

"She's good."

"It's just I thought that she would have uh… been the one… to collect the groceries." He could hear movement outside. Gravel. It sounded like she wasn't alone. Multiple footsteps moved around the house. He saw shadows behind the curtains. He'd closed all of them to prevent anyone from looking in.

"She's working. A lot of overtime right now."

"Huh. That's odd. Isn't that her SUV?"

"A work colleague picked her up. She'll be home later."

He heard movement behind him and turned to see Lily standing there. Josh glared at her. He mouthed the words, *go back.*

"And your sister? Lily okay?"

This woman was sure persistent or... acting as a distraction. He heard the doorknob rattle. "Well, I brought your mother an apple crumble. I heard about the incident in town. Poor thing. She must still be in shock."

*Shit.* She knew about it. Who else did? Word traveled fast.

"Mrs. Banks. I appreciate it. Just leave it outside."

"I'd prefer not. The bugs and all. Couldn't you just open the door, Josh?"

"I'm not dressed. I just got out of the shower. Sorry." It was quick thinking but that still didn't deter her.

"Then maybe Lily could take this."

"She's asleep."

"In the middle of the afternoon?" Her voice was deadpan. She wasn't buying it for one minute. The door rattled hard. Mrs. Banks banged on the door. His phone buzzed. It was from his mother. Her text told him not to open the door.

"Open up, Josh. This is very rude."

He said nothing and backed up, making his way into the kitchen, where he considered taking a large knife from the holder on the counter then opted not to. If whoever was with her was infected, an open wound, well, that wouldn't be good. Instead, he set his rifle down and collected his metal baseball bat from the closet. The banging persisted as did her demanding he open the door. She was even threatening to tell his mother. He found that humorous. Life with her must have been hell. He pitied her son. That poor bastard.

"If you don't leave, I'll call the cops."

A pane of glass shattered and he darted through the

kitchen to the side door where a hand was reaching in to unlock the door. Josh brought up the bat and in one fast downswing, he broke the guy's hand. One strike, that was all it took. The man fell backward, howling like a banshee.

The front door sounded like it was being kicked in. He pulled back the drapes from the side door and saw the man groaning in agony. It was her husband. A council member in town. What an asshole. He was nursing a swollen, battered hand. He scurried away while at the front door the banging increased. Someone lobbed a brick at the window of the living room, smashing it. That was it. He snatched up the rifle and didn't think twice. He aimed at the front door and fired a round, then darted into the living room and squeezed off two more rounds. He didn't know if he hit anyone as the curtains were blocking his view, but he certainly made his point clear. He fully expected them to turn tail and flee but they were driven by desperation.

It went quiet for a minute or two, and then they started unloading slugs at the door. It was a pump-action shotgun.

"Open the door, Josh. We don't want to hurt you."

"Oh, no, you just want to give me a VIRUS!" He returned fire, squeezing off two more rounds through the door, and then ducked back behind the wall. That's when he heard more glass break. This time it was coming from the sunroom at the back of the house.

He knew if they got in, that would be it.

Moving fast, he peered around the doorway and saw their oldest son Brad, who now looked even older. Oh, yeah, that's why. This was about him. Josh didn't want to kill him. He wasn't a murderer, at least not yet. Instead, he fired off one round shattering the glass. The bullet struck Brad in the leg. He hit the ground and cried out in agony, clutching his thigh. His parents came around and wanted to help but touching his body, getting close was a death sentence.

So much for parental sacrifice.

All that talk at parent meetings, city hall, helping the youth of our generation.

What a crock of crap.

They valued their own life over his.

Josh fired another round, this time they got the message.

Their son hobbled away, gripping a bloody leg, while the husband nursed a broken hand. That would teach them to think twice about coming around here again. He waited and watched them get back into the vehicle and reverse out at high speed. That was the moment he knew his mother was right about leaving. He couldn't stay here. It wasn't safe anymore. He might have been able to hold them off this time but others would eventually show up and when they did, he might not be as fortunate.

## CHAPTER ELEVEN

July 6

"There's strength in numbers," Tommy said, trying to convince Ryan that they should let the few remaining people at the motel tag along. Josh knew where his uncle was going with this but he agreed with his father. It held too many problems. Besides, trusting strangers went against everything his mother had said before they left. *Don't trust anyone.* He'd already broken that rule with Ryan and now Tommy but he figured they were family and she'd sent him here.

"If we were staying, maybe, but traveling together? C'mon Tommy, not only would that attract a lot of attention, I didn't come here to turn this journey into a damn convoy. Besides, we don't know these people. When did you see them last?"

He shrugged. "A few days ago."

"Yeah, and they probably have family, loved ones, people who are expecting them to return. Now we open this thing up to them and they might want to take a detour and collect other family members. No. We don't have time for that. We have until the tenth of this month to reach St. George Island. That's five days from now, bud." He took a deep breath. "And there is no telling what the roads are like out there, or how much room they have on those boats."

"Then why go? What do you even know about this island, brother? Who owns it?" Tommy shot back.

"I don't know. Look, if Elizabeth felt it was safe enough for our kids, I trust her."

Tommy laughed. "You trust her now," he muttered. "At the very least the people here deserve to know."

"So leave them a note," Ryan added.

"I can't do that."

"Of course you can."

Tommy groaned. "I still think having them with us is better than not."

"Too many people means too many mouths to feed, too many who could disagree. Too many things that could go wrong!" Ryan replied. "I'm sorry, it's out of the question. I have these two to think about. I'm not endangering them."

Tommy ran a hand over his face and opened the door of the RV and stepped out.

"Then I need to stay."

Ryan lifted a hand to his face and ran it over his head. "This is about this damn motel, isn't it? It's not even about them."

"Ryan, I built this place from the ground up. My entire life is in this motel."

"Yeah, and if you don't get to safety soon, you won't be alive to enjoy what little days remain."

"That's you. Not me."

Josh frowned. *What was that supposed to mean?*

"You really don't make life easy, Tommy," Ryan said.

Tommy went about emptying the black and gray tanks on the RV. He opened up the side of the RV and took out a green tube and attached it to the RV and then prepared to use a large black slinky to guide the hose into the hole in the ground. He continued talking while he worked. "Forgive me, brother, if you think I'm being ungrateful but the way I see it... you are talking about not trusting strangers, and yet that's exactly what you're suggesting by heading down to a place on the word of your ex-wife. At least here, I know how things work." He dropped the hose into the hole then yanked on the black tank valve to empty it. It made a flushing noise as it emptied. "I'm far enough outside of town that the few people heading this way are probably travelers trying to get out of Texas or Louisiana."

"Yeah, and where do you think they'll stop to look for supplies?"

"I'll deal with that if it happens," he said, not looking at Ryan.

Ryan knew it was a losing game. "You got enough food?"

"Do I have enough?" He laughed as if it was obvious.

"Josh, Lily, get your things, we're leaving."

"Nice meeting you, Uncle Tommy," Josh said as he led Lily out of the RV.

"You too, kiddo. I'm sorry it wasn't under better

circumstances." He ruffled Lily's hair. "And you, butterfly, you take care."

Josh could see it bothered his father. He couldn't let it go. Gesturing for them to get in the truck, he handed the keys to Josh and then returned to Tommy's RV. Within seconds the two of them were in a heated argument. Josh couldn't make out what they were saying as Tommy waved him off and went inside the RV. Ryan followed. Josh expected it was stuff he couldn't or didn't want to say with them around. Lily peered around her brother.

"Why won't Uncle Tommy go with us?'

"No idea, Bean."

It was easier for them as they had nothing to go back to, but this was his uncle's business, his career, his life.

Josh fired up the engine and turned on the air conditioning while they waited. He surveyed the office, and some of the suites off to the right that looked like newer additions to the lodge. He turned the radio on and scanned stations looking for an update. There was nothing except white noise. It was an older model truck with a cassette player. There was one part sticking out so Lily leaned forward and pushed it in. Country music blared out of the speakers so he turned it down. Josh turned to his phone while Lily bopped her head from side to side, enjoying the tunes.

He'd been hoping to get hold of Callie but had gotten no response in the last few days. He could only hope that she hadn't suffered the fate that so many had. Over the past week, more people were realizing the only key to their survival was to infect others. No other virus acted like that but this did. It brought a whole new meaning to spreading infection.

Staying abreast of what was developing, he searched for news on Louisiana and the outbreak. Within twenty minutes they would be crossing into another state and he figured it would be wise to know what lay ahead.

It was more of the same.

The situation was only getting worse.

Why would anyone self-isolate when there was a way to stop the aging by giving it to your neighbor? The images were gruesome. People defending their homes. Shooting anyone who tried to get near them. The infected tackling unsuspecting people to the ground. Driving vehicles into other vehicles only to get out and pass it to the unconscious. Riots erupted in major cities as the National Guard tried to gain control of looters taking advantage of the chaos.

Josh had his head down when he was startled by a gun erupting.

Glancing sideways, he saw Tommy lunge at some strangers, forcing them to the ground with a rifle in hand, as another lay on the ground not moving. Several more people were trying to get into the RV, pulling on a closed door. A second later, his father emerged, clambering out of the top of the RV, a gun in hand. "JOSH!" he bellowed. The gaze of several people turned and they began running toward them.

His eyes bulged.

Fear spread.

Josh dropped his phone and slid into the driver's seat, hitting the lock.

He told Lily to do the same as he shifted the vehicle into reverse and backed out, swerving the truck around. There didn't seem to be more than six. They dashed forward, one dived onto the hood, and began cracking the front windshield with a tire iron.

Lily screamed.

Josh punched the gas and the truck lurched forward barreling into the group, knocking them over like bowling pins. The truck bounced, sending the guy on the hood off.

Adrenaline surged through his veins as he yanked the wheel to the right and then the left to get another guy, who was bleeding from his nose, off the top of the truck. A second or two and the man slid sideways, disappearing out of view.

"Hold on," he shouted to Lily as he brought the truck around the back of the RV and slowed just enough for his father to jump off into the back of the truck bed. Ryan smacked a hand on the side of the truck.

"Go!"

He turned the wheel, coming around the RV, but then the unthinkable happened.

Josh swerved to avoid hitting a young child, and as he did, the truck went down an embankment just beyond the parking lot and the engine died. "No, no, no," he said, turning the key. It spluttered. The engine coughed.

All the while, Ryan was shooting at those dashing toward them. "Any time now, Josh!"

"What do you think I'm doing?"

The engine caught and roared to life. He jammed into reverse and the wheels spun.

The back end smashed into two people, sending them underneath.

Behind them, gunfire echoed. A woman plowed into the passenger side of the vehicle, taking a brick and hitting the window. Lily screamed, leaning toward Josh, staying away from the window. The glass cracked, then the truck bit into the dirt and bounced onto the asphalt. In his rearview mirror, he saw his uncle swinging on several of them.

It was too late for him. He'd been touched.

Josh jammed the gear stick into drive and tore out of the lot, never letting up on the accelerator until Ryan smacked on the window and told him to pull over.

When they were far enough away, he slowed the truck.

As soon as it stopped, Josh got out. Ryan was pacing. "Shit. Damn it." He slammed a fist into the side of the truck. "If he'd just listened to me." Josh looked up the road. It was empty. No one was following.

"What the hell happened? Where did they come from?"

"Where do you think?" he asked, revealing his frustration.

Still clutching his rifle, Ryan lowered to a crouch at the edge of the road, running a hand over his head. Josh could hear him cursing under his breath. He looked back in the vehicle. Lily looked traumatized. This was becoming all too real for her. Tears streamed down her cheeks.

"I want mom."

"Hey. Hey," he said, reaching across the driver's seat to her. "I'm here. What did I say?"

She struggled to get the words out.

"Bean, what did I say?"

"You won't let anything happen to me."

He held her hand tight. "That's right."

Glancing out of the rear window at his father pacing, he closed the driver's side door and went around. Ryan was trying to come to grips with it all.

Josh didn't know whether he should say something or not. It was his father's brother after all. He'd seen Tommy make contact. Throwing himself at the two individuals trying to get in. He'd put himself before his brother long enough for him to climb out the top and escape.

"It happened so fast," Ryan said, not even looking at Josh. "I was talking with him. Finally getting him to see reason when one of them entered the RV."

Ryan ran a hand over his beard.

There was a long pause. Josh continued looking warily up the road. "Did anyone touch you?"

"No," Ryan shot back.

Josh nodded and Ryan placed a hand on his shoulder. "You did the right thing, son."

Hearing that didn't sit well with him. It didn't feel right.

"We should get moving," Josh added, tossing the keys to him and then getting in the passenger side. His father waited out there a minute longer before he got in and they took off heading south down U.S. 190 toward the border of Louisiana. It was quiet. As they drove, Josh glanced at his father then back at the road.

"If you have something to say, say it," Ryan said.

"Uncle Tommy said you were adopted."

Ryan nodded. "It's a long story. Let's just say my parents weren't the best. My father, well... I ended up in the foster system and Tommy's parents took me in and eventually adopted me. I was young. Not much older than Lily."

Josh nodded.

The road was barren for the most part in the short drive across the border.

Ten minutes down the road, Ryan turned on the radio. It was mostly static but now and again, it would pick up a station. As they saw a large "Welcome to Louisiana" sign, they tuned into KM27.01. It was a local station coming out of Merryville, a tiny town near the border about eighteen miles southeast of Newton, Texas. An older-timer came over the speaker. "And to y'all out there. I can't say much because the infected are listening but there are safe zones out there. Remember. When in doubt, get out. If they're bleeding from the nose. If they have the rash. Don't go near them. For you who are infected. Godspeed. Stay safe, folks."

Ryan shook his head as he turned it off.

"What did your mother tell you about Florida?"

"Not much."

"She must have shared something. She wouldn't have asked me to take you down there without divulging the situation you were heading into."

"All she said is it's where our grandparents are. That they were alive. That they have a boat. That others have boats and they're using them to stay out on the water and keep their distance from others. That there is some island or islands that are being used as safe zones."

They passed through Merryville with relative ease. Ryan kept off the main stretch and took some of the side roads. The few people they passed were either making a run to get food from whatever was being distributed from stores or they were carriers of the pathogen out to spread it, trying to gain some years before the virus robbed them of what little they had left.

"How much gas do we have?" Josh asked.

"Enough for a while."

"I need to use a washroom," Lily said.

"You'll have to hold it," Ryan said.

"I can't."

"Why didn't you say something back in the last town?"

"I didn't need it then," she replied.

"The next town is ten minutes."

"I can't hold it," she said, crossing her legs.

Josh looked at Ryan. "Pull over to the side of the road."

They were in the middle of nowhere. A lonely stretch of road between two towns where homes were absent and all that could be seen was miles of road and thick forest on either side. "Ryan! Pull over!" Josh said.

Ryan sighed.

After what they'd just been through back in Newton, he understood Ryan's hesitation to stop even if there was no one around. He eased up on the gas and swerved to the edge of the road.

"Okay, make it quick."

Lily hopped out and Josh shuffled over.

"I can't do it with you looking," she said.

Lily squatted at the side of the truck in the knee-high brush while he and Ryan looked at the road ahead. "How long have you been sober?" Josh asked.

"Eighteen months, two weeks, and four days."

"I read the material in the folder."

"And?"

Josh didn't say anything.

Ryan chuckled. "You wouldn't be the first to not believe me. It's okay."

"Is that why you and mom separated?"

"That and other things. But you could say that was the straw that broke the camel's back." He brought his window down and a gentle breeze blew in. "Did your mom ever talk about me?"

"Not really."

"Smart. It was such a mess, Josh. I wanted things to work out but it just all collapsed in on itself. And these things aren't resolved quickly. Your mother tried. I will give her that. We both did. I don't hold any animosity toward her for what she did. She did what was best for you in light of the situation. A new start. A place where no one knew her, you or me."

He was too young to remember. The memories were vague, fragmented, like trying to make sense of a kaleidoscope. He was about to reply when Lily let out a bellowing scream. He jumped out of the truck, expecting to see someone, but it was just her, gripping her leg, her pants still down. A snake slithered away into the brush. Josh caught sight of it. Its pattern was unmistakable.

"What is it?" Ryan yelled, coming around the other side.

At first, there was panic. Confusion even.

"Copperhead."

Then it turned to terror when Lily turned and showed the bite on the back of her leg. She was crying uncontrollably, her anguished screams piercing the air. Josh scooped her up and double-timed it back to the passenger side. He pulled up the pant legs to cover her as he placed her in the vehicle. With not a second to lose, Ryan crushed the accelerator and the truck took off speeding toward the next town of Singer, Louisiana.

Lily screamed as venom coursed through her young body.

# CHAPTER TWELVE

5 days earlier
July 1

No one was prepared to lose a parent before their time. Before this, you were lucky if you got eighty years, now, depending on a person's age, it was days. It wasn't meant to happen this way. She was meant to watch them graduate high school, cheer them on in their chosen career, be there to see them get married, and become a listening ear if they got divorced. Then, when it came time, when she was too old to take care of herself, the roles would reverse and they would become the caregiver. Eventually one day she would take her last breath and they would bury her in a plot that they could visit.

That was the natural order.

That was the way a parent goes out.

The way life was meant to end.

Not like this.

Not this soon.

"No. Absolutely not," Josh said, walking away from his mother's bedroom door. He couldn't believe what she'd said, let alone what she was suggesting. He went into the kitchen and looked out the window. His mother called him back but he refused to listen to her reasoning. He didn't want this on his conscience. It was hard enough thinking of how they would cope without her. Josh went outside and lit a cigarette as he wrestled with the inevitable. She was dying. They all were. Just she was arriving at death's door quicker than most.

"Josh, where you going?" Lily asked. He turned and blew out smoke.

"Go back inside, Lily."

"You're not leaving, are you?"

"No. Just go in." His frustration shone through. Her fears too.

She went inside and he walked the length of the driveway to the road, pushing the thoughts of his mother's request from his mind so he could finish the cigarette in peace. Gripping the handgun, and surveying the woods, he was aware that his neighbors might not be the only ones looking to get inside. Since they'd tried to break in, he'd covered the windows with panels of plywood. It wasn't perfect but at least they were able to sleep at night without fear of someone barging in. He didn't figure his neighbors would be back anytime soon.

In the weeks after the original incident in town, the situation had only gotten more out of hand.

As the way to slow the aging and stop symptoms

through infecting others became known, more people were taking matters into their own hands despite orders by state officials to self-isolate and notify them. While not everyone resorted to spreading the pathogen, the greater majority did. Desperation superseded morals and ethics when faced with imminent death.

Josh looked back at the house that had once been a sanctuary to him, a safe place. It was no longer that. If he ignored his mother's pleas she would be dead in days. Reports varied widely but most died when their heart gave out; others suffered excruciating agony as their body was unable to deal with the rapid pace of aging. He saw photos online of the dead. The worst cases had blood trickling out of their eyes, nose, and ears. It was a gruesome, slow and painful death that he wouldn't wish upon anyone.

That's why his mother wanted to go out on her terms.

She'd accepted that death was the outcome. Suicide just circumvented the suffering. She wasn't the first to do it. Suffering was the reason why some chose to take their lives. Online videos showed people after having shot, hung, or offed themselves in other creative ways. That's what that lady had tried to do the day of his release. She'd stepped out in front of a truck to end her life. Although she'd transferred the virus to his mother, it was too late for her.

Her internal injuries were too severe.

So, his mother wanted him to set a revolver outside her door, and then she would take care of the rest. Sure, he wasn't the one pulling the trigger but it still felt like he was playing a large role in killing her. She wouldn't come out and get the gun herself. She said she was too weak. The damage was done. Exposing him or Lily to what she now looked like would have scarred them for life. She didn't want them to remember her that way.

And yet she was more than prepared to let him have the memory of playing a role?

Was he meant to be cool with that?

Was he meant to just say yes without hesitation?

Of course not. She was asking for something that no mother should have to ask, and yet in many ways, how different was it from those who experienced long-term illness and decided to pursue physician-assisted suicide?

That's how she'd approached the conversation with him.

She wanted him present. She didn't want to die alone and yet she would.

His mother had sent him articles on assisted suicide and euthanasia followed by videos of loved ones there in those final moments. But this wasn't the same. She wasn't going to down a drink that would send her into a slumber. She planned on shooting herself in the head.

He pulled out his phone again, and looked at the articles, scanning each one.

Seven countries were allowing assisted suicide although it was still fiercely debated. As many argued for their right to die, more countries and states were now green-lighting it, including California. These were people whose quality of living had diminished to such an extent, and were in so much pain, that they no longer wanted to go on. He watched another video that revealed what his mother would endure if he refused. The images were hard to forget. They were filmed by those who had contracted the pathogen and were now in the final days of its grip. Josh turned down the volume as the noise of a woman's cries was too much to bear. The final moment was brutal.

He didn't want that for her.

Neither did others who chose to help them.

It was like putting a family pet out of its misery.

For those who refused, the afflicted took matters into their own hands.

Josh turned off his phone, he felt sick to his stomach as he made his way back into the house. He wouldn't give her an answer that day. Who could? His mother knew that. She'd texted him to say she understood if he wouldn't do it but asked him to think it over.

And what of Lily?

So oblivious to it all. The horror around them. The pathogen sweeping across the nation and the infected spreading it to gain extra years. Could he ever expect Lily to understand if he said yes to his mother? Would she resent him for the rest of her days?

Three weeks since his release and the TV was still broadcasting. Like any virus, they thought they could reel this in, contain and even cure it if given enough time. But time was against them. Against all the experts. People couldn't ride this out or wait a year for them to roll out some miracle vaccine. People were dying within thirty to forty days, others spreading it to buy themselves more time. What should have ended with the death of those infected didn't, and it wouldn't as long as people continued to spread it and infect others.

The closest anyone could get to understanding what it was, came from articles on Werner Syndrome and the use of nanobots in medicine. But where did it come from? Was it a biological weapon that got away from its creators? Was it the result of a failed human trial paid for by an anti-aging company? That remained unknown.

Josh monitored the news reports and stayed in contact with Callie via video conferencing and texting. Her family had like many others barricaded themselves inside and were expecting things to change.

Josh never told Callie about their mother. That would have only brought the EIS to his door. His mother had instructed him to say nothing. That when it was time, when she had mustered the courage to go through with her plan, she'd give him strict instructions.

"You're to burn the house. I don't want anyone stumbling across me."

He believed it was more than that.

It was her final wish. Her desire to make sure he couldn't return.

She didn't want him or anyone to get anywhere near her body after death. There was still a chance that when the body died, the infection would spread if it was touched. That's why virus victims were being buried in mass graves by health officials in BSL 4 suits because the strain on morgues and funeral homes would only pose a threat for further transmission. The choice was based on previous experience from the Ebola outbreak in West Africa. They'd learned then that when someone died, the body was still highly contagious.

As the days wore on, and the longer they stayed indoors, Lily's curiosity piqued and her questions increased:

Why was mom ill?

What caused it?

Couldn't their mother go to the doctor?

When could she come out of her room?

And finally, was she going to die?

Fortunately, his mother never made him answer those questions. She did it herself, in a way that only a mother could. Arms folded, Josh leaned against the doorway, listening to his mother's calming voice as Lily pressed her ear up against the door and listened. Now and again, Lily would look at him and he would smile.

He felt sorry for her.

He'd had sixteen years with his mother. She wouldn't be so fortunate.

In those final days of deciding what to do, Josh spent a great deal of time sitting outside his mother's bedroom talking with her. In many ways, he was grateful for the chance to be there when so many in life weren't with their parents at the end. Despite all she was facing, his mother didn't complain. It was as if she truly understood the value of those last days and instead allowed him to ask questions that he wanted to know. Life, love, marriage, and every-thing in between. Some of it seemed meaningless when looking down the barrel of an uncertain future but his mother believed he would survive, and one day look back on this and see the blessing.

How? At that moment he saw nothing but bleak prospects.

"Did you get all the items on the list?" She asked.

"Yes."

She'd been very specific about making sure he had certain things in the backpack, survival gear, you could say, in preparation to ride out several days on the road. A map and compass, a whistle, a first-aid kit, a signal mirror, a fire starter, a knife, cordage, fishing line and hooks, a flashlight and headlamp, a solar blanket to stay warm, food, sanitation items, tape, water filters, and a multi-purpose tool. That wasn't all, either. The bag was bulky.

He'd collected the items from other homes to avoid going into the town now that local radio had said that Vidor, Texas, was in the grip of the mysterious virus.

The CDC had released a statement saying they were doing everything in their power to find a cure. They were still advising people to stay away and notify them. But few did that. Until then the temporary cure was spreading it to others, a selfish act that was terrifying to witness as people went to great lengths to pass it on by touch, blood, or other bodily fluids.

"Mom, why won't you tell me who this is?"

He didn't think that it was his father she was sending him to, as he'd been out of their lives for so long that he wasn't even a blip on the radar. At first, he'd gotten birthday cards and Christmas gifts from him but no telephone calls, no visitation once or twice a month. Then even that stopped. After he'd found the information about his father, he'd simply accepted it was what was best. That his mother was doing what was right by them.

"I did."

"RW. What does that even mean? Who is it?"

He was six when his father exited the house. It didn't stand out in his mind as very few things did at that age. Nor did his mother nurture any memories he had. It was like his father was wiped from the slate. He never existed.

"Trust me, Josh."

She wasn't one for being vague. That wasn't her. And despite his misgivings about it all, he did trust her. He figured it was a work pal, a friend from the past, someone who could keep them safe. At that time, Florida was a secondary plan, a last-ditch effort to survive. Nothing more.

His relationship with his grandparents had been close but they were old.

The only upside to the event was that the power was still on. How long it would stay that way was anyone's guess. He couldn't imagine what it would have been like in those weeks confined to that house if they had to endure the brutal heat of Texas without air conditioning. It was the small things now that held meaning, that he and others appreciated.

Eventually, even that would be gone.

As Josh crawled on top of the bed that evening, his mind turning over what would happen to the two of them, Lily was already under the covers. Under the glow of a small hand-held lantern, Lily held out a book. He snorted. "Come on, Lily, you're too old for that."

"Please. It helps me sleep."

His mother had always done it. Although she was reaching an age where she was transitioning out of the stage of being tucked in, she liked having stories read to her or having someone there when she fell asleep. She would ask their mother. Now, she asked him.

He relented and opened it wide. Lily curled in beside him and he wrapped an arm around her. It was a picture book called *Are You My Mother?* She'd gotten it when she was five. She'd held on to it because it made her laugh.

Josh hadn't made it three pages through the book when he heard knocking.

At first, he thought it was a tree branch brushing up against the front of the house but then he heard a distinct knock as if someone was testing how firm the plywood was.

He shut off the light and told Lily to be still.

She immediately became scared.

"Josh, don't leave me."

"I won't let anything happen to you."

The house was as secure as he could make it in the days after his neighbors tried to get in but that didn't mean it was Fort Knox. He slid off the bed and made his way over to the hallway. Moving quickly he made it down to his mother's room, to where he could hear the noise.

"Mom?" he whispered through the door.

"It's someone outside," she said back.

The front doorknob rattled. Someone tried to force their way in but Josh had added additional security using wood that could slide down behind the door. Even if they managed to break the hinges, they wouldn't get in.

Had his neighbor come back to finish the job?

He didn't dare make any noise.

Whoever it was, they went around the house trying

each of the doors. When that didn't work, they smashed one of the windows. He heard them curse when they saw that behind the curtains was thick plywood preventing entry. They kicked at it but Josh had considered that and drilled into the brickwork.

He saw shadows moving outside.

From what he could discern, it was one person. Probably doing exactly what he'd done nights before — searching for supplies in other homes.

He could have shot through the wood but the stranger might not be as willing to leave as his neighbors had been. He had Lily to think of now. His mother had told him that until he left, the best course of action was to pretend as if no one was there. If someone entered, then fair enough, he could take action but otherwise, silence was their greatest defense.

Keeping the gun trained at the plywood, expecting it to explode inward any second, relief washed over him as the stranger gave up. They cursed and walked off, their footfalls growing more distant. No doubt they would end up at their neighbors' and God help them then.

"Josh?" his mother asked.

"They're gone. We're okay."

*Okay?* They would never be okay again.

He returned to his room to find Lily peering over the sheets. "Now where were we?"

He never told her what the noise was. The less she knew, the better. He would soon become the only barrier of protection between her innocence and a world that was getting darker.

# CHAPTER THIRTEEN

July 6

*S*he could die. Though deaths from copperhead bites were rare, her body could still go into anaphylactic shock as a result of the snake bite. It was the worst possible situation they could be in next to getting near people, and trusting someone, and yet that's exactly what they would have to do as they rushed to get medical help and antivenom. Josh did his best to keep Lily still and calm to prevent the spread of venom but she was in agonizing pain.

"Bean, here, here," he said, bringing up an inhaler to her mouth.

Ryan glanced at her.

"She's asthmatic," Josh said.

Lily took a few hard inhales and then returned to crying hard.

"Damn it. Bring up the list of hospitals in the area on the GPS,"

Josh stared at Ryan for a second. With everything that was happening, hospitals were the worst place to be. Anyone and everyone who was infected but didn't understand the magnitude of the situation would have headed there. "Josh. Hey! Did you hear me?"

"Yeah, but those places are a death trap."

"We don't have much choice."

The forest rushed by in Josh's peripheral vision. They were topping ninety down that stretch of road. Josh pulled up a list of hospitals on the Garmin GPS device. "There's a hospital in DeQuincy that's twenty-four miles away and another hospital in DeRidder, eight miles away, or we can swing back to Merryville where there's a medical center but I doubt that would have what we need."

"Singer?"

"Nothing."

They were already close to Singer, a tiny community.

"Then DeRidder it is." It was a slight detour from their southbound route but all that mattered right now was getting her the antivenom as soon as possible. It would take roughly ten minutes to get there at a normal speed, Ryan was flooring it so they made it there in seven.

Beauregard Health System was in the southernmost part of the city, just off the main stretch. "Listen up. When we get there, I'll carry her in, you watch my back," Ryan said.

"Yeah. Yeah, sure thing."

As they made their approach, the hospital looked like a ghost town. Garbage rolled across the street like tumbleweed. Homes they passed were fortified with plywood. There were only a few regular cars in the parking lot. Abandoned or part of a skeleton crew?

Making their way around, they noticed a few burned-out vehicles. Bodies lay strewn across the lot. Executions? The city of DeRidder had just over ten thousand people. Where were they? For an event of this magnitude, Josh figured the place would be crawling with infected seeking help but it had gone far beyond that now. No one knew who to trust. A touch. That was all it took to pass it on and with the attacks in cities and small towns all over the country, sifting through those who needed real medical care and those looking to pass on the pathogen would have been more than a challenge. It would have been practically impossible.

Ryan swerved into the lot outside the three-story brick building. The truck bounced over a speed bump and stopped beneath the porte-cochere. He hopped out, hurrying around to the other side to get Lily out. There was no one around, no staff ready to come out and help. Josh was already out, handgun at the ready, holding it low.

Lily hadn't stopped crying the whole way. The pain had to be excruciating. "All right, sweetheart, we're going to get you help." Ryan shuffled her out and held her in his arms as he approached the automatic doors. Josh led the way.

The doors hissed open.

Inside it was dark and barren.

Not a soul to be seen. It smelled of death.

Someone had taken all the chairs in the waiting room along with gurneys and formed a huge barrier in front of doorways and one of the corridors. It was a tangled mess of metal.

"Hello! Anyone?" Ryan bellowed. No answer. His voice echoed.

They waited for a second or two.

"I told you. These places are like morgues. Nothing but a final resting place."

Unlike other viruses that might slowly sweep across a nation or the world, allowing emergency services to continue to run, this was far different. By the time people knew what was happening, too many were infected, too many dead, and others were passing it on without even knowing. The rest, well they spread it on purpose. Hospitals and retirement homes would have been the first places people might have gone to transmit the infection. Those here wouldn't have stood a chance. Stuck in beds. Staff run off their feet. By the time anyone realized, it would have spread like wildfire.

Ryan set Lily down and he and Josh began moving obstacles out of the way to get through. The barrier seemed more of a message to anyone entering that the area was off-limits or no longer being used than a deterrent for entry, as it didn't take them long to clear the way.

They hurried down the corridor. Ryan eyed the signs, looking for a medication room. As they turned a corner onto the next hall, Ryan slowed, looking at the blood smeared on the wall. There was dry blood splatter, large and small droplets. A sign of people coughing. Succumbing to the pathogen. Ryan adjusted his N95 mask. He tried to remember fragments of what Elizabeth had said when she was on shift at the hospital. It varied from hospital to hospital. But besides pharmacies, medication was kept in secured areas, locked drawers, and medication carts on each nursing unit. Those were often inside a medication room. That room would also have a cart, and a safe or an automatic dispensing machine that required a biometric scan to access. Those contained Class I through IV meds. All of them were signed out for patients when nurses gave them out. Again though, it depended on where the medications were needed with the majority kept in the pharmacy. "Do we even know what we're looking for here?"

"Secured areas."

"Great. That helps."

He didn't have a clue where those might be so he was looking for a sign for the pharmacy. Stopping and moaning would have been no use. At least if he could find something, anything, he could find some medications, and antivenom might be among them.

"Keep your eye out for locked drug trolleys, crash carts, or a..."

"Can I help you?" a voice bellowed from behind them. Ryan turned to see a fair-haired female in bright colorful scrubs. She was middle-aged, tall, but most importantly, healthy-looking. She was a good hundred yards away from them and must have come out of a room they'd passed or one of the many corridors. Josh immediately lifted the gun at her.

"Whoa, whoa, put that down," she said.

"You a doctor? A nurse?" Josh asked.

"A nurse."

"Yeah, then where are the others?"

"A group of us are running a skeleton crew here."

"Why are you still here?" Ryan asked.

She shrugged. "Someone has to be."

He nodded. It made sense. Not everyone would run for the hills though most had.

"I need some help. My daughter has been bitten by a copperhead."

"Bring her this way."

She turned to lead them and Ryan began to follow when Josh placed a hand on him, stopping him. "How can we trust her?"

He nodded. "Hey. Lady."

She turned.

"You wearing any ID?"

"Oh, sure." She took off her photo ID and slid it across the floor. Ryan stamped his boot on top of it and Josh shone a flashlight beam on it. They looked back at her. "What's your name?"

"Ella." She reeled off her birth date and told them her age.

The woman in the photo looked the same age. The details matched. Still, it didn't mean that she hadn't just been infected. The first week would barely register for someone her age. A wrinkle here, a gray hair there, the real damage came later.

"How come there is no one else here?"

"We're over on the east wing of the hospital. I came over to collect some supplies. We've had to barricade ourselves in."

"Is that right," Ryan replied skeptically.

She nodded.

"How can we trust you?"

"You ever had any woman tell you their real age?"

"Many, since this started."

A smile tugged at her lips. Ryan kicked her ID back to her. It slid across the polished floor and she picked it up and put it back on again.

"You want our IDs?" he asked.

"In a minute. You've got a young girl in a lot of pain. How about we deal with her first?"

Ryan followed and Josh kept close. He was right to have a healthy skepticism. People could turn at the drop of a hat, act as if they were your friend, pretend as if they didn't have the pathogen only to pass it on.

"You seem very trusting," Ryan said.

They kept their distance. She replied over her shoulder. "If you wanted to infect me, you would have done it by now. After all, people don't shoot the breeze. They act first and justify it after the fact."

"And you know this because?"

"I was here when all hell broke loose. If it wasn't for some of the locked areas, and some fast-acting security guards, I don't think we'd be having this conversation." She led them along a hall, through multiple doors that she unlocked with a scan of her card.

"Are you treating the infected?"

"No. Only those who have been injured."

"How do you know they're not infected?"

"As I said, we've been at this a while now. There are ways to check. We follow protocol." They reached another set of doors. Ella looked up at the camera. "Three for quarantine."

"Oh, hey lady, we are not quarantining."

"It's just temporarily. You want your daughter treated, right?"

Ryan glanced at Lily who was still writhing in pain. She came first and neither Josh nor he was going to let her out of their sight. Ella placed her hand on a biometric scanner. A second later the doors hissed open and they entered a secure area where nearly everyone inside was wearing similar outfits to her. Through a long window, they could see another area. Medical experts clothed in hazmat suits were treating patients.

"How many here?"

"Twenty-eight people."

"Who's running the place?"

"Local health officials and the military."

She hit a button on the wall and the doors hissed open and she gestured for them to enter.

Inside they noticed one soldier talking to a nurse.

"National Guard. Not as many here now though."

Ryan was hesitant to enter at first.

"You can take your daughter in with you. You have nothing to worry about. I'll get a doctor and be back in a moment."

They entered and the doors closed behind them. Through the glass window, they watched her stroll down a corridor out of view. Ryan laid Lily on a bed. Josh stood by the window, watching the activity. Most were covered from head to toe with overalls, and face shields.

"You trust her?" Josh asked.

"Right now I don't think we have any other choice."

"But the military..."

"I imagine they're doing whatever they can to help."

"Yeah, like killing anyone infected. You saw those videos online."

"That was in the larger cities and they were being threatened."

"Still doesn't make it right."

Ryan turned to Lily who was grimacing in pain. "You're a strong girl. Just like your mother." She gripped his hand tight. Ten years. Never seeing her birth. Not watching her grow up. All those birthdays, Christmases, special moments at school.

The doors hissed open and a female Indian doctor and Ella entered.

The doc kept her distance but was wearing a BSL 4 suit

"Hello there. My name is Doctor Ravish. And who might you be?"

"Lily."

"Lily. That's a pretty name."

"And you would be...?"

"Her father. Ryan Davenport."

"Okay, well, Lily, let's take a look at that bite and give you something for the pain."

Ryan turned away while she was unclothed and they began to examine the area. The doctor stepped away for a moment and then returned and explained she would administer an antivenom. From there she approached Ryan.

"So? Will she be okay?" he asked.

"Yes, while nasty and painful it's rarely fatal. Nearly all patients with snakebite experience pain and swelling. While it varies depending on the bite, in most cases, children can completely recover and resume activities within one to two weeks, though it can be longer in some cases. I would like to keep her here for at least twenty-four hours, so we can monitor her blood pressure. If her blood pressure drops we may need to give her some IV fluids but besides that, it's mostly monitoring her. Hopefully tomorrow you should be able to go on your way."

"Hopefully? Twenty-four hours?" Josh said. He looked at his watch. "But we've got to get moving."

"I'm afraid you won't be moving anywhere fast if she doesn't rest." She looked back at Lily. "That's a very brave young girl. Fortunate to have you, dad."

Ryan replied, "Thank you, doctor."

"You're welcome. Oh. We would like to run a few precautionary tests on you. Just to be safe."

"We're not infected."

"That's what an infected person would say." She smiled.

"We're not."

"I understand but there are those who are asymptomatic. They're not showing symptoms. It's precautionary, I'm sure you understand. It's for the others. We accept people in for treatment but that is the one condition we have. Your call."

Assessing the situation, Ryan knew they weren't getting out of there any time soon, at least not until the morning. And if this place was under the military, he didn't want to lock heads with anyone and find himself staring down a gun barrel. Not that it would happen, but the news had shaken them up. "Sure. Okay, whatever you need."

"Very good. I'll have Ella take some blood and we'll run those tests."

The doctor walked out while Ella finished up with Lily. "That wasn't so bad, now was it?"

"I don't like needles."

She was calmer, in a better state of mind. Not only had she received the antivenom but she'd received something to help with the pain.

"I'll tell you a secret. Neither do I." She smiled and gave Lily a happy face sticker from her pocket. She told them she'd return in five minutes to take their blood. As she went to walk out, Ryan made his way over to her, making sure he was out of earshot.

"Ella. Do you think you might be able to get me a refill on these?"

Josh looked his way. He knew his son was curious but he wasn't about to tell him what they were for. Ella looked at the label on the almost empty bottle. She glanced at Lily then back at him. "I'll see what I can do."

# CHAPTER FOURTEEN

July 7

Ryan had been sleeping for close to two hours. He awoke to the sound of something hitting the ground. His eyes fluttered open, and he jerked forward to find Ella picking up a bottle of pills. "Sorry. My fault. I tried to be quiet and place them on the table. It's the meds you requested."

Out of breath, he replied, "Oh. Right. Thanks."

He looked over and saw Josh staring. He was on one side of the bed, Ryan was on the other sitting in a chair. He didn't mean to fall asleep but he hadn't slept well the night before. Lily was still asleep. Ryan pocketed the pills.

"You think I could speak with you for a moment?" Ella said.

"Sure."

"Alone."

Josh's gaze bounced between them. "Yeah, yeah, sure. Josh. You'll be okay?"

"Of course," Josh replied.

Ryan got up and walked out of the room into the hallway. The soldier he'd seen earlier was standing by the main doors, looking out the thick, protected glass in the door. Unlike before, he looked more vigilant. "How long has the military been here?"

They walked off down the hallway.

"A couple of weeks. A unit from the National Guard was passing through on their way to Lake Charles. If any hospital is still operating, they leave a couple of soldiers to offer some additional protection. We have three here."

"Has it worked?"

"So far."

Ella led him into a room and closed the door behind him. "We got the results back from your bloodwork. I know it's none of my business, but do your children know?"

"No. I plan to keep it that way."

"You know things are going to get rough."

"The story of my life," he said, making his way to the window. It was dark outside. The clock on the wall said it was just after two in the morning.

"Is your wife dead?"

"Ex," he said. "And yes."

"Sorry to hear that."

"Not as sorry as I was to hear how she died." He cast a glance over his shoulder. "She took her own life." He shook his head.

"Do you blame her?"

"It's hard not to. You know, leaving them without a mother. Involving Josh in her suicide. I mean that kind of thing stays with you. I mean who asks a sixteen-year-old boy to place a gun outside their room?"

He took a deep breath.

Ella leaned against a table. She looked different from his wife and yet similar in that he remembered Elizabeth coming back from work in the early days of marriage wearing blue scrubs. Back then things were different. There was an urgency to spend time with each other. How quickly that changed. "She was a nurse like you."

"Oh?"

"Community based for a while and then she went to work in the hospital."

"Where are you from?"

"Houston originally but I was living in Jasper."

"And the kids?"

"Vidor with their mother."

"That's quite a ways south. What are you doing in Louisiana this far north?"

Ryan perched himself on a table and ran his hands over his tired face. "They came up to me." He yawned. "I haven't seen Josh in ten years. Lily, I didn't even know she was mine."

Ella shifted from one foot to the next. "On top of every-thing that's happened and what's going on in you, that's a lot to take in."

He smiled. "I guess. What about yourself?"

"Born and raised in DeRidder. No kids. Married but that's..."

Ella looked away and ran her hand over her ring finger. She quickly shifted the topic back to him. "It's quite common, you know."

"What is?"

"What your wife did. The end-stage of this is horrific to witness even worse to endure. It's not like regular aging. The body wasn't made to age this quickly. It can't adapt. That's why you see rashes, frequent nosebleeds. It progressively gets worse from there. They experience a lot of pain. You see, the body is under an extreme amount of stress." She got up and walked over to a wall and pressed a button. A light lit up a separate room. All that divided them was thick glass. On the other side was a body laid out on a table with straps over the wrists and ankles. The skin on the face looked almost mummified, dry, and wrinkled beyond comprehension.

"Originally a thirty-nine-year-old male. By the time he died he was in his late eighties but to look at him you would think he was over a hundred and twenty. In the final stages of death, they can't stop the bleeding. The capillaries burst. It ends up coming out of the eyes, and other orifices. The pain they go through is unbearable."

Ryan gestured to the dead man. "Didn't you give him morphine or something?"

"Wouldn't be much use."

"So who is he?"

"This was a doctor who worked here. After contracting the virus, he wanted us to document his experience of death, study him so we knew what we were dealing with."

"And do you?" He asked.

"Somewhat."

She reached down and pulled up a table and tapped the screen, used the biometric thumb lock to gain access to it, and then pressed play. It was a time-lapse of the days leading up to his death. In excruciating detail Ryan listened to the sound of the man groaning in pain, begging to be put out of his misery.

"They wouldn't intervene?"

"No. He gave strict instructions that no matter what to keep filming. Eventually, a soldier was sent in to end his life but before he had a chance to squeeze the trigger the man died." She turned off the video, not showing it completely. Ryan could see it affected her deeply. As she turned away, Ella said. "That was my husband."

Silence stretched between them and in that moment he realized that he'd been hasty in his judgment of Elizabeth. As anyone with a background in medicine, she knew what was coming. She'd done her homework, no doubt witnessed a similar video, and had concluded that she wanted to go out on her terms rather than suffer. Could she have retrieved the gun herself instead of asking Josh to put it outside the room? Maybe. But she didn't. Was she too weak or trying to make him stronger? Make him ready to do whatever was necessary to survive?

"I'm sorry," Ryan said. "Is that how it ends for everyone?"

"No, some don't reach this stage. Their hearts give out on them. Like anyone who dies of old age, not everyone goes out the same but many suffer as my husband did."

"Were there many others here like him?"

"Many."

"Is there a cure?"

"If there is, we haven't discovered it yet," she said, glancing at him. "I mean, of course spreading the pathogen to a host that doesn't have it will help the infected but that is still..." she trailed off, shaking her head. "Uncharted territory."

Ryan nodded. It raised all kinds of moral and ethical issues.

"Do they know what it is? I mean, it doesn't act like a typical virus."

"That's because it isn't. From what we can gather it was created in a lab. Where? Who knows. We've analyzed the infected blood under a microscope and it appears to be using some form of nanobot technology. Like the kind used to fight cancer. Except it's doing the reverse of its true purpose."

"To prevent aging?" He asked.

"Something like that."

She lifted her face and clenched her eyes closed. "Come, let me show you something." Ryan glanced one last time at the man on the table and grimaced.

Ella led him out and down to the stairwell, where they went up several floors until they reached the roof. As they exited, a soldier having a cigarette tossed it down and lifted his rifle.

"It's just me, Heath."

"Ma'am." The soldier gave a nod. Ella led Ryan over to the other side of the building, past large air vents and snaking wires. "We isolated everyone who came in. The first casualties were staff unaware of what was happening. Within a matter of days, as news reports flooded the airwaves, the rest of us took precautions. I wasn't on shift at the time. I had the week off. After learning about my husband contracting it, I decided to head into the hospital and offer my services."

"But you could have stayed home."

"You're right, but, it's what my husband would have done. It's what he wanted."

"So you spoke with him before he died?"

"Through a pane of glass. Yes."

She gave a strained smile.

They made it to the far side of the building. "We stored the dead in those until they were filled." Down below were large 18-wheeler trailers that were often called reefers, refrigerated trucks that had been brought in. "After that, they were piled over there," she said, pointing across the lot to a large, tangled mass of bodies. "A tractor was used to open the ground up and roll bodies in but it became too many."

"Dear God," Ryan said as the weight of loss hit him hard. It was a unique virus that spread fast, killed quickly, and offered zero mercy. Young, middle-aged, old. It didn't matter. They were all down there. A mass grave of the infected.

"It's quite a sight and that's just this small town. I can only imagine what it's like in the major cities of this country. And that's not the worst of it." Ryan shot her a sideways glance as she continued. "The threat isn't just from those choosing to spread it, or unknowingly spreading it, it's from those fearful of being infected. Unless someone makes it known that they have the virus, unless they show a rash, or are bleeding from the nose, it's hard to tell who has it. Our world is surrounded by people of every age. Is that sixteen-year-old over there, ten? Is that thirty-year-old, twenty? Is that sixty-year-old really forty? It's a guessing game and one that some aren't leaving to chance. If in any way they feel threatened—"

"They're killing them?"

"You got it. And of course, then you have those hunting down people for the heck of it. Like a sport. Taking whatever they want, killing under the guise that everyone is infected. It's a freak show out there."

"That's happening?"

She nodded. "If the military is to be believed. I mean, it's not like anyone is going to stop and inspect the bodies of those shot. The risk is too great. People are keeping their distance."

"You didn't," he said.

She scoffed and dropped her chin.

"You weren't coming for supplies, were you, when you saw us?"

Her lips curled at the corner of her mouth. "No. I saw you on the video monitors. You have to understand, the people they have inside here are from weeks ago. Some have left but they're hesitant to take anyone else in. The last person we took in was eight days ago."

"So why did you let us in?"

"That's the question, isn't it?" She took a deep breath and placed both hands on the lip of the roof's wall. "Probably for the same reason you are helping your kids despite your situation." She looked at him and was about to say something when a gun erupted, a flurry of rounds igniting.

Ryan whipped around to see the soldier firing at someone down below.

"Ma'am, you should get inside, now," the soldier said.

"Is it the same ones?" Ella asked.

"The same," the soldier said before unleashing another slew of bullets.

Confused, as Ryan followed her back into the stairwell, he asked, "What's going on?"

"Lynch mobs. Well, they're not exactly lynching people but the outcome is the same. You think the ones spreading the infection are selfish." She chuckled. "These folks don't care who you are, if they see you, you're getting a bullet. I guess some think it's their job to wipe clean the landscape and put the nation back in order."

"I heard that's what the military is planning on doing in the major cities."

"That's not what I heard."

"Yeah, well, they keep changing the story. How come we never saw this mob?" Ryan asked.

"They were probably around the east side when you entered from the west. As I said, we don't have many entering as of late."

"Explains the torched vehicles outside, and bodies strewn across the lot," he said.

As soon as they were inside, Ella was back to acting as if nothing had happened. "So where are you heading?"

"What?"

His mind was still on the gunfire outside.

"You said you were from Jasper. Where are you going after this?"

"South. To Florida. Franklin County. There's supposed

to be a haven somewhere out in the Gulf Coast. Refuge boats, they're calling them. A way to get away from infectious areas."

"You believe that's what you'll find?"

"My wife believed so."

She stopped on the stairwell and looked up at him. "Do you have room for one more?"

# CHAPTER FIFTEEN

*J*osh was a little taken aback when his father told him. She was a stranger. He wasn't against Ella going with them but he had his reservations, as did Ryan. "She's definitely not riding in the cab with us."

That was one of the conditions.

"I didn't say she would."

"Good," Josh replied.

Although it was an odd request, having a nurse with a bag of meds to watch over Lily after the snake bite was helpful.

But why them?

Why now?

His questions weren't without reason. He didn't trust anyone.

Had his uncle gone with them, the arrangement of having him travel in the rear of the pickup truck would have been the same at least for a few days, while they monitored him.

Curious, Josh probed for an answer.

Ryan said Ella wanted out. She was tired. The situation wasn't improving and they'd lost more people than they were able to help. His father had shown him the dead from the roof. Mounds of bodies piled up like trash.

It was terrifying.

So, it was agreed. She would go with them.

Under the cover of darkness, they'd exited while the lynch mob on the far side were kept busy by soldiers. They made it as far as Acadia Parish. It was a good two hours, and a hundred miles later before they had to stop for gas. They'd traveled south down Highway 26 and east along Interstate 10 without issue. The roads were for the most part barren as the threat of infection forced people back into their homes. They'd passed a group of students whose broken-down sedan was at the edge of the road with steam pouring out of it. They thumbed a ride but his father didn't stop.

No one in their right mind would as there were only three types of people now on the streets.

Those trying to get somewhere safely.

Those trying to spread the pathogen.

And those seeking to kill.

All three were equally dangerous.

The rest were the dead. Those whose lives were ended by themselves or others.

That's what made stopping a last resort.

Safety was an illusion. And what made it even more challenging was they couldn't trust the graffiti announcing "safe zones" seen on barns and walls along the way, as there was no way of telling if those were legitimate or a means of luring in unsuspecting victims.

Traps were set for the infected, and the infected set traps for those who weren't.

Both had the same agenda. To kill and survive.

The truck started coughing, and Ryan tapped the fuel gauge.

"I thought you said we weren't out yet?"

"I know." He tapped it again. "Damn thing must be broken."

The truck rolled to the edge of the road just on the outskirts of Rayne, a place known as the Frog Capital of the World. Ryan reached over and brought up a list of gas stations on the GPS. He got out and collected a ten-gallon gas canister. "It's only half a mile walk from here to a Mobil station. I'll get some gas and bring it back."

"And leave us here?" Ella asked.

"There's no point all of us going"

"Or..." Josh said, pointing down the road to several vehicles that were in a ditch. "We could try and siphon gas."

"Why do I get the feeling you did that before the outbreak?"

Josh exited with a mischievous smile. "Give me the tank, I'll get it."

"I think not."

"You don't trust me?"

Josh looked at Ella. Maybe it was her Ryan didn't trust. If so, it was a little late now to be second-guessing. They'd placed Ella in the back of the truck to be sure she wasn't a carrier of the pathogen. Her appearance didn't send that message but they couldn't risk it. Even though she was in nursing scrubs, hands and face covered when they first met, the only way Ryan would agree to take her was if she got a blood test. That's what she'd done in the early hours of the morning at the hospital. Apparently, the infection showed in the blood. It was all clear.

Still, Ryan wasn't ready to let his guard down. They had no way of knowing if the results were from earlier. For all they knew she could have been infected the day they arrived. Hence the reason she was riding in the back for a few days. "Come on," Josh said. "I'm gloved, masked, my eyes are covered." He was wearing shades, an N95 mask, and his hood was up. Lily was still wearing her motorcycle helmet even though she'd been offered a mask. His helmet was on the motorcycle when the barn burned down.

"No, I'll do it," Ryan said.

"Suit yourself. At some point, you'll have to trust me."

Ryan stopped and looked back at him. There was a moment of reluctance then he said, "All right. Here you go. Just make it quick."

Josh grinned as he took the gas container and hose and made his way over to a black Mercedes SUV. It was a good fifty yards away. Another vehicle was near it, the back end crushed. The windows on the side were smashed. One of the doors was open on the passenger side. Josh looked back at them and left the road, pitching sideways down an embankment to get to the vehicles. Cars run off the road were common. The infected used their vehicles to collide with others head-on, others they'd clipped and forced off the road, then swarmed the occupants.

Holding the empty gasoline canister and tubing in one hand, and the Glock in the other, Josh made his way to the side and peered through the window. A woman was slumped over the steering wheel, face sideways, features turned away from him. Her one ear had dry blood coming out of it. A crusty red stain was spread over her face and neck.

His thoughts went back to his mother. The videos she sent him of those who had succumbed to the virus. The passenger seat was empty. Nearby was a young boy who'd been shot in the back multiple times.

Josh scanned his surroundings.

It was quiet. No one around.

The gas cap was locked.

To open it meant reaching in and pulling up the latch on the floor of the vehicle, he wasn't that stupid. Josh set the gas cans down and slipped off his backpack.

"You okay?" Ryan shouted.

Josh gave him the thumbs-up. He fished through his bag for the knife and stuck the tip of it in the thin gap to pry open the cover. It didn't take much force to get it to pop. He unscrewed the gas cap and stuck the tubing inside and began the process of siphoning out the gas. Gasoline flooded out and he spat it off to the side before letting it flush into the gas can.

The world around him was peaceful even if it was dangerous.

The can was almost filled when the sound of birds chirping and breaking away from the trees caught his attention.

He squinted at the road which had heatwaves vibrating across the top.

He heard the rumble of the engine before he saw what kind of vehicle it was.

"C'mon, c'mon," he said under his breath, looking down into the canister.

While they had passed other vehicles along the way, the ever-present threat from the infected or those taking matters into their own hands was at the forefront of his mind.

Ryan had seen it.

"Josh. Let's go!"

"It's nearly full."

"Leave it."

He wasn't about to do that. Not now. If he left it, there was a chance whoever was driving would take it. Without that, they weren't getting anywhere.

With nowhere to drive, Ryan, Ella, and Lily got out and made their way down into the ditch and across to the tree line to take cover. All the while he was calling to Josh to leave it.

As he got the last few drops into the canister, he tore out the tubing and pulled back behind the rear end of the SUV.

Ryan kept beckoning him to come but the vehicle was too close.

He would have been spotted if he hadn't been already.

Josh waved at Ryan to step back into the tree line as he lifted the unlocked trunk of the SUV just enough that he could climb in. Inside, it smelled rancid, like someone had vomited. He could hear flies buzzing around the driver's rotting body at the front.

He found a blanket in the rear and covered himself,

looking up at the dark-tinted windows. Listening intently, his hand on the gun, he waited for the vehicle to drive by. "Keep going, keep going," he said.

They didn't.

Gravel crunched and two doors slammed. Hooting and hollering followed.

"Jimmy, we got a live one over here."

He thought the man was referring to him but there must have been someone alive in the next vehicle farther down. What followed next, startled him.

A gunshot rang out then someone started singing the chorus to the song by Queen, "Another one bites the dust."

"She was a good-looking girl. Such a shame."

More laughter followed. They were heartless. Lacking any empathy.

"Niles, shut up and check the next vehicle."

Heavy footfalls got closer. A shadow lingered near the front. The driver's door opened at the front of the vehicle he was in. "Oh man, this is rank. Geez, Louise. It's a no-go here unless of course, you're into necrophilia." The guy laughed.

The door slammed shut and he heard him come around to the rear. Josh's heartbeat sped up. He wouldn't think twice to shoot the guy if he opened the trunk.

Sure enough, the rear opened but only a crack and for just a second before whoever was at the back let it go. "Oh, what do we have here? Hey, Jimmy!"

Had they seen his father? He wanted to pull off the blanket and steal a look but by the sound of the conversation outside there were at least three of them, two males and a female.

Three rounds erupted in rapid succession.

For a second he thought that maybe his father had opened fire on them.

Taking them out. Ending their pitiful existence.

But when he heard the strangers' voices outside he feared the worst.

As he was about to take a look, the vehicle shifted ever so slightly. Through the thin blanket, he could just make out the shape of two individuals pressed up against the side. Were they making out? Sick. How could anyone get turned on around death? He could hear them slurping up a storm.

"Hey!" A woman said.

"Shut up."

"Don't grope so hard."

"Stop fussing."

A slap followed. "I told you I don't like that!"

Josh stifled a laugh. The female wasn't taking any shit.

"Remind me again why I put up with your crap?"

"Likewise," she shot back. "Asshole."

Movement at the back of the vehicle. A hand pressed against the window.

"Did you find anything, Niles?"

"Oh, just a little something."

*Little?*

He heard their footsteps get faint, then doors slam shut and an engine growl as a vehicle tore away at a high rate of speed. Josh waited there for a second or two before he pulled off the blanket and peered around.

They were gone.

He got out of the vehicle and double-timed it over to

the tree line where he last saw his father. He expected to find all three dead, the victims of strangers. "Lily! Ella. Dad?"

"Josh," his father said.

He whirled around to find them coming out of the forest, just a short distance from where they had gone in. Relief washed over him. "You okay?"

Josh lifted the canister. "Got the gas."

"Next time let me do it."

"Be my guest," he said, thinking about the smell in that vehicle and his heart pounding. "Which way did they go?" Josh asked.

Ryan pointed in the opposite direction. He took the canister from Josh and emptied it into the truck. They collected some more from the second vehicle, extra so they wouldn't have to stop again for a while. Josh got back into the vehicle and Lily leaned into him, holding him tight. It wasn't easy for her. This was no life for a child.

Ella climbed into the rear.

Ryan turned on the radio as they rolled out. Some preacher came on talking about the event being God's way of punishing the world for their sins.

# CHAPTER SIXTEEN

*L*afayette was a bust. It was to be expected, they'd been lucky so far. A clear shot down from the city of DeRidder, they'd seen a few blockades but none they couldn't get around. Now with gas in the tank, they were willing to wait until they reached a small town to find food rather than stop in a big city, but that wasn't to be.

The sky was blue but with heavy dark clouds rolling in from the west.

Interstate 10 was the main artery that cut through the city heading east. The wide road had suffered one crash after another. It had to have been the largest multi-car wreck he'd ever seen. It stretched for miles, covering parts of the grassy median.

"You have got to be kidding me," Ryan said.

He eased off the gas, bringing the truck to a crawl at the sight of the tangled mess. He scanned openings. Was it possible to get through? Maybe, maybe not but getting stuck wasn't the only thing that concerned him. "We'll have to go around."

"But that'll add hours onto the day," Josh said. "Can't we try to weave through it?"

"We could try but if there are carriers among that wreckage which more than likely there are, we'd be trapped. No, we can..." he tapped the GPS, narrowing his eyes as he concentrated. "Come off here and join Highway 725 then wing it north on 723 and join Mouton Road east." He reversed, swung the SUV around, headed across the median, and took them back a mile down the road before coming off an exit ramp.

Ella tapped on the rear window.

Ryan didn't want to explain it again so Josh told her.

They hadn't been traveling for more than ten minutes when Lily said, "I'm hungry."

"Here." Josh gave her a granola bar. "Ryan, we'll need to stop at some point and get something to eat."

"It's dad, not Ryan. And until we make it past this city we aren't stopping."

"If the roads are anything like that back there, we might not have a choice," Josh replied, thumbing behind him. "It might be best to ride out the night somewhere, eat and continue rather than burn fuel and veer all over the state."

"Josh, this is the first exit we've taken."

"Just saying. It might be the..."

"I'm driving, okay?"

"All right." He waited for a second or two before he added, "You didn't get much sleep last night, did you?"

"I got enough."

Ryan was irritable. The heat of the day felt stifling. Then of course that close encounter with those freaks on the road had unnerved him. It was one thing agreeing to travel to Florida, another to face the risks. He noted several cars and trucks pass them. He scanned the scared faces inside. Not everyone was out to hurt others, the majority were trying to avoid people, not face them.

Still, the detour wasn't all clear sailing.

While they didn't come across a multi-car pile-up, some roads were blocked, though this time it felt as if someone wanted to steer the traffic in a certain direction, for a reason other than construction.

The problem was, it was either go back or follow the detour signs.

"How are you feeling, Lily?" Ryan asked.

Lily grimaced then offered back a brave face. "All right."

She'd been given medication and by the time they'd left, the doctor said she should be good in about a week but to keep monitoring her.

"You sure you know where you're going?" Josh asked.

"Worry about your sister, not me."

There was a long stretch of silence.

"Why didn't you ever call?"

"What?" The question blindsided him. He was too focused on the road, the signs, some of which didn't look right. They were normal road signs, the kind that any road construction might use, but too many, too close together. What reason would any city have to lead people into a residential area? Ryan shifted his gaze to the rearview mirror and saw a truck swing out of a road behind them. His muscles tensed and his anxiety elevated. He immediately thought the worst.

He continued for another few minutes before he pulled

into a driveway of a home and watched the black Ford 4 x 4 roar past.

Josh looked over his shoulder. "What are you doing?"

"Quiet," he said, focused on the mirror.

Seconds passed. The truck didn't return. Ryan didn't turn the engine off but he got out, rifle in hand, and headed over to the road. In the distance, farther down the road, he saw the black truck come to a halt, then reverse fast. It smashed into a parked van but managed to break away. As it turned and headed back his way, he assumed it was returning for them.

It wasn't.

Vehicles on either side of the road shot out, blocking its path.

Adults got out and before the occupants of the truck could even respond, rifles were drawn, handguns aimed and an onslaught of rounds lanced the vehicle.

It was a trap.

Whether they were doing it to take what the driver had, or killing anyone who might pose a threat to their neighborhood, that was unknown. Ryan wasn't sticking around to find out. He ran back to the truck, got in, jammed it in reverse, and tore out heading back the way they came.

"What is it?" Josh asked.

He didn't answer. Instead, he swung a hard right and then a left and weaved his way through the streets away from any detour signs until they were in the northern end of Lafayette. When they were in the clear, he explained what happened to Josh.

As they came out of the suburb, it wasn't long before he came across a supermarket. They'd eaten their way through their supplies. While he didn't want to stay in the city any longer than needed, he knew that it was best to stock up because they didn't know when they would get another chance.

Ryan veered into the lot and pulled up beside other vehicles. The window in the store was smashed. There were shopping carts toppled over. Bags of groceries split open and rotten fruit everywhere as if someone had dropped bags in a hurry.

"In and out. Let's not linger. Get what you need and when I say it's time to leave..."

"It's time to leave," Josh replied. "Yeah, yeah, I got it."

He shut off the engine and the four of them made their way into the store. Inside it was dark. It smelled gross, like sour milk and rotting produce. The chances of finding anything were slim to none but it was worth a look around if only to satisfy Josh's need to guide the boat, so to speak.

"Here, you might need this," Ryan said, pulling a SIG Sauer from the holster and offering it to Ella.

"I wouldn't know what to do with it."

"You never used one?"

"Why would I?"

That was another thing different about her and Elizabeth, who'd grown up around guns. She was familiar with them and comfortable having one on her hip. Ella stared at it like a live bomb. "It's easy. Look..."

She lifted a hand. "Thank you, Ryan, but I'll leave it to you."

He nodded as she walked on.

"I'll take it," Lily said.

"You will not."

Josh chuckled as they ventured further in. Glass crunched beneath their boots. There were smears of blood on the checkouts. A few bodies lay in various states of decomposition nearby. Ryan lifted a fist. He stopped walking. As Josh went to walk on, Ryan placed a hand on his chest. He brought a finger up to his lips, thinking he heard something.

"What is it?" he asked.

"Shhh," Ryan replied. He could have sworn he heard movement.

They remained frozen for at least a good minute. Convinced that it was safe, they snagged several bags from one of the clean checkouts and began fishing through what was on the ground. Shelves were practically wiped out. Anything that still existed was on the floor. Squashed, dented, or torn open. "Let's make this quick. Josh, you go with Ella. I'll take Lily."

They split, wading through a sea of debris. Most of the products were of no use.

Like a bird pecking at the ground, Ryan sifted through the trash looking for gold: packets of noodles, canned goods, anything that would tide them over for a day or two. "How's that leg of yours, Lily?"

"Sore but not like before."

She was unusually upbeat. He wished he'd been there to see the first ten years. Those were the most impressionable. That's when it dawned on him. He didn't even know her birthdate. Elizabeth had kept that from him. "Lily, you said you're ten, right?" he asked as he rolled a can in his hand only to find a hole in the top. He tossed it and continued.

"I'll be eleven next year."

"What month?"

"April 17."

"Then I guess we'll have to throw you a big party."

"Really?"

"Why not?"

There was a pause.

"You think I could have ice cream cake?"

"You can have anything you…" He lifted a hand.

It was that sound again. It was too light for a human. Paying close attention, he thought it sounded like slurping. The strap of his rifle was slung over his head and around the back of his shoulder to hold it in place. He opted for the handgun.

Lily, unaware, continued talking. "Mom used to always say that…"

He placed a hand over her tiny mouth and her eyes bulged. "Shh."

The sound shifted. With all the trouble they'd run into so far, he couldn't help but wonder if it might have been safer staying at his home. Out here, there were just too many variables. Too many things that could go wrong. It wasn't all about making smart decisions. Like when you were driving a car. It didn't matter how good you were, if a drunk driver ended up veering into your lane, you were screwed.

His instinct was to call out to Josh and Ella but he didn't want to give away their position.

Then again, if they were close enough to hear whatever was making that sound, surely it could hear them? Backing out was the best option but they were already close to the end of the aisle. Curiosity got the better of him. Ryan scooped up Lily with one arm and threw her over his shoulder as a fireman might. He moved a few more feet, then turned on the light attached to his gun. A wide beam sliced through the darkness as he got close to the corner. He kept the gun low, illuminating the ground before him. As he craned his neck and lifted the gun, the light fell upon a dark mound. It took a second to realize what he was looking at, then a head lifted.

It was a mangy dog licking blood from a dead body.

It growled then continued devouring the body.

Sudden movement off to his right revealed two more dogs.

They emerged from the darkness, sauntering forward in a threatening manner.

These were bigger.

One a bullmastiff, the other a German shepherd.

*Okay. Okay.* He thought as he took a slow step back.

All three growled, baring gleaming teeth, all drooling blood.

In the breakdown of society, as people became victims of the virus, or were murdered or took their lives, it would have left open a wide door for pets to turn feral out of a need to feed. And right then he and Lily must have looked like lunch.

Lily twisted on his shoulder and caught sight of them.

She screamed.

He didn't have much time to run before the dogs leaped over the body, scuttling through blood toward him. They might not have been carriers of the virus but with them licking blood that might be infected, one bite and there was a possibility they could contract it.

The transference from humans to animals was still a big unknown.

Ryan squeezed the trigger, taking out the one closest to him.

One of the three must have seen Josh or Ella as it darted down the next aisle, leaving the mastiff lunging forward in a threatening manner. It barked like a rabid dog. Hackles up. Head low. Its body was half the size it should have been for its breed. It was starving. Desperate. Who knew what the blood had done to it. Unlike the other, it was hesitant to follow suit but that didn't mean it wasn't about to attack.

Although she was only ten, the weight of Lily was beginning to make his shoulder ache.

Ryan lowered her and told her to slowly make her way down the aisle while he kept an eye on the dog. The mastiff reached its dead friend, and sniffed at the dog, nudging it with its snout before baring teeth.

"All right, boy. There's a good dog. We're going. Okay."

He backed up a little and the dog took a few more steps forward before charging.

With his left arm free, Ryan grabbed the shelving close to him and pulled it down as he backed up. The dog collapsed beneath it, its paws scraping the ground until it managed to slide out from it, pushing forward, eyes locked on him, snarling.

Finger on the trigger, he gave that dog every chance to back away but it never did.

As it came at him, he had no other choice.

He managed to get three rounds into it before it dropped near his feet.

By now Lily was screaming at the top of her voice but it wasn't fear from another attack, it was what she was seeing. Piercing screams filled the store. Ryan's heart leaped in his chest as he rushed down the aisle and burst around the corner just in time to hear a gun go off.

## CHAPTER SEVENTEEN

rozen, Josh still had the gun poised, aimed at the dog.

Beside the dead animal, crying out in agony, Ella was on the floor clasping a torn pant leg. In the dim lighting, it was impossible to see the full extent of the damage.

Instantly, Josh sloughed off his backpack, unzipped it, and fished out the first-aid kit, coming to her aid. Before Ryan could intervene, Ella did.

Abruptly, she lifted a hand to him.

"No. Stay back!" Ella said in a firm and clear tone.

Josh looked up at his father, perplexed for a second. Ryan nodded in agreement. Ella knew just as Ryan did what it could mean. If infected blood lapped up by the dog had made its way into her bloodstream, she might be infected.

Grimacing, tears of pain rolling down her cheeks, Ella used both hands to tear away at the pant leg. Ryan shone his flashlight down and his stomach sank. The leg didn't just have a bite, the flesh was torn from the bone. She struggled to catch a breath between the pain and the realization. Josh took out some hydrogen peroxide and unscrewed the cap.

"Maybe it hasn't made its way in…" Josh said.

"It has," she said angrily.

"But at least try washing the wound," he offered. "You might not be infected."

"Hold on, he's right. Wash the wound, I'll be right back." Ryan hurried up the aisle to check on the dead body. The man whose blood had pooled around his body might have had nothing more than a defensive wound. There was a chance he wasn't infected. That he… Ryan jogged to a slow pace, as the light before him shone on what was left of the man.

*Damn it!*

She was screwed.

Regardless of his age, he had bloodshot eyes and dry blood trickling around the nose, eyes, and ears. His open shirt revealed a massive rash, one of the clearest symptoms that carriers of the pathogen would show.

He turned back, slowly making his way to the front of the store.

"So?" Josh asked, now with Lily standing beside him, clutching his coat.

Ryan's eyes averted down.

When he met Ella's gaze, she already knew.

She sighed, nodding as if accepting a terminal diagnosis given by a medical professional. Ella clenched her hands and released the emotion. Lily began to cry too.

"There must be something we can do," Josh said.

"Josh, take your sister out to the truck."

He stared at her.

"It's okay, Josh," Ella said. "Go on."

There would be no hugs. No heartfelt goodbyes, just a painful separation.

Ella grimaced in pain, shuffling back against one of the shelves, blood seeping out.

Ryan waited until he was out before he dropped down nearby. "We can wait and see."

"Ryan. I've worked long enough with this virus that I know how it works."

He was at a loss for words. His mind churned over the what-ifs, the could-haves, the unknowns. Anything that might give her some hope, but he wasn't dealing with the average joe, someone gullible or ignorant. She was on the front lines and had witnessed the devastation up close and personal.

"How old are you?" he asked.

"Ryan, no." She shook her head.

"You're still young."

A strained smile broke through the pain. "I guess I should say thank you."

"What I'm saying is it takes time. I mean, they could still find a cure for the—"

She cut him off, shaking her head. "It won't be the virus that kills me." She pulled back the pant leg higher up and revealed more of the wound. She was bleeding profusely, far more than someone might from a regular bite. The dog had torn into an artery and she was bleeding out faster than she could stem it with her hand. He shone the light on her face. It wouldn't be long before she'd turn a pale gray, her body going cold, and then she'd slip to the other side. Everything in him wanted to reach out and touch her, put on a tourniquet, offer some reassurance but it wouldn't have done anything and would have only infected him.

"Damn it!" he bellowed, rising to his feet. "Shit!" He ran a hand around his jaw.

"It's okay, Ryan."

"No, it's not. None of this is," he said, looking around him. "None of this is!"

"Listen to me," she said, showing an unusual acceptance in the face of something that would have angered, and scared the hell out of anyone else. "Every day, after I lost my husband, I thought, will this be it? Every day people came into that hospital seeking help and there was always this small voice in the back of my mind telling me this would be my last day." She paused, looking out the door. "I've seen this coming for a long while. All right, I didn't think it would happen this way but hey, none of us saw it going… this way."

"It's still not fair."

"Is anything fair?"

"I barely got to know you."

She smiled. "Probably for the best," she said. "I would have reminded you of your ex, and you wouldn't have lived up to my husband." She grimaced again, her face contorting as the pain squeezed her. Ella gritted her teeth and let another smile seep through.

"Well, I'll stay with you," Ryan said.

"No. Go. I'm good."

"Bullshit. I bought what you said before but not this. I'm staying. And that's that. Just let me… uh…" He pointed to the door, feeling choked up. "Let me just tell them I'll be a moment longer."

"It won't be much longer," she said. "These things don't take more than five minutes."

He looked at the leg. "I can…"

She knew he was referring to a tourniquet. "No, you can't."

"Then you do it."

"I'm not going to delay it. "

Ryan sat down across from her, holding in his emotion. He stared at her, sitting on his haunches. "Then tell me about you," he said.

"What do you want to know?"

"What food do you like?"

She couldn't hold in a chuckle. "You're asking me that now?"

"Well, we are in a grocery store. Who knows, I might be able to find it."

She snorted through her pain. "Right. Last meal and all. Well, chef, I'll take a rib-eye and fries, with a pint of your finest."

"Coming right up," he said in a joking manner though they both knew it was anything but.

There were no moments of silence. Time was slipping by as fast as the life force leaving her. "You know, Ryan. The one we often find the hardest to forgive is ourself. Ten years is a long time to hold on to the past. If I've learned anything in the twenty-plus hours I've talked to you, it's that you love your kids. No one can deny that."

"I sometimes wonder if I'm a good father."

"You're a good father."

"You don't know me. You don't know my past."

"Actually I do."

He gave her a confused look, then a wave of humiliation came over him. It always did even though the charges had been cleared. But that wasn't what she was referring to.

"Josh told me," she said. "About the separation."

"Oh. Right. That." He nodded. "Yeah."

"He seems like a good kid. A little lost but isn't every sixteen-year-old."

"And you would know?"

"Just because I didn't have kids, it doesn't mean I wasn't around a lot of teens. My sister had three. Besides, a woman has a strong intuition. You mean a lot to him."

"Well if I do, he has a funny way of showing it."

"It's not for him to show it."

"What are you saying?"

"I'm saying we aren't guaranteed x number of years so what time you have left, show them how much you care."

"I'm trying."

"I know but..." She tapped her ear. "Listen. Listen to him. Trust him. He's come this far without you, hasn't he?"

He smiled and nodded.

"Now how about you tell me about a good time you remember. A moment when he was younger, a memory so vivid it feels like yesterday. Something good."

She clenched her teeth as a wave of pain rolled over her.

"Um. Well..." He looked down and thought about it. The first time he took Josh fishing. The pride he felt seeing him reel one in. Ryan smiled as he retold the events of that day. Ella's eyes closed and opened as she grew more tired due to the loss of blood. As he was finishing, Ryan looked up and she was gone.

"Ella?"

No response.

His stomach sank.

Ryan got up and looked around for something to cover her body. He found a tarp out back and lowered it over her. He stood there for a moment longer thinking about the risk she'd taken to help Lily. She was the best example of humanity in a world that was falling apart.

He lowered his head and said a silent prayer.

"Godspeed."

Ryan stepped out of the store and pressed his back against the wall, bringing a hand to his face as the emotion crawled up into his throat. He covered his eyes, blinking hard. As he removed his hand, he saw Josh staring at him from inside the truck, concerned.

He sniffed hard and blew out his cheeks and wiped one of his eyes.

Her death came far quicker than he expected.

Everything was moving faster than he expected. Like the sands of time slipping through an hourglass, reminding him of what lay ahead, and the risk that could snatch any one of them from this world.

# CHAPTER EIGHTEEN

$a$s the truck rumbled along the highway, the atmosphere in the cab was somber. Ryan pulled his shoulders back and rolled his head around, to work out the tension in his neck and back. They hadn't spoken a word to each other in several hours. He'd been unable to put the image of Ella out of his mind. He kept circling back to the moment they walked in. He played out the what-ifs. It was hard not to feel responsible for her death.

"Do you want me to take a turn driving?" Josh asked.

"It's okay. I'm good for now."

"Just saying, if you get tired. I'm here."

"I'll keep that in mind."

He wasn't opposed to him taking over. He'd seen the way he handled the truck back at Tommy's. But after everything that had happened, he was struggling to let go of what little he could control.

Lily had fallen asleep to the vibration of the truck. Her head was in Josh's lap, her legs curled up on the passenger seat.

"You did offer her a gun," Josh added as if trying to find sense in the tragedy. He nodded but wasn't sure what he was supposed to say to that.

"It happened so fast," Josh said. "One second she was beside me, the next wrestling on the ground with that dog. I would have shot it sooner but it kept moving."

"You're not to blame."

"I just wish I could have reacted sooner."

Ryan had been chewing over the threat of animals. It hadn't even entered his mind until today. They'd have to be more vigilant. With so many now running stray and eating whatever they could find, they were another potential carrier of the pathogen. A thought dawned on him. Had it started in animals? Elizabeth often talked about medicine, new trials, and how companies would test out viruses on animals first before creating a cure.

"Do you mind me asking about the girl?" Josh asked.

"What?"

"The accusation. The articles didn't go into great detail. I mean, you don't need to if you don't want to."

"It was a long time ago."

Ten years to be exact.

He hadn't given much thought to her since his charges were cleared because so much of his energy before that was consumed by lawyers, court, and accusations. It had upended his family, destroyed his career, and ruined his reputation. Media outlets widely published his name and face, adding more fuel to the flames. His passport had been revoked. His work had put him on paid leave and he was no longer able to help at his local church. It had a ripple effect that spread far and wide beyond what he imagined it would. He thought he would be treated fairly but from day one he was seen as guilty by everyone around him, and his lawyers had the difficult task of proving his innocence.

Naturally, it didn't take long for anxiety and depression to kick in and for him to suffer panic attacks when he left his home to do simple things like grocery shopping.

In many ways, it was akin to having someone drop a bomb on his house. In the aftermath, he was left to pick through the pieces of what remained, alone, with an entire circle of friends, family, and community watching with accusing eyes.

For a while Elizabeth was supportive. She didn't believe it. Not for one minute.

That soon changed as she came under the microscope and those around her made it seem like she was covering up for him. And it really came to a head when other parents no longer invited Josh to birthday parties.

The accusation against him was tainting them too.

That's why he couldn't fault her decision to leave, as Elizabeth was human after all. She could only handle so much and the case was dragged out over several years.

Within weeks of being cleared of charges, he'd moved away from the town. It wasn't just to escape those who sought him out, it was to put distance between them so he could find a reason to go on.

And go on he did, finding solace in a bottle as he struggled to deal with life. Then, his drinking only got worse when it came to fighting for his right to see Josh.

After all was said and done, he had very little energy left to fight. He also didn't expect to have to explain the situation to Josh later as Elizabeth had done a great job of shielding him from it all.

Although he didn't have visiting rights, he was allowed to phone but after a while, Elizabeth had said it was probably best he didn't. Not until he got back on track. Until he got a handle on his drinking problem.

He agreed.

It took time. He eventually did overcome his demons, but by then it was too late.

"Her name was Natasha. She was a student of mine from high school. She asked to take one of my private classes. I wish I'd never started them. I was teaching music at the local high school in the day but offering additional one-on-one lessons at our home a few evenings a week. Piano."

His thoughts went back to her. The conversations they had. Natasha opening up about her struggles at home and school. "The offenses of sexual abuse were supposed to have taken place over two years."

"When mom was around?"

"Yes. I mean, for the most part, she was at the house but there were times when she stepped out to be with friends. That point was brought up. When I was arrested and heard the charges, I was blindsided. I didn't want to believe it at first. Not this girl." He shook his head.

Even thinking about it put a bad taste in his mouth and a knot in his stomach. "I'd been teaching at the high school for almost ten years, and offering private lessons for close to four without fault, and then I get one person with an ulterior motive accusing me and it essentially made those years mean nothing. After that, the community shunned me and your mom."

"So that's why she left you?"

Ryan nodded. "And I get it. I don't blame her one bit. Anyone in her position would have buckled under the strain. I know I did. It destroyed us emotionally. I ended up losing my job and then it just spiraled down from there."

"So how did your lawyer manage to disprove it? As it seems it would have been her word against yours."

Ryan sighed. "From what I recall it was a matter of credibility, inconsistencies, and her version of the events. A point that was made clear was that Natasha had continued to come out and take lessons for almost two years in the time she claimed the assaults occurred."

"Yeah, that's odd. I mean, no one would put themselves deliberately in that position when it was outside of school hours, right?"

"Exactly. Anyway, my lawyer was able to prove I didn't do it. The judge didn't believe her."

"It might have been different today with the Me Too movement and cancel culture," Josh said.

"Maybe," he said. "Look, I believe these things happen to people. I truly do. And I think every one of them should be taken seriously, however, in this case, I didn't do it."

Josh nodded. "Did everyone not believe you?"

"No. I had colleagues and lots of private students who vouched for me, but when these things happen, even the best of people will want to distance themselves from something like this. It doesn't look good on them, right?"

Josh glanced at him. "The articles didn't say why she accused you."

"She never said why. They never found out."

"But you have an idea?"

Ryan exhaled hard. "That's a question I've chewed over and over." He stared off into the distance as they sailed past one farm after another. "If I had to take a wild stab, I would say it was her home life. You know, students used to open up about what they were going through. I mean, somewhat. Some of them did. Not all had it good. She didn't have a good home life. Her parents weren't around much and when they were, they ignored her and basically treated her like a child. I think she resented that."

"Right."

Ryan noticed the way Josh replied but let it slide. "Who knows, maybe she did it to get her parents' attention as believe me, she had their full attention after that. But again, I'm just speculating."

"And yet you were left to deal with the aftermath."

"Not just me. Your mom. Even you."

"I don't remember much about those early years."

"That's probably best."

"But I do remember a few things."

Ryan smiled. "Really?"

"I mean, somewhat. It's a little hazy but yeah, I think. I mean sometimes I question my memories."

"You and me both, kid."

As they journeyed on and night fell like a dark blanket over the land, Josh fell asleep. With only his thoughts to keep him occupied, and pondering the conversation he'd had earlier, Ryan thought back to that time, that last night before Elizabeth left the home.

It had reached a boiling point.

Nothing he said made her feel any better.

They were at the table one evening, eating. Josh had been with his grandmother for the past week while he'd been dealing with lawyers. "I was at the store today," Elizabeth said, picking at her salad.

Ryan looked up at her and took a swig from a bottle of beer. Beer that he'd have on occasion but would eventually own him. "Yeah?"

"I bumped into Helen Ethridge. You remember her?"

"Somewhat."

"You know what she said?"

He clenched his eyes tight, knowing where this was going. He knew because they'd had multiple conversations just like that over the past month. Each one was worse than the last. Each time, Elizabeth revealed her frustration, her embarrassment.

"I think I can guess."

He chewed and looked at her, waiting for the CliffsNotes.

"I can't do this anymore, Ryan," she said, setting her fork down.

"Elizabeth. When the truth comes out, everything will go back to the way it was."

She scoffed. "No, it won't. You don't bounce back from this. It's like a stain that you can't remove. And it's not just on you, it's on me, it's on Josh. You know how many parents don't want him coming to their kids' birthday parties because of this?"

She got up and scraped food from her plate into the garbage. Elizabeth collected her glass of wine and leaned back against the kitchen counter. "I was reading about another case like this. It got dragged out for years, Ryan. Years. We've only been at this a month and it feels like a year. People look at me differently. They treat Josh differently. Like we're covering up some dirty secret of yours."

He set his cutlery down. "I'm sorry. I get it."

"No, you don't. I love you, Ryan. I believe you didn't do it."

"Do you? Because I'm not feeling that support."

"What do you expect me to say?"

"I don't expect you to say anything. Just be there with me. Isn't that why we married, to be there for each other?"

His words hung out to dry.

"This isn't going away, Ryan, and it's only getting worse. I'm thinking of heading to my parents' for a while. I have some vacation time that's owed to me. It's just to take a break from the town and…"

"I understand."

He should have known then where it would lead. A few weeks turned into several months, and heated conversations on the phone only ended one way, with her in tears and him listening to a disconnected tone.

# CHAPTER NINETEEN

July 8

*I*t was two in the morning on the day following Ella's death. The journey so far had been a series of stops and starts. What should have taken only a few hours was much longer. Blockades, detours and multiple attempts by those seeking their vehicle or to kill them had forced him to opt for a less direct route and weave all over rural Louisiana. With every passing hour, the fuel in the gas tank got lower and Ryan's stress level increased.

Lily remained asleep, only waking a few times to ask if they were there yet.

Josh had bundled up his jacket and was using it as a pillow against the passenger window.

In a landscape that had succumbed to a virus that spread rapidly, he imagined it was only a matter of time before their luck ran out.

However, stopping was no longer a question but a must.

They were somewhere west of Robert, Louisiana, just off Highway 190 when he veered off to the side of the road. The truck bumped over uneven ground that cut through a heavily wooded area that he believed took them into a farmer's field.

It didn't.

At the end of the long stretch was a two-story white clapboard farmhouse, and off to the right a huge red barn. There was a tractor nearby. No cars out front. The lights were off in the house.

Most of the homes along that road were spread out a good distance from each other, which in his mind meant there was less chance of them running into anyone. As Ryan swerved around to head out, because he figured someone was home, the headlights of the truck lit up the front of the house. He noticed the front door was wide open.

No one in their right mind would do that.

He stopped, and let the truck idle as he stared at the home. He honked on his horn a few times. If anyone was sleeping, a light might come on or the owner might come out. There was no movement. Josh stirred, rubbing his eyes. "Where are we?"

"Just outside the town of Robert."

Josh looked around. "I thought you said we weren't stopping for a while."

"You've been asleep for two hours, Josh. We're running on fumes and there is no gas left in the canisters."

Josh sat up in his seat and looked out. "Looks sketchy to me."

"Everywhere is like that. I'm going to take a look."

"Can't we just find another place?"

"They'll all be the same."

"So we find a farmer's field. It has to be safer than this." He looked at Lily as she stirred.

Rubbing her eyes she said, "Are we there yet?"

"We're somewhere," Josh said, pushing out of the vehicle and expecting a large dog to come barreling out of the darkness. On one side of them was a large cornfield, on the other two sides, forest. The property was several acres. The house, modest in size.

"Stay with Lily," Ryan said.

"Don't you need someone to watch your back?"

"I need you to watch her back, okay?"

Ryan turned on the light attached to his handgun as he approached the house. The beam spread wide, making it easy to see so he wasn't locked into tunnel vision. It was a Surefire XH35 with 1000 lumen, offering more than enough illumination.

He eyed the ground, the railings up to the porch, and the door.

There was no blood which was a good sign. The door didn't look as if it had been kicked in. The wooden frame was still intact as were the windows. Still, that didn't mean it wasn't a trap. They'd seen a few homes along the way offering people sanctuary for the night. They didn't stay. Anyone with a lick of sense knew that no one would offer that if they didn't have some hidden agenda.

Standing in the doorway, he peered into the darkness,

shining the light over the hardwood floors. At the far end was a kitchen. He began thinking of the numerous things that could have led to the occupants abandoning their home, or worse — that could go wrong if they were still here. Using his fist, he banged on the door then listened. "Hello!?"

No movement.

No floorboards creaking.

He eyed Josh one last time over his shoulder. He made a gesture to him to turn off the headlights. They blinked out, cloaking him in darkness. The last thing he wanted was to have anyone in the vicinity drawn up from the road to the house by the sight of bright headlights.

Ryan slowly went into the home, calling out to the occupants.

"Anyone here?"

He could have stayed silent but he didn't want to spook anyone.

"If you can hear me. Make yourself known. We're not here to harm anyone. Just need some gas, and a... place to... lay down for the night," he said, trailing off. Immediately off to his right was a small living room, across from that a dining area. The décor looked modern. It was clean. Nothing was damaged. Certainly, if someone had broken in, they were the tidiest home invaders in Louisiana. He quickly swept through each room on the lower level before heading upstairs. He glanced at family photos on the walls. His heart hammered in his chest, expecting someone to get the jump on him, but if there was anyone there, they weren't coming out.

The last place he checked was the attic.

There was nothing but lots of brown boxes.

Convinced that it was safe, he made his way down and told Josh to come inside. He went into the kitchen and searched the drawers for candles. He lit a couple and set them on the table. Then he went to the cupboards to check for food.

They were bare.

Josh entered the kitchen. "So what's the plan?"

"We'll stay a few hours. I need to find some gas. Get fueled up and we'll continue."

Lily came out of the bathroom. The toilet had rattled the pipes in the house as it flushed. "Are we staying?" she asked.

"For a little while." She took a seat at the table and stared at the flame.

"I'm going to check the barn. You good here?"

Josh gave a nod as he lifted his gun.

Ryan went out the back of the house and crossed the large grassy area between the two buildings. All the while he scanned the terrain. It was possible the family had heard them coming up the driveway and had hidden, so he wasn't taking any chances. He held the gun low as he entered the barn. There were no horses inside. He went from stall to stall, shining the light around.

That's when he saw them.

He stepped back, startled.

Hanging from the rafters. High above him. Two bodies. Both aged beyond their years. They look mummified. Ryan's jaw clenched. He was glad he came alone to spare Josh and Lily the horror. He grabbed the rung of the ladder and was about to climb to the upper tier when he heard a scream.

Ryan bolted out of the doors and hurried over to the house.

He burst in. "Lily?"

She was no longer screaming.

They weren't in the kitchen. "Josh?"

"Up here."

He bounded up the steps two at a time until he found them in the master bedroom. Josh had his hand over Lily's eyes. On the far side of the room, there was a dead dog. It had been shot in the head. He hadn't seen it when he cleared the room as he'd only checked the closet, which was immediately to the right of the door, and seen the bed was made. It was on the far side, hidden in the darkness by a thick blanket.

"Did you touch it?" Ryan asked.

No reply.

"DID YOU TOUCH IT!" he bellowed.

"No," Josh said.

There was blood splatter on the wall behind it.

Ryan beckoned them outside. He'd hoped to spare her the horror of witnessing that.

He crouched down in front of Lily. "Hey, butterfly. Don't be going in there again, okay?"

She nodded. He led them downstairs.

"Look, I need to see if I can find some gas."

"Should we go with you?" Josh asked.

"No, you're probably safer here."

"Probably? Were you just in the room with us?"

"Look, whoever did that is probably long gone. Lock

the doors and stay out of sight. I won't be long. Oh, and don't go in the barn."

"And what if you don't come back?"

"Nothing will happen to me."

"Yeah, I expect Ella thought the same."

"That was different. Look, Josh, you wanted me to trust you. This is me trusting you. Okay?"

"You know what. Just go. We'll be fine." Josh walked into the kitchen and fished out of his bags some snacks they'd collected from the grocery store. Ryan stood in the hallway contemplating staying, but they needed gas. They still had miles to go before reaching Florida and if today was anything like the previous ones, they could find themselves arriving just as the boats were leaving. "I won't be long. Lock the doors."

Ryan exited and collected the ten-gallon canister. First, he checked the tractor that was nearby. It was bone dry. There were no other vehicles on the property. He glanced at the house then took off at a jog, cutting through the tall, green sugarcane field as he headed to the closest neighbor's home. If he couldn't find any there, he would head back and wait until morning and see if they could find some vehicles on the way.

The truck wasn't entirely empty but it was close.

In the quiet of the house, Lily chewed on a granola bar, then stuck her hand into a packet of gummies, pulling them out and filling her mouth. Josh had collected a couple of cans of soda pop from their stash and was listening intently to every sound. Outside, there was only the chorus of crickets. "Do you think he'll leave us?"

"What makes you say that?"

"Because mom did."

"Bean. Ryan's not mom. He's got our backs."

"You didn't think so back at the barn."

"That was different."

"How so?"

"Just eat up." He needed a cigarette, or a beer, something to take his mind off things. He opened the pantry and went inside, shining a small flashlight around. There were some bags of flour, and the rest was pickles. Whoever lived here had gone on a canning spree and had put everything but the kitchen sink in a jar. He unscrewed the top and took a whiff. His eyes widened, and his face twisted. "Shit, that is bad."

"Do you think about her?" Lily asked.

"Who?"

"Mom."

"Of course," he said, peering out the back window. It was pitch dark outside. If anyone was lurking he wouldn't have been able to see them. He turned. Shadows danced on Lily's face from the flicker of the candle's flame.

"You don't talk about her."

He set the can down. "You talk too much. Aren't you tired?"

"No. Can we go upstairs?"

"We're not going back to that room."

"No, the other one looked like a girl's room."

"No. We stay here," he said, feeling agitated.

Lily lowered her chin and he caught the expression on

her face. "All right. Just for a few minutes." A smile spread and she got up and hurried up the stairs.

"Bean. Hold up."

He blew out the candles and used his flashlight to light the way. Lily had stopped halfway up, waiting for him. As soon as he had made it a few steps up, she raced to the top and ran into a room on the east side of the home. When he entered, he shone the light around. There were posters of TV shows and movies, and guys with their shirts off. There was a stack of records against a vintage record player. Lily made a beeline for some makeup on a table. She opened it and unscrewed some lipstick. He snatched it out of her hand before she could put it on her lips.

"Hey!" Lily protested.

"You don't know where that's been," he replied, putting it back.

"I just wanted to..."

"Look, don't touch. That's the deal."

"We can't get the bug by touching things."

"Lily, just listen to me."

"You ate from that can. Someone touched that."

"Yeah, but they didn't smear it on their lips."

"How do you know?"

"Bean, you ask a lot of questions. Do I look like I've aged?"

"I don't know. In this light, you look kind of scary."

"I do, do I?" He pulled a face, shining the light up under his chin, and she chuckled.

As Lily looked through a series of books using a mini light, Josh roamed the room shining the beam over shelves of collectibles. He opened the closet. It was full of clothes on hangers. There was only one palette. Black. He was shining the light up when he caught a glimpse of something moving. That's when he jumped back. On the top shelf contained within a glass cabinet were two tarantulas. "Who the hell keeps spiders and especially ones that size?"

Lily whirled around. "What? Let me see."

Josh closed the closet. "I think not. You have bad dreams as it is."

He took a seat on the bed and scooped up what looked like a diary. He flipped it open and began reading the first few pages. It mostly contained small snippets of the person's day. What they did, where they went, how they felt. It was only when he flipped through to about halfway that he began reading accounts related to the outbreak.

*Dad had to bury Keith today. He lit his body on fire. God, I miss him.*

*We're running out of food. I took a trip to the grocery store with dad. People were fighting over the last remaining items on the shelves. It's getting scary out there.*

*The news keeps showing images of people spreading the pathogen. Mom wants to head north to her parents in Canada. Dad won't go. He thinks it's safer here.*

*Dad got sick today. He sleeps in the barn now. Mom won't stop crying.*

*I had to go into town by myself. I barely escaped. I had to leave the truck behind.*

*Every day is harder than the previous one. What happens if the power goes out? I'm losing hope.*

*Mom is sick now. She won't say how it happened but I think she touched him. They're aging fast and at this rate will be dead before the week is over.*

*I can't handle listening to them groaning in pain. It's unbearable.*

*What will I do when they are gone? Where will I go?*

*They hung themselves today. THEY HUNG THEMSELVES!!!!!!*

*I cried all day today. I haven't gotten out of bed. I just want to die.*

*There's so much I haven't gotten to do with my life yet.*

*Why is this happening? If it wasn't for Jasper I don't think I could get through each day.*

*I hate him. I hate him so much. I wish he was dead.*

*Three times I put the gun to my head today, considering pulling the trigger. I can't do it. I'm such a chicken shit.*

Josh was about to turn the page when he heard a noise downstairs.

A clunk. The door groaned open.

# CHAPTER TWENTY

*H*e'd locked it. His father didn't have the key, he did.

Lily was humming while reading a book when Josh closed the diary and put it back where it was. He clasped a firm hand over her mouth. She dropped the book on the bed. He spoke quietly in her ear.

"Don't make a sound. Someone's in the house."

Lily tensed.

He released her and without making a sound crossed the room to close the door. Before he did, Josh paused and peered into the darkness. He could hear movement. One person. They weren't trying to stay silent. Every footstep was heavy. Did the person even know they were here? The stranger strolled into the living room and stopped. Were they listening?

He heard something get picked up and placed back down.

What were they doing? Who was it? They headed into the kitchen.

"What do we have here?" a deep booming male voice said. "Oh, Ren, I thought you were smarter than this." Josh's brow furrowed. "Leaving your gun behind?"

The gun. He reached around to the small of his back.

*No. No. NO.*

It was gone. *Shit.* He must have set it down on the kitchen counter when he was pulling items out of the pantry. Josh squinted as he shut the door, trying to stay quiet. He brought a finger up to his lips as he made his way over to the window. He was about to shimmy it up when he saw movement outside. Under the canopy of the blackest night, he couldn't see the face but the person stopped and looked up at the window. Quickly, he stepped back, hoping not to be seen, but his hip nudged a low shelf and a snow globe toppled off. Time seemed to slow. Almost bending backward in a *Matrix-style* pose, he caught the globe before it hit the hardwood.

His heart raced as he registered Lily's reaction. Her mouth was wide, her hands cupping the lower half of her face. Josh set it back down.

"C'mon Ren! Are we going to keep doing this? Look, I know you're mad about Jasper. Maybe I took things a little too far but you wouldn't listen. What I suggested is only fair. You know, being siblings and all."

More silence.

Plates shattered, a glass hit a wall and what sounded like the kitchen armoire being overturned put both of them on high alert. "Ren, you are pissing me off!"

Josh didn't dare look out the window again, out of fear of being spotted. Or had he already been?

*Think. Think!*

If the person was infected, he couldn't get near them to fight.

One touch, that's all it took and he'd have a different battle.

His eyes scanned the room for anything that could be used as a weapon — something long, firm, and liable to cause massive damage — a baseball bat, an award trophy, or... He snatched up a tall floor lamp. He took the end off, unplugged it from the wall, and wrapped the wire around the pole. It was solid metal. A good six feet long. It wasn't ideal but it might keep whoever was out there at a distance at least until Lily could climb out the window.

Out the corner of his eye, he caught a dark mass move past the pane of glass. He glanced at it but there was nothing there. Was his mind playing tricks on him? Was fear getting the best of him? The stranger continued to bellow. "You and I both know how this ends. Now be a good sister and come on out. I'm getting a little tired of your games."

Josh inched over to the window. Part of the lower half of the roof jutted out. At least Lily stood a chance. He could hold off the stranger if it came to it. He stared into the ink of night. No one was out there. Whoever was on the ground was gone.

He scanned the sugarcane field.

What the hell was taking Ryan so long? This was just like him, leaving them in their hour of need.

Josh heard footsteps coming up the stairs.

He couldn't wait any longer.

He set the lamp down and rushed to the window and

was just about to lift it when on the other side a girl shuffled into view.

Their eyes locked.

Behind him, outside the room almost at the top of the landing, the stranger cried out.

"I can hear you, Ren!"

What was probably less than a second, felt like minutes.

In an instant, he locked the window.

The girl slapped a hand against it, shaking her head.

Josh stepped back and snagged up the tall floor lamp not taking his eyes off the girl. "Lily. When I say open the door. Open it and run over to the master bedroom. You hear me?"

She nodded and didn't hesitate.

Even at her young age, she knew the inherent danger.

Josh adjusted his grip on the lamp, wielding it like a jousting spear.

Lily stood behind the door, gripping the handle and waiting for the word.

The stranger on the other side got closer. "I knew you'd eventually come back. I knew you'd come to your senses." A steady knuckle rap on the door. Josh gave a nod and Lily pulled back the door. Josh was already in mid-sprint. Had she not opened it fast enough, he would have driven that lamp through the door. He burst out, driving the tip into the stranger sending them reeling back.

"Lily. Go!" he yelled.

It was too dark to make out who it was but they were an adult, that's for sure.

Caught off guard, dealing with the pain of having a lamp jammed in their gut, they didn't stand a chance. Josh drove the individual back to the top of the stairs only a few feet away. They struggled to clasp the banister before they toppled backward down the stairs.

Behind him Lily shot by, entering the main bedroom.

Josh followed, closing the door and hurrying over to the window. He set the lamp down and tried to open it but it was locked. He fumbled with the latch but it didn't matter what he set it to, it wouldn't budge.

That's when he noticed nails.

Someone had hammered nails into the outside frame. Even if it was unlocked he wouldn't have been able to open it. Had the other window been the same?

Outside the room, he heard groaning.

"You didn't tell me we had guests, Ren! I would have baked a cake, put on a clean shirt, brought a welcome gift."

Lily was staring at the dead dog.

Doing the only thing he could, Josh took the lamp and smashed the windowpane. Shards of glass exploded outward, rolling across the lower roof like tiny pebbles. All the while he heard the stranger struggling to climb up the stairs.

"All right, Lily, out you go."

"But that girl..."

Josh stuck his head out. There was no one there.

"I want you out the window. Now!"

"What about you?"

"I'll be right behind you."

As he helped her out of the window, she caught her skin on some glass, cutting her hand.

"Are you okay?"

She grimaced, clutching her hand. Josh was just about to follow her when the door burst open. The stranger filled the opening like a dark, looming demon of darkness. "Going somewhere?" Josh had no choice but to snatch up the floor lamp. He wouldn't have made it out in time. He jabbed it at the guy as he entered the room, slamming the door behind him.

"Stay back," Josh said.

"Oh, I can't do that."

The stranger darted left trying to get around the tip, but Josh was quick and flipped the end piece around like a dragon's tail, whipping him across the top of the head and knocking him onto the bed. "Stay back or I'll kill you."

The stranger brought a hand up to his face. "So will I."

As quick as a flash, the stranger bounced up, this time trying to go under and tackle Josh's waist. It failed. Josh sidestepped and kicked him in the face.

Circling him, Josh now had his back pressed to the door, he went for the handle, planning to go out that way, but the stranger had another idea.

Desperation drove him up and forward.

Josh lunged again, this time driving the stranger back toward the window. The upper half of his body bent out of the opening, leaving only the lower half inside. That's when he got a better look at him.

He was black, middle-aged, and clearly infected. A rash had spread over the left side of his neck and face, and there was blood trickling out of his nose.

Pinned, the stranger reached for Josh, trying to touch him.

But he kept his distance.

Crying out loud, it took every muscle in Josh's body to hold him. He knew he wouldn't be able to hold the position for long.

Then it happened.

"Do it!" the stranger said.

From out of view a gun erupted and the stranger went limp.

Blood oozed from the side of his temple. For a second, he thought Ryan was back. Then the girl appeared. She looked at him then at Lily who was crouched, arms around her knees, hands over her ears. "Don't you touch her!" Josh shouted. "Don't you go near her."

"Believe me. I don't plan on it." She looked despondently down at the stranger one more time before backing away. Josh released his grip on the floor lamp and hurried out of the room, down the stairs, and outside. The air was thick and humid. He made his way around to the front and raised both of his arms. She hadn't moved from the spot and was staring at the stranger.

"Jump, Lily."

She looked over her shoulder. "It's too high."

"I'll catch you."

She hesitated for a few seconds and then launched herself off the porch roof. Josh let out an "Ooof!" as he caught her. They crumpled. He ran a hand over her face. "You okay?"

She nodded. Josh looked up again, wondering where the girl had gone. She wasn't on the porch roof anymore.

"Come on, we need to find dad."

"You should put a bandage on that hand of hers," a voice said.

He looked back to find the girl standing in the doorway of the house.

Josh didn't respond. He tightened his grip on Lily's hand and hurried to the truck.

"I'm not infected," she said.

He stopped just as he was about to open the passenger side and put Lily in. Josh looked back and saw the girl had come out and sat down on the step. She lit a cigarette and blew out smoke. It drifted in the breeze. Under a starless sky, he still couldn't fully see her features. Just her form. She was black. The same as the stranger. That he could tell from when he locked eyes with her.

Before he could reply, Ryan came running out of the field, rifle at the ready. He tossed the gasoline can down and lifted the rifle at the girl, unaware that Josh and Lily were on the other side of the truck. "What did you do?"

"Dad," Josh said, coming around the truck.

"Josh?"

Lily ran toward Ryan and clung to his side. "You okay? You hurt?"

Lily showed her hand. He looked back up again at the girl who still hadn't moved. She didn't seem fazed by the rifle. She leaned back on the porch, puffing away, legs outstretched, ankles crossed.

"What happened?" Ryan asked.

Lily pointed up to the roof where the man's body was hanging out of the window.

"No one was touched," Josh said before he could ask.

"You shot him?"

"No, she did," Lily said. "Josh's gun was downstairs."

"What?"

"We're okay," Josh said firmly, noting the look of judgment in his eyes. "Besides, where were you?" Maybe he shouldn't have tagged the last bit on the end but he figured it would put things in perspective, especially since his father looked as if he was about to dish out a lecture.

"I came as soon as I heard the gunshot."

"Yeah, well, obviously not soon enough."

"And I thought my family was messed up," the girl said without a hint of amusement as she rose to her feet and headed back inside. "If you're hungry, feel free to come in."

"Who are you?" Ryan asked.

Not even looking at him, she replied, "The name's Ren. I live here."

With that said she walked into the house.

# CHAPTER TWENTY-ONE

"Isaac. He was my younger brother," she said, sliding a steel-framed family photo across the table. Ryan stared at it under the glow of a lantern and several candles around the kitchen. In the family portrait were the parents, whom he believed were hanging in the barn, then there was Ren, two other boys, and a younger brother that had to be three, maybe four years younger than Lily.

"How old?"

"In that? Seven," she said, stopping to take a swig from a can of Coke before continuing to clean Josh's gun. She was wearing latex gloves, an N95 mask, and goggles. She had a red bandanna around her head to keep a huge mass of hair in check. He noticed she was wearing a black crop top, and another bandanna around her neck to protect any exposed areas of skin. She had tight black jeans and ankle boots. There was an air of confidence to her, the way she dismantled the gun. It certainly wasn't the first time she'd seen one. "He was that age until he got sick. By my estimate, he must have aged around thirty years in just over two weeks. Give or take. If the reports are right, people are aging around two years every day. He got sick a couple of weeks ago."

Josh sat at the table, eating some of the food she'd offered. Surprisingly it was good, more than they'd come across in a while. It was packets of beef jerky. Her father had the good sense to run out and get as much as he could when the first wave of news hit outlets. She'd stored the supply outside the house in an insulated container that was hidden.

"How old are you?" Ryan asked.

"Is that a trick question?" she replied with a deadpan expression. "Seventeen. Give or take a few days."

"Happy birthday," Lily mumbled with a mouth full of soda pop.

"Lily. Not with your mouth full," Josh said.

Ren's eyes darted between them. No smile. It was to be expected. Only moments ago she'd had to kill her brother. "So, you all family?" she asked.

"That's right."

"Where you from?"

"Texas."

"A little out of the way. What brought you to our neck of the woods?"

Neither of them replied.

"Ah, it's secret. Okay. I can respect that. You don't know me. I don't know you."

"So what's the deal with your brother?" Josh asked. "I mean obviously he was trying to stop the aging in himself but it sounded like you two had been at it a while."

"Hide and seek. Yeah, you could say it was something like that."

"Why didn't you just leave?"

"And go where? It's not like there are any safe zones out there."

"I mean, why did you stick around here?" Josh asked.

She stopped cleaning the gun and looked out the window, thoughtful. "I don't know exactly. I thought about killing him sooner. But I just couldn't bring myself to do it. Figured he'd eventually get too old and die."

"And your other brothers?"

"My father killed them; Keith first, Martin, after that. Then when he got sick, he asked my mother to squeeze the trigger but she wouldn't. She stuck him in the barn and told him that maybe they would find a cure. That didn't happen. He hung himself. My mother lost it. After losing two of her sons in a month, she couldn't bear the thought of living without him. Two days later I found her hanging beside him."

"You mean she purposely killed herself?"

She nodded.

"But she still had you two?" Ryan said.

Ren looked at him. "She touched him. She was infected. Still, I think if she hadn't, she would have hung herself anyway."

"Why?"

"Does that surprise you?" Ren asked.

"It's just not what I would do."

He didn't say anything so she continued. "You might not but others are doing it. Families. Taking their kids' lives and then their own rather than face this. Crazy, right?" She chuckled but Ryan could tell that she didn't find anything funny about it. It was a mechanism, a response to dealing with the situation.

The problem was that she was telling the truth.

There were so many fears surrounding getting old as it was, but now with the virus increasing the speed, and the videos circulating online of the horrific and painful manner in which people died, for some that was too much of a gamble. They didn't want to bury their kids any more than he did. He hadn't considered what he would do if Josh and Lily were exposed to the pathogen. He'd been so focused on keeping them alive that this had reminded him — that even in the most isolated areas, danger could be lurking. Even though he wanted to trust Josh, he couldn't drop his guard for one minute.

"After that. It was just me and Isaac. We kept the lights in the house off at night. I ventured into town for supplies and he would hide in the attic while I was away." She stopped cleaning and got this faraway look in her eyes. "I came back from a trip to collect supplies and found him on the porch. They'd used rope to tie him to the main post. He told me that he saw from the attic a small girl crying. She was alone. At least he thought she was." She clenched her hand and closed her eyes. "I'd told him countless times that under no conditions was he to leave the attic. No matter what he heard or saw. Anyway, that's how they got him. Apparently, the young one was infected. As soon as he stepped outside, the father scooped Isaac up. And that... is that. I mean I get it. I understand. No parent wants to bury their child, but..."

They sat there listening intently as she resumed cleaning the gun.

"Anyway, I cut the rope and isolated him in the house. He asked if I was going to shoot him. I never gave him an answer. After a week, he was older than me, and that's when the problems started. He wanted out."

"So he chased you to transmit it?"

"Yes and no. He wanted me to kill him and I wouldn't do it. At least not until today."

"That's why he said, do it," Josh added.

She nodded.

Ren cast a glance at Ryan. "He didn't have the nerve to take his own life. He felt it was only right that I take it because I'd left him behind. Left him alone." She paused. "He blamed me. That's why he killed Jasper. My dog."

She splashed the gun with more bleach and continued cleaning.

"I've never seen a gun cleaned with bleach," Josh said. He chuckled.

"You are aware of how the pathogen is transmitted, right?" Ryan asked.

Ren nodded. "Of course."

"Then you know people are exposed to it through direct, not indirect contact."

"Right. Blood, saliva, vomit, diarrhea, sweat, semen, breast milk, shit, urine, a kiss, and from anyone who has died. Yeah. I got the memo. Hence the reason assholes are chasing people instead of just vomiting on park benches, playgrounds, or over door handles."

She continued scrubbing, not looking at him.

They offered her a puzzled look.

Ryan continued. "So then you would know it's not transferred indirectly by way of touching contaminated surfaces, or objects that were held by carriers, or even through mosquitoes that have bitten an infected."

"Well, that last part is still up for debate. I mean, it's not like society has had the time to sit around on talk shows shooting the breeze and working out the fine details. My motto is when in doubt... don't believe a damn word people say," she said, continuing to scrub.

Ryan considered the dogs back in that grocery store. They had blood from the infected on their teeth. If Ella's leg hadn't been torn so badly, could she have survived? If any one of them had been bitten, would they have begun aging? It was food for thought. There was still a lot about the virus that they didn't understand. Even Ella said it wasn't a typical virus.

Ren finished and set everything out in pieces on a clean cloth. "It should be dry soon. You know how to put one back together?" she asked Josh.

He nodded as she walked out of the room.

Ryan nudged him. "Eat up. We aren't staying."

"Did you find gas?" Josh said.

"No. There was none."

"I have gas if you need it," she said, appearing in the doorway. Ren peeled off latex gloves and tossed them into a basket before squirting sanitizer over her hands, and rubbing them, then squirting more. She followed that by putting on another pair. It was like she had OCD. She was working on a whole other level and was making a point not to come near them even though they'd told her they weren't infected. "The gas. It's from the

Sommers property. Our neighbor. Where you went, I assume."

"So you took it?" Ryan replied.

"Well, she is our neighbor." She leaned against the doorway, a smirk lingering at the corner of her lips. For someone who had just taken out her brother, she seemed a little too calm about it, almost removed. Was it shock? A form of PTSD from witnessing her entire family wiped out? "It's yours under a few conditions."

"What?"

"Where's the safe zone?"

"What makes you think we're heading to a safe zone?" Ryan asked.

"What other reason would you jeopardize the lives of your two children?"

Ryan stared back at her. He knew where she was going with this. Another hitchhiker, another one to think about.

"Josh. Lily. Get your things. We're leaving."

"But the gas," Josh said.

"We'll find some on the way."

"And the gun? It hasn't even finished drying."

"Leave it. It wasn't much use to you anyway." The words slipped out without him thinking. It was an innocent mistake anyone could have made. He didn't want to make him feel like an idiot but he had.

"I'm not going yet, it's the dead of night," he shot back.

"Josh. Get in the truck!"

He glared at him.

They collected their belongings and made their way out. Josh caught up with Ryan. "She's just offered us gas. Food. Hell, even a roof over our head for tonight. We need it. Lily needs it. Why won't you tell her where we're going?"

"Because the next condition she'd have is to come with us. And that's not happening."

Josh looked back at Ren who was leaning against the porch. "Why not? She can go in the bed of the truck like Ella did."

"Think about what you are asking."

"I am."

"No," he said. He tossed his bag and the empty ten-gallon canister into the truck then made his way around to the driver's side. Josh spoke to him across the back of the truck bed.

"You don't want her to come because of what happened to Ella. Right?"

"Get in the truck, Josh."

"No. Answer the question."

"I said get in the truck. I'm not having this conversation."

"Well, I am. If anyone should feel to blame for her death it's me."

"No. You don't get to do that."

"Yes, I do. I was on the other side with her. Not you. There were a few seconds I could have shot that dog before it latched on to her. I didn't. I froze. That's on me. Not you. Now, that girl saved us. Okay? If it wasn't for her, there's a good chance both of us would be infected. So I'm going to tell her where the safe zone is. And if she wants to come, she's coming."

He walked off. Ryan shook his head and let out an exasperated sigh. All he needed was to be responsible for one more life. It was hard enough as it was. He already felt like he'd let them down in the past, and almost lost them searching for gas.

Lily stood there, holding her small backpack in one hand, and a bear in the other.

"Does he argue often?" Ryan asked.

"Josh? All the time. I've just learned to tune him out," she said with a flicker of a smile before climbing into the truck. That made him chuckle. "Well? Are we going?" Lily asked. Ryan looked back at the house to where Josh was talking to Ren.

# CHAPTER TWENTY-TWO

*E*xecutions were a daily occurrence.

The numerous dead bodies strung up with blame-filled placards draped around their neck served as a warning to anyone not to linger. It wasn't the first time they'd seen it. This morbid display had become an all too familiar sight, dotted throughout the landscape, in cities and small towns.

As local radio broadcasts became the breeding ground for misinformation, the color of a person's skin, sexual orientation, disability, religion, or race no longer mattered. No one group was blamed for the outbreak. Everyone was a target.

In the eyes of town lynch mobs, fear was the justification for hatred.

And in a pandemic, nothing spread faster than fear.

Now, fear was firing on all cylinders.

After spending the night at Ren's home in Robert, Louisiana, they rolled out at the break of day, hoping to put in as many miles as they could before dark. The plan was to not stop until they reached Alabama, one state over. That was foolish thinking.

Mississippi proved to be far more challenging than he had banked on. It seemed they weren't the only ones who were heading for the safety of the water. Interstate 12, which offered the most direct route east along the coast, was controlled by quasi-military and blockades. They were checking for those who were sick. With traffic bumper-to-bumper, the chances of his truck's engine overheating in the soaring temperatures were high.

As drivers got out to see what was holding up the line, a slew of gunfire answered that. While he didn't see the carnage unfold, he didn't have to — word spread fast down a line of trucks, RVs, and cars. Those found to be infected were being pulled from vehicles and thrown into the back of wagons to be quarantined. Anyone who opposed was dealt with in a deadly fashion.

It was a sifting of the chaff from the wheat.

For better or worse, he saw his opening and took it before it was too late. Ryan swerved out of the traffic down an off-ramp and headed north on Highway 21 to merge with Highway 26. From there they would head south on US-98 which would take them across Alabama. The downside was the route led them away from the southerly shore and through an endless slew of small towns and rural settings.

If the GPS was anything to go by, they had just under four hundred miles ahead of them. It would have been a steady six and a half hour journey if they didn't stop and the roads were clear, but they weren't and now with a detour, realistically they were looking at another two days, factoring in sleeping at night, finding gas, avoiding the sick, and lynch mobs.

In one sense it was good to be away from the crowds. The roads were better and the odds of contracting the aging were less, but even in isolated towns danger wasn't absent.

Lawlessness was rampant.

That only became clearer when they stopped in the city of Wiggins, Mississippi.

Food wasn't the issue. They could go days without that. It was water. In this heat, thirst could make a man go mad. Each time they stopped, they would fill up one five-gallon jug from abandoned homes or businesses while one of them searched for extra gasoline.

His old clunker wasn't getting the best miles to the gallon so it was burning through what they had faster than they could find it. He'd seriously considered dumping it and stealing another vehicle as it wasn't like the cops were checking license and registration, but that meant finding one, or carjacking someone and he wasn't ready yet to cross that line.

Since their arrival, Ryan had felt an overwhelming sense of responsibility to set an example, to lead and prove to his kids, specifically Josh, that he was more than a recovering alcoholic stained by a false accusation. That was behind him. The past. He'd done better things since. He held down a regular job, paid his bills on time, and even volunteered at a local shelter. Not that any of that mattered anymore.

While they collected water from a restaurant where the

front windows had been shattered, Ren said she wanted to do her part and find some gas.

It was quiet in the downtown near the crossroads of East Pine Avenue and First Street North. The few people they'd seen as they rolled through town were quick to scurry away. They figured the stop would amount to no more than ten minutes. What they didn't bank on was what would come next.

A horn honked.

It sounded like the General Lee from *The Dukes of Hazzard.*

Ryan stepped out onto the street, Josh, and Lily behind him, only to find the street empty. That changed as two people with children burst into view to the right of them, they wheeled around the corner near the crossroads if they were being chased by a bull.

There was no time to duck back into the store.

Instantly they dropped behind a station wagon, taking cover.

Following close behind, a 1991 red Chevrolet Silverado 4 x 4 swerved into view and tore down the street after them.

In the back three men were standing up, holding on to the roll bars and bearing hunting rifles. Ryan watched as one of them opened fire, dropping the male who was carrying a young girl.

The two of them hit the ground hard.

The girl let out a scream.

Still alive, the guy gestured for his wife to keep running but she slowed to help.

A young boy waited nearby as she tried to get the guy up but another round to the back of the leg dropped him.

The truck swerved diagonally, stopping a few feet away.

"Who are they?" Josh asked as the ruthless group pursued its prey, hooting, and hollering.

Two growling ATVS came barreling down the street from the east. Even if the family had managed to elude the truck, they would have been cut off by the rest of the mob.

The three men jumped out of the back.

All of them looked like your typical small-town residents. Nothing jumped out to him as a hate group, militant, or having any affiliations.

There were no symbols. No patches on their clothes. They bore no signs with messages.

In fact, their lack of protection was the only thing that set them apart. They wore muscle shirts, jeans, plaid shirts, no gloves, no masks, no eyewear. It was as if they were toying with fate, unafraid to die or immune.

Was anyone immune to this? To date, there had been no reports of such people. All those who came in contact with the aging were dealt a death sentence unless they could transfer it to others.

"Please. Leave us be," the woman said.

"Put the young one in the back of the truck."

"No!" the mother howled as they scooped up the boy. The child screamed bloody murder as he was taken to the truck and his mother had a rifle butt thrust into the back of her head.

The father couldn't help. He was in agony from his

gunshot wounds. He was bleeding out and only able to claw forward enough to grasp his wife's hand.

The men didn't take the girl who couldn't have been more than eight years old.

He couldn't hear what the men were saying but they forced the three at gunpoint onto their knees. The two parents began praying, hands clasped together, eyes to the sky.

The look of anguish was unlike anything he'd seen.

Were they being given a chance to make peace with their maker?

Were they begging for their child's life?

In an instant, the men executed all three of them in cold blood with one round to the head.

Why had they killed the one child but taken the other?

"String them up."

A heavyset man with a bald head and a goatee seemed to be in charge. Nooses were brought out and wrapped around the deceased's necks and the other end slung over the top of street lamps. A placard was placed over the head of one of them. Two men pulled on the other end and lifted them high. Ryan squinted trying to make out what it said.

As the rope was tied off and the bodies twisted in the air, the bald man surveyed the road, his eyes washing over the buildings. He turned away then for a second looked back as if he'd seen something. Ryan froze. Was it their reflection in the window? All that stood between them and these men was a line of parked cars at the edge of the road.

"What is he staring at?" Josh said, his hand wrapped

tightly over Lily's mouth as if expecting her to give away their position.

Sweat beaded on Ryan's face, rolling down his cheek.

No. He wasn't looking at them.

He tapped one of the men and pointed to their truck that was parked on the other side of the road farther down. Ryan had made a point to never park outside the building they went in. It gave them a way out, it would serve as a distraction. He didn't expect someone to recognize the difference on the road but that told him they were locals. Familiar with the area. Folks who had been down this road enough times to know what was out of place.

"Shit, he's seen it."

All they could do was watch as one of the guys made his way down. He figured they would check inside, see it was empty, maybe explore a few of the stores in front of where it was parked before returning and leaving.

The sound of the engine made his stomach drop.

"Did you leave the keys inside?" he asked Josh.

Josh nodded. He replied in a low voice, "There was no one on the road. We didn't see anyone passing through."

"Josh."

"I thought we were getting water and going."

He closed his eyes, pushing down the urge to argue. It wouldn't serve them now.

His truck rumbled up the road to meet the others.

There were a few tense moments as Baldy eyed the stores. Would they search for them? All it would take was for them to cross over to the other side of the street and they'd be exposed.

The wait was killing him.

Instead, the bald guy twirled his finger in the air and the rest got back on the ATVs and hopped into the other truck, and peeled out of there.

They remained where they were for what felt like an hour but was probably only five minutes before they emerged. Ryan listened intently for the sound of vehicle engines as he crossed the street to read the placard.

He grimaced at the sight of the young child. No mercy was shown. She was just a kid. The body of the woman twisted. The rope making a creaking sound.

*And these signs shall follow them that believe; in my name shall they cast out devils; they shall speak with new tongues; they shall take up serpents.*

"What do you make of that?" Josh asked.

He noticed that all three of them were showing signs of infection, and yet the group had got close to them. Were they even aware of the danger? A month into this and those they'd met so far knew how it spread.

"I think we should find Ren and leave immediately."

Easier said than done now they were without wheels.

He turned away from the macabre sight. "Check the vehicles. See if any of them are open, or have… keys," Ryan said emphasizing the last word to make it clear that he was not impressed or expecting them to have keys.

"I'm sorry. Okay."

"Just search while I check on Ren."

Ryan jogged to the corner of the block and looked up the street to see if she was returning from the Marathon station on the corner of College Avenue.

She should have been back by now.

There was no sign of her.

He regretted agreeing to have her come with them. Even though she was traveling in the back of the truck. It was just one more person that he had to think about. One more reason they couldn't just up and leave. Besides, gasoline without a vehicle wouldn't be much use now.

He looked back and saw Josh and Lily going down the line of parked cars, peering in, checking handles. The two of them locked eyes. If he was hard on him, it was because he was trying to keep them alive. But on the road, not everything would go right. A decision here, a mistake there, a lack of judgment, no one was immune to oversight.

"Come on, Ren," he muttered, holding his rifle and expecting any minute now the same bizarre group to circle back.

In the distance, he could see movement through the trees. He was too far away to see the station. Ryan jogged a little further up the road, darting from one vehicle to the next.

The downtown was run-down.

By the looks of it, many of the stores were empty long before the event had hit.

Ryan pulled out his compact high-power binoculars and crouched behind a minivan. As he adjusted the focus and tried to get a bead on the gas station, he spotted the two trucks and ATVs. Locked on to them, he observed them swerve into the gas station. Outside were large signs that read: GAS FOR TRADE.

That was a first. The gas stations were one of the first to be hit after the pathogen got out of control. The price per gallon had skyrocketed as long lines of vehicles bled them dry. Ren hadn't said where she'd go for the gas, only that she'd be back soon. The Marathon was the closest, and with a sign like that, he imagined she would have approached it versus siphoning from vehicles. Siphoning wasn't as easy on new models. Many of them had anti-siphon valves. They commonly used a mesh screen.

Ryan watched the men stop their vehicles, and climb out. They disappeared out of view as they entered the station. He shifted the binoculars to the back of the truck. The young boy was in tears. Not only had he been torn away from his family but he had to watch their execution. Who were these men? And did they control the town?

A moment later, they re-emerged though now with another captive. Thrashing in their grasp was Ren.

She elbowed one of them in the stomach, and stomped on the other guy's foot, and tried to make a break for it. She didn't get far. A swift jab to the side of her face from Baldy's rifle and she hit the ground. Limp.

They dragged her to the truck and loaded the new cargo.

## CHAPTER TWENTY-THREE

*L*ily stared wide-eyed at the bodies while they waited in a rumbling Jeep Cherokee.

"Stop looking at them, Bean," Josh said. The vehicle had just over a quarter tank of gas. He'd waited until his father was gone before he shattered the driver's side window and hotwired it — a trick that could have landed him in juvie. He'd once taken a neighborhood car on a joyride with a group of friends. One of them had shown him how to do it.

Conversation soon shifted to the family. Lily had questions. She wanted to know why those men had killed them, if they were bad, and what would happen if they caught her.

"They won't get you."

"But how do you know?"

He shifted in his seat, looking into the back. "You're alive, aren't you?"

She nodded and stared ahead but he caught her eyes

darting over to the victims. Josh twisted in his seat. "They had the virus." He just came out with it. It was the only justifiable way of explaining what they had done. He didn't want her to think that they'd killed in cold blood without a reason.

"Does that happen to everyone?"

"No. Just them."

"That's a lie."

"How is it?"

"I saw the others. Along the highway."

He sighed. "Look, people do bad things to others when they are scared. Don't worry, because we'll be long gone before they come back. Okay?" He reached over and shifted her face away from it. It was everywhere and only getting worse by the day. Eventually, she'd understand the full scope of it, if she didn't already.

But like him, she wasn't one to let things go until she got an answer. "So are they bad people?"

"No. I mean, yes but…" As the words came out of his mouth, Ryan burst around the corner, running at full sprint down the strip of stores. Josh honked the horn and put his hand out. Ryan's eyes widened as he approached and got in the passenger side. His eyes went to the ignition, probably expecting to see a set of keys. Instead, wires were hanging down, a tangled mess connected to get the engine started.

"Should I even ask?"

Josh looked puzzled. "Where is she?"

"She's gone."

"Gone? What? Where?"

"It doesn't matter. Put it in drive, and let's go."

"Does she need picking up?"

"Josh. I told you. Drive. We're leaving the town now before we can't."

"Where is Ren, Dad?"

There was a pause.

"All right. I'll drive." Ryan got out. As he made his way around, Josh reached down and unattached the wires, shutting the engine and pocketing the small clip that was used to connect the wires. Ryan opened the driver's side.

"That's not cool. Start it up."

"No. I'm not leaving without her."

"You don't even know her!"

"I know enough. I know she wouldn't do this to us."

"You don't know what you're talking about so start the engine and go around. We're leaving."

"You want to start it. Go ahead. I'm not doing it."

He got out and Ryan grabbed him and pushed him up against the vehicle. "Do you think this is a game? Look over there. Did you see what they did to them? Do you want that to happen to us?"

Josh stared back defiantly but said nothing.

Lily began crying.

As if coming to his senses, Ryan released him, turned, and ran a hand over his head.

"It's okay, Lily," Josh said. "It's all right."

Ryan looked back at him and then up the road. He could see real fear in his eyes, unlike anything he'd seen before. He was scared. Scared of them. Scared of what would happen to the two of them. "The same men. Took her. Okay? So when I say she's gone. She's gone."

"Took her where?"

"I don't know, Josh. I didn't go and ask them. Look, you knew this could happen. This is why I didn't want her to come with us. Now, I appreciate what she did for you back there but we are dealing with something that is over our head. We don't have long to reach Florida. Every hour we waste here could mean not getting on a boat. Now I promised your mother I would get you on that boat."

"You never promised her anything. She's dead."

"That changes nothing."

"It changes everything," Josh snapped back. "She's not the one facing this now. We are. And I'm not driving away from someone who helped us. Who knows what they'll do to her. Even if we make it to Florida, there's no guarantee we'll find safety any more than here."

"Josh. Josh."

"Stop speaking to me like I don't know any better. For the past sixteen years, I've had to grow up fast. I've had to deal with things without your help. At times even without mom's."

"Think about Lily."

"I haven't stopped thinking about her since this kicked off."

"Then you know trying to find Ren is madness. We don't know where they've taken her. For all we know, they could be from out of town, out of state even."

"And yet they recognized a single vehicle on this street that shouldn't have been here?" Josh replied. "They are locals. Someone must know who they are and where they are."

Ryan shook his head, pacing. Josh could see he was

losing his patience. His hand clenched and then he ran it over the front of his mouth. "You are killing me here, Josh." He looked up the road again. "Even if we found her. Do you honestly think they're just going to let us waltz in there, la-de-dah, and take her out? I won't risk losing you two for a stranger."

"Well she's not a stranger, is she? She's a friend."

"For a friend then. You mean far too much to me."

"If that was so, you would have fought harder years ago," Josh snapped back.

"Josh, I would like nothing more than to right the wrongs of the past and give you the answers to where it all went wrong but I can't. I can't undo the past. I can't roll back time. All I can do is move forward. And right now that's what we need to do. So get in the Jeep. Please. And let's go."

"Sure. I'll start it."

Ryan clapped his hands together, relief appearing. "All right. Good. Finally."

As he made his way around to the passenger side, Josh added, "But I'm not going. Not until I find her. I owe her that."

"You have got to be kidding me. You are as stubborn as your mother!"

Josh shrugged. He waited. It took a minute or two for him to chew it over before he gestured for Josh to get in. "All right. You win. We'll go see. But if things get hot. I'm driving us out. Even If I have to throw you in the vehicle. You hear me?"

Josh declined to hit back with sarcasm. He knew it was

best to strike while the iron was hot. While he had the upper hand. The rest was just dad talk. It was to be expected. After he started the vehicle, Ryan told him to hang a right at the end of the road and to drive up to the gas station. He pulled out and while he was driving, Ryan checked the ammo in his rifle as if expecting trouble. They drove up to College Avenue and crossed the railway tracks. Josh turned into the four-pump gas station and parked right outside the main doors. Ryan laid his rifle down and checked how many rounds he had in his handgun. He opted to take that in with him.

"Wait here."

"I'm coming in with you." Josh leaned around the seat toward Lily. "Close your eyes."

"Why?"

"Just do it."

Lily screwed up her face, then opened one eye.

"Bean."

"All right."

He got out and skirted around the vehicle and followed Ryan into the station. There were two men inside, that weren't a part of the group they'd seen earlier. One of them had a pump-action shotgun, the other was behind the till smoking a cigarette without a care in the world. He barely registered them as Ryan strolled up to the counter.

"What have you got to trade?" he said from behind a car magazine.

Josh made his way around the aisle, not taking his eyes off the armed thug. He was a white dude with dreadlocks tied back, a muscle shirt, and tattoos down the side of his face and neck. His arms had swirling ink that wrapped around his bulging biceps. The guy's eyes flitted between the two of them, his trigger finger shifting from the side into the trigger guard. Josh let him see he had nothing in his hands.

The Glock was in the back of his jeans.

The shelves contained a sparse number of grocery and convenience goods. Chips, cans of food, soda pop, cigarettes, mostly items that had been traded. There was a large sign that read: DON'T TOUCH!

A plexiglass barrier prevented anyone from getting to the high-ticket items like alcohol, weed, boxes of bullets, and even a few handguns.

His father asked outright. "A black girl came in. Some men in two trucks took her. You know them?"

"If you don't have anything to trade, kindly leave."

"I think you misunderstood me," Ryan said.

The man lowered his magazine to reveal a sawed-off shotgun pointing at him. "Oh no, I understood you but perhaps you didn't read the sign on the way in. So let me spell it out for you. It says trade or fuck off."

"Okay, we don't want any trouble. Josh, let's go."

Ryan backed out slowly, Josh did the same. As soon as they were outside, they got back in the Cherokee. "Well, that didn't go the way I thought it would. So that's it?" Josh asked.

"Pull out of the station."

"We're leaving?"

They drove a short way down the road and Ryan had him pull off into another road before telling him to get out of the vehicle. He got into the driver's side. Josh went to get in but he told him to stay there with his sister.

"Like hell. If you're going back so am I."

Ryan clenched his jaw. He stared up the road. "I'm trying to keep you safe."

"And who's doing that for you?" Josh asked as he got in.

"I'm an adult."

"So am I."

"All right but don't say I didn't warn you. You want to be an adult so be it. Put your seatbelt on."

"What?"

"Seatbelt."

"But there are no vehicles on the road, it's..."

"JOSH!"

He groaned as he put it on. "You too, Lily."

Ryan waited then tore out and drove the needle up above seventy. At the last minute, he swerved into the gas station lot. The Jeep bounced. Josh's eyes bulged as he drove straight through the thin outer exterior of the station. There was no concrete, it was all fiberglass and drywall. The walls exploded, dust, shelves, goods, drywall going everywhere as the Grand Cherokee tore in like a hot knife through butter. The vehicle pinned the shotgun thug against the wall. His body slumped over, blood gushing from his mouth.

"Can't beat American-made!" Ryan said, tapping the steering wheel. "You okay, butterfly?" he asked, looking at Lily in the rearview mirror. She was shaken up but other-wise fine.

Josh looked at him in astonishment.

This guy was crazy.

Before Josh could react, Ryan pushed out his side and clambered over the rubble, and jammed a handgun in the face of the prick behind the counter. Josh slid out to hear the conversation. A chunk of folded metal from the counter was lodged in the clerk's lower stomach, the cigarette still hanging out of his teeth.

"You really should make your signs clearer. Especially the SLOW DOWN one. Now tell me who they are and where they've taken her?"

"Screw you, man."

Ryan reached over and pushed the metal lodged in his stomach in, making him cry louder. "Let's try that again, shall we?"

"The water park! North. They took her to the water park."

He withdrew his hand. "See, that wasn't hard."

"And who are they?"

Blood trickled out the corner of his mouth, the cigarette dropped and that was it. He was gone.

"Shit." Ryan turned and got back in. He revved the engine a few times until the tires bit and pulled out taking a good portion of the gas station exterior with them, but it got stuck on the way out. He tried again. But that sucker wasn't going anywhere.

"Get out."

Ryan got out and went outside, he went around to a white truck and got in. Josh observed him as he looked around. He flipped the visor down and keys dropped into his lap. He met Josh's gaze. "All right. Some people leave their keys inside. It's still stupid."

Josh grinned.

Before they left with the new truck, Ryan collected as many full gas canisters as they could find and put them in the back, along with handguns, ammo, and two walkie-talkies. Josh and Lily snagged food and various items that might come in handy and tossed it all in the back. He turned to Ryan as they rolled out. "You know, you're starting to grow on me," he said. Ryan rolled his eyes.

# CHAPTER TWENTY-FOUR

*S*eeing the lynch mob sent a cold chill through him. Ryan adjusted the focus on the binoculars until he could make out the tiniest details on a face. They were a mixed crew of various ages. It was hard to tell how many. That alone gave him pause for thought. The aroma of pine, damp earth, and moss lingered in the air as a warm breeze blew against his skin.

The state-run water park located off Highway 29 covered thousands of acres around the banks of the Flint Creek Reservoir. A myriad of campsites and cabins were shrouded in a heavily wooded landscape close to a glistening body of water. Its proximity made sense — two miles from the downtown, a central hub close to a lake full of fish, yet still far enough away to avoid the infected.

He peered at the lodge, observing quietly.

Occasionally the reflection of the sun glinted off the surface, making him squint.

"What do you see?" Josh asked.

The three of them were laying on their stomachs,

JACK HUNT

propped up by their elbows. Ryan had parked in a secluded spot far enough away from the lodge to not be heard when they approached. He also wanted to be sure they could make a quick exit. "The reason why this is not a good idea."

"What?" Josh tore the binoculars away from his eyes and looked. "You still want to walk away?"

"I want to keep you two safe."

"Well, you're a little late. Have you forgotten about the gas station?"

"It is one thing to go up against a couple of thugs, another to approach a crazed lynch mob and ask for a girl back."

"Hold on," he screwed up his face, "that was your plan?"

"Of course not, Josh."

"Then what are we talking about?"

Ryan turned his head. "Look again."

Josh shrugged. "And?"

Ryan groaned and laid on his back looking up at the sky, hand covering his face.

Lily scrambled over. "Can I take a look?"

Josh handed the binoculars to her.

"I don't get you. One minute you say you'll help and now you're back-pedaling."

"No. I let you talk me into this. I'm just realizing again why I didn't agree in the first place."

Josh threw his hands up. "How did you suppose this would go?"

"I figured if an opportunity presented itself, maybe, just maybe... we might be able to get her back safely. Emphasis on safely. Sticking my neck out for a girl that I barely know, Josh, isn't smart. She's not the first nor will she be the last person we come across."

"So you would leave if that was me or Lily down there? Is that what you're saying?"

"No. That's different. We hardly know her."

"How is it? You barely know me. You sure as hell don't know Lily."

Ryan stared back at him. "I'm not playing this game, Josh. I have one job and that is to get you and Lily to Florida. That's it. Now I'm sorry Ren got grabbed but getting caught or killed ourselves wouldn't be helping her."

"So we don't."

"Geesh. You really don't listen."

"I listen just fine."

"Why, then?"

The question caught him off guard. Josh looked back at him confused so Ryan continued. "Why do you want to help her?"

"I already told you."

"Josh, she had one person to deal with, the odds here are very different. It's like night and day. So why? Why risk our lives? Do you have a thing for her?"

"No."

"Then give me one good reason why?"

There was a long pause. Lily looked at Josh, waiting for him to say something. She brought the binoculars up again.

"Exactly. Let's go," Ryan added, trudging away.

As he was walking the short distance back to the truck, Lily said, "They're leaving."

"What?"

Josh grabbed the binoculars and looked through them. "Well look at that. That opportunity has presented itself. There it is," he said, turning and handing him the compact binoculars. Ryan made his way back and took them and peered through.

Sure enough.

There was movement. Lots of it.

Now he was able to get a better idea of how many there were.

By the looks of it, it was the same number of men they saw in the street, around seven. Though he imagined there had to be at least one or two inside to watch over the place.

"They must have gotten wind of the gas station," Josh said. "Which means we have a limited window to get down there."

Ryan scoffed. "You're not going anywhere. You're staying here with your sister. I'm going."

"What? No."

"Listen to me. Now I allowed you to talk me into this but if you want my help, then we do things my way. Understand?" He reached for his bag and pulled out the two walkie-talkies they'd snagged from the gas station. He fiddled with the knob on the top and handed him one. "You keep an eye out for them, and an eye on your sister. Got it?"

He groaned and nodded. They did a quick test to make sure the line was clear.

Ryan waited a few more minutes for the trucks to roll out before he pitched sideways down the grassy embankment they'd taken cover behind. The terrain was muddy, covered in leaves. There were multiple cabins dotted through the woods as he made his way down to the lodge. Ryan moved fast, handgun at the ready, expecting trouble. He didn't think for one moment they would leave anyone behind without someone watching over them.

It was quiet outside.

Only the sound of water lapping up against the shore and birds chirping.

Above the property was a huge sign that read: PREPARE TO MEET GOD.

Ryan listened intently and scanned the windows for movement. Nothing. No one.

He ascended three steps to a wraparound porch that led to two double wooden doors. It was unlocked. Ryan stuck his head in and listened again. No sound. It smelled musty inside, like a closet full of mothballs. As if it had been sitting unused for over a decade. The entire site had fallen into disrepair. State-run, they didn't have the budget to shell out for renovations.

The sprawling lodge was weathered, with 1960s style wood panels and stucco ceilings.

At the far end of the hall, it opened up into a large dining area with cathedral ceilings, thick wooden rafters, and ceiling fans. There were multiple long tables covered with white sheets and chairs tucked beneath. There was a kitchen off to the right. Ryan checked the back of the lodge and discovered a dirty bathroom with shower stalls. The sleeping area was filled with bunk beds and there was more religious décor.

His walkie-talkie crackled. It was Josh.

"You found her?"

"No. She could be anywhere. There are cabins all over this lake. Any sign of the men?"

"Not yet."

Ryan continued through another series of corridors until he entered a room that must have been converted into a church sanctuary. There was a large cross on the back wall with a crown of thorns over the top of it, and a piece of purple cloth twisted around it. He made his way down to a small podium, and a low step. There he found boxes with plexiglass on top. As he got closer he heard a rattling sound. "What the heck?" He peered through the glass to see it was filled with rattlesnakes. They had stacks of them.

He backed out, going into the corridor and making his way down to the next room. Inside there was a projector and a white screen on the back wall. It was turned on but wasn't playing. He approached it and touched the play button.

Without sound, a black-and-white video began playing showing men and women hoisting rattlesnakes in the air, others dancing around while the same guy he'd seen earlier, the bald one, lifted a Bible, and held a microphone to his lips. Behind him, the same scripture he'd seen on the placard.

*And these signs shall follow them that believe; in my name shall they cast out devils; they shall speak with new tongues; they shall take up serpents.*

Ryan couldn't hear what was being said but he had a good sense of what was going on. He'd heard about these snake-handling churches. They weren't as common as they were back in the day due to deaths and legal issues but they still existed. He watched as a child was brought to her knees and had venomous snakes placed around her neck. The kid was terrified but it didn't stop them from continuing.

It was another level of crazy.

Ryan sniffed. It smelled like tobacco.

Out the corner of his eye, he caught sight of an ashtray. There was an almost burned-out cigarette perched on the edge.

Making his way out, he continued to check room after room. It was empty. Nothing but storage. Stacks of chairs, boxes, toys, and... he reached one door that was padlocked from the outside. All the other rooms were open. Ryan put his ear to the door. At first, he didn't hear anything, then came a cough.

He stepped back from the door and considered shooting the lock but if there was anyone here that would only draw attention. He turned and went back down the corridor and pulled a red fire extinguisher off the wall. Moving quickly, he returned and struck the lock once, twice, four times with the bottom of it but that didn't even put a dent in it.

"Ren?" he said.

"Ryan?"

"The key to the lock. You know where it is?"

"No. Please get me out of here."

"I'm working on it."

He raced back up the hallway and began checking each of the rooms. Just as he entered the main foyer where a large living room and fireplace was, he heard someone approaching.

"I swear I heard something."

"It's probably just them trying to get out."

Ryan ducked behind a doorway and waited as two men came into the lodge, out of breath. One of them was huge, overweight, T-shirt barely covering his bulbous gut. He wore jean dungarees over his white T-shirt. "The lock is still on, Jerry."

"Go down and check it out while I get the keys."

As the large one passed by the door he was tucked behind, Ryan got a waft of bad body odor. He peered out as the other, a thin rail of a man, went around a counter and took some keys off a hook where there were many for different rooms. He wore a baseball cap, a striped shirt, and pants that an old-timer might have worn.

The thought passed through his mind to choke him out while the other was distracted but that meant laying hands on them and he couldn't tell if they were carriers of the pathogen. Killing them outright was the only other way. He had to do it once, back at the barn, but that was because he had no other choice. It was either that or Josh and Lily would have burned up. His actions felt justified. But killing two men for a set of keys?

He withdrew the handgun, preparing to do the unthinkable when the guy bellowed back. "It's locked, Jerry. Nothing wrong."

He heard the big fella rattle the padlock down the hallway.

The stringy fellow strode over. "You sure?"

"How many times do I have to tell you?"

He watched him return and place a set of keys down. Sweat trickled down Ryan's face, his heart thumping hard at the thought of being seen. The two of them grumbled as they exited the lodge leaving him alone.

Not wasting any time, he dashed across the room and scooped up the keys, and made his way down. The ring which held the keys must have had upwards of forty keys. They were color-coded. Without knowing the codes he would have to try every single one.

"I've got the keys."

"Please hurry," Ren said.

He had managed to try eight different keys and was on the ninth when the walkie-talkie crackled. "Ryan. Ryan! Come in, Ryan."

"What's up?" he asked.

"Have you found her?"

"Yes, but I need a few more minutes."

"You don't have it. They're back. Get out of there."

# CHAPTER TWENTY-FIVE

*C'mon, c'mon... he wouldn't make it.*

Josh saw them before he heard the engines. The heat of the day had turned the roads dry, cracking the mud. That worked in his favor. Through the trees, farther down the road, a plume of dust and grit rose above the trucks as they approached. They were hauling ass and fast. All he could think was someone had raised the alarm or the group had been tipped off to them entering the park. He felt safe where he was, as they were out of the way, off the beaten path, but Ryan wasn't. He was in the lion's den.

*Think, think!*

Lily looked as anxious as he felt. He got back on the walkie-talkie.

"Hurry up, Ryan."

This time he didn't get a response. He tried again. Nothing.

*Shit.* He scrambled over to the truck that was heavily shrouded by branches. He pulled two of the five-gallon canisters of gasoline out of the back and lugged them back over to Lily. He handed her the walkie-talkie. "If dad answers, you press this button and speak into this."

"Why can't you do it?"

"Because I've got to go and help him."

"And leave me here?"

Josh looked again through the binoculars. "Lily. I don't have time to do this. Just take this, press that to speak to him. But don't do it unless he speaks to you." With that said, he hurried, stumbling over large roots, and sliding down the grassy embankment. He took off at a full sprint toward a cabin that wasn't far from where Ryan had gone in. He peered inside to make sure no one was in there before he unscrewed the cap off the gasoline container and entered. He splashed the contents up the walls, creating a trail that came out the front. He took out a lighter, and a scrap of rag. Josh lit the end, then dropped it.

He stepped back as the gasoline burst into color, a tongue of fire that crawled quickly into the cabin and up the sides. He didn't linger. He ran to another, doing the same again. Within seconds he had three cabins engulfed in flames. Smoke billowed through the trees, dark and thick, swirling in the wind.

Breathing hard, he ran to the rear of the lodge with the second canister. He began dousing the back of the walls and creating a trail that led away into the woods, far enough that he wouldn't be spotted.

He waited, lighter in hand, preparing to send the whole damn lodge up in a blaze of smoke.

*C'mon, Ryan.*

He closed the Zippo and took out the Glock.

On the western side, two guys came out with fire extinguishers in hand. It wasn't going to be much use. The easterly winds had picked up, carrying the flames beyond the cabins to the overhanging trees.

# CHAPTER TWENTY-SIX

*D*esperation kicked in with every failing key.

Ryan's chest tightened at the thought that he might have to abandon her — that this might be all for nothing. He'd tried at least eighteen keys before the padlock gave way. He dumped it fast and twisted the handle, sending the door wide open.

It was a cramped space.

What he found inside was hard for him to see.

Jammed into that tiny room that couldn't have been larger than a café's storage area was a collection of people shackled. Young, old, middle-aged. There had to have been over thirty. They were being housed like cattle. Most cowered back. What were they doing to them?

Among the dirty faces of the scared, Ren emerged, moving toward him only to be yanked back by a shackle clasped around her ankle. The chain that restrained her was looped through hoops to the others like inmates on a transportation bus. It snaked away into the midst of them, the end looped around a huge iron hoop on the far wall and back out to the next group. When one moved, they all did. It was a simple yet clever way to keep them in check.

Ren beckoned for the huge set of keys in his hand.

The color codes were associated with small stickers on the restraints. Individual keys. No one key could open them all. This would take forever to get them out.

He tossed the keys and Ren quickly found her color and unlocked her ankle.

As she began working to unlock the others, loud shouting farther down the hallway alerted him to the arrival of the men. They were shouting to one another, something about a fire, and getting more extinguishers. Ryan closed the door behind him. "Ren, we don't have time to get them out."

"I'm not leaving them here."

"Are they infected?"

She never answered. He scanned their faces, every bit of exposed skin. Unless he'd known them personally and seen them for days or saw blood trickling from their nose or the common rash, there was no way of knowing. "Ren. Let's go!" She'd managed to unlock six people's restraints before she understood. She tossed the keys to an older man to let him continue and then turned to leave. Ryan cracked the door open just a notch. When he saw it was clear, he exited and turned right down the hallway, heading for a secondary door at the far end of the hall.

"It's locked," a blond guy said.

"How do you know?"

"We passed it on the way in."

"Then it's only out the front," Ryan added.

Loud voices made it clear that direction was out of the question.

"No, this way," he said, guiding them down another passage into the huge lodge that would make any hotel chain seem small. Ryan was a little hesitant to follow. He didn't know these people and he sure as hell didn't want to find himself being indebted to them.

As they doubled back and crossed the hallway that led down to the main foyer, one of the men must have come in to collect the extinguisher he'd used earlier. It was no longer on the wall. For a second when they crossed that hallway, he looked their way. Whether it was shock to see the door open or fear, the man froze.

They didn't.

"Go. Go!" Ryan said, beckoning them on.

Moving through the hallway, the blond guy led them to another doorway only to find that one locked as well. Though instead of having a chain on it as the previous one did, it was locked from the outside. "Now what?"

"Out of the way!" Ryan took out the SIG Sauer and fired at the double-paned window. The glass shattered, and he reached outside only to find the chain that was holding it in place was padlocked. An alarm rang out, and lights began flashing all down the hallway. The guy in the hallway must have alerted the others or pulled the fire alarm as it let out one hell of a shrill.

Undefeated, he was about to extend the gun outside the door and fire at the padlock when Josh came running out of the smoke that was drifting through the woods.

"I've got it. Out of the way."

Ren, Ryan, two adults, and a child moved back as Josh

fired several rounds at the padlock. A moment later, it was open. They burst out and turned right into heavy smoke. Wheeling around the corner of the extended portion of the lodge, Ryan was able to get a better idea of the fire. It was blazing out of control, chewing up cabins and the forest. It all crackled and popped, releasing a mass of smoke high into the air.

No sooner were they out than they heard rounds erupting.

They weren't being fired at.

The other survivors, the ones in the room, had managed to free themselves and were making a break for it out the front. Adults and children darted between the trees on the far side, pursued by armed men.

Some were tackled. Others shot.

There was nothing they could do for them even if they wanted.

It was a chaotic scene.

People running. Screaming. Shouting. The blaring of an alarm. And a fire burning out of control. Heavy smoke moved like a wave through the woods, making them cough. "Which way?" Ren asked. Josh pointed but before he followed, he used his Zippo lighter and tossed it. Ryan saw it hit the ground, roll and then a second later a tongue of fire snaked quickly across the earth until it reached the lodge. A sudden burst of orange, yellow and red spread, eating into the wood like a billion termites.

With the world ablaze, they sprinted.

Lily looked like a scared rabbit peering out from its hole above the embankment as they made it to her. There was no time for embracing. No time for questions. If they didn't move fast they would become trapped by the fire. As they worked together to pull away the branches, Ryan got in the driver's side and fired up the engine. Lily and Josh were in the front, while Ren and the family that came with her jumped in the truck bed.

He jerked the wheel, stuck it in gear, and peeled out, coughing hard.

The truck tore through the woods, bouncing over the uneven ground until it swerved out onto the main road. In his side mirror, the reflection was an inferno.

The truck rumbled along Highway 29 south until he veered onto 26 heading east and leaving Wiggins behind.

Grateful to be alive, Ryan caught Josh looking at him. "Thank you," he said.

"For what?"

"Helping her."

"I didn't do it for her."

Josh stared.

Their faces were blackened by smoke. A heaviness fell over them at the thought of those that didn't escape. How many were shot? He glanced in his rearview mirror, through the pane of dividing glass to the family in the back huddled together, a blanket wrapped around their child. The question he'd had earlier lingered in his mind.

*Are they infected?*

# CHAPTER TWENTY-SEVEN

The truck aggressively swerved to the edge of the road, sending up a plume of dust.

Ryan slammed the brakes on and everyone lurched forward. They'd made it a few miles outside of Wiggins. He'd held off until he was sure they weren't being followed before he addressed the elephant in the room.

He hopped out before Josh could ask why they were stopping.

Even at the lodge, he'd kept his distance. N95 mask on, sunglasses to protect the eyes, a bandanna around his throat, and blue latex gloves covering his hands.

"Get out," he said, gesturing to the family.

"What's the matter?" Ren asked.

"And you."

When they didn't move fast enough, he took out his handgun and gestured. "Let's go."

He wasn't playing around.

Josh was observing it play out through the pickup

truck's rear windshield. He slid open the glass to hear. Lily was on the far passenger seat blocking the side door.

The four in the back climbed over the side, each having an expression of concern.

"Ryan, what is this about?" Ren asked.

"You already know. I asked you back at the lodge, you never answered."

Ren looked at the family who he still didn't have names for. There had been such a mad panic to escape, there was no time for introductions let alone to refuse to give them a ride. It wasn't that he wouldn't help, but with their lives on the line and the risk he'd already taken allowing Ren to tag along, he wasn't going to take any chances.

"We're not infected," the father spoke up.

"Yeah? And how do I know that unless you strip out of your clothes, or I watch you for the next few days?" A rash showed up often on infected individuals, nosebleeds followed after. It was the clearest visual confirmation.

"They're telling the truth," Ren said, coming to their defense.

"And you would know that because?"

"I just do."

"I'm afraid that doesn't work for me. No one puts a group of strangers in a room and locks it unless they want something or are trying to protect themselves from something. So which is it?"

They offered back blank stares.

"Answer the question or I'm leaving you all here."

Even Ren looked at a loss for words.

"Fine." Ryan turned to get back in the truck, preparing to leave them in his rearview mirror when Ren spoke up.

"They're immune."

With a hand resting on the door, Ryan shot them a side-ways glance. "All of you?"

The family nodded.

"And the others, in the room back at the lodge?"

"Yes. I mean, they were, too," Ren said. He thought back to what he'd witnessed in the downtown of Wiggins. The lynch mob chasing that family, tearing the one boy away while killing the others who were showing the signs of the infection. Logically it made sense. They wouldn't take him if he had been exposed to the infected.

But nothing about the way this event had unfolded made sense.

The aging shouldn't have been able to slow in anyone, but spreading it to someone who didn't have it, if the reports were to be believed, proved this was the case. It made him wonder who had created the virus.

Josh had mentioned that he'd heard it was a form of nanotechnology being used in medicine by companies in the health field. It had been reported that thousands of tiny microscopic machines were designed to travel through the body, repair damaged cells and organs, wipe out disease, cure cancer, restore memory, and slow aging. That it had been used to treat the very real Werner Syndrome, a disease that made people age fast for which there was no cure. However, in this case, something had gone wrong and instead of slowing aging, it sped up the process in those initially exposed to it, but then left or slowed in their body after they passed it on. Like pouring water from one cup into another, instead of copying, it left the original host which in turn slowed the process, allowing the once infected body to return to its normal state. It brought a whole new meaning to the term "spreading an infection."

"Then why lock you all up?"

Ren looked at the couple. The mother had her arm around her child, the girl clung to her, distraught. She was covered with a gray blanket that went around her shoulders and was held in place by her small hands.

The father stepped forward, and Ryan took a few steps back.

"When a venomous snake bites you, it injects its venom which courses its way through your body, swelling limbs and changing the blood cells, preventing blood from clotting and causing blood vessels to leak. You can then experience all manner of organ failure. The treatment for a bite is anti-venom, a way to neutralize the poison. That's why they were holding us."

"What? As some form of anti-venom for the aging?"

He nodded.

"Yeah, right. An entire family immune. Sorry, I don't buy it."

"It's true, Ryan," Ren said.

Josh got out of the truck and made his way around. "That's why you stayed at the house, wasn't it?"

She nodded. "Once, my brother managed to touch me. I assumed that was it but when I didn't begin to age, I knew something was different."

"Why didn't you tell us?" Ryan asked.

"Would you have believed me? You certainly wouldn't have let me go with you."

Ryan stared back at them, unsure of what to believe.

He sighed.

One thing he'd learned was not to take anyone's word. Josh nudged him and jerked his head away from the group. He followed his son to the front of the truck a few feet away from the grille. Out of earshot, Josh leaned into him. "We can keep them in the back of the pickup truck. If they have it, we'll know within a day."

"I don't know about this, Josh." Ryan looked at them.

"We can keep our distance. Like we have since this kicked off," Josh said.

"It's not worth the risk."

Josh pointed at them. "If they're truly immune, this could be exactly what is needed to stop this event. Whatever is in their blood or DNA could be the key. Leaving them here might help us, but if it's true, it won't help the rest of the world. This is bigger than us now, Ryan."

"God, I wish you would stop calling me Ryan. It's dad."

He breathed deeply and wiped his lips with the back of his hand.

Ryan took a moment to consider it then nodded. "We keep them in the back of the pickup truck. We keep our distance. Don't touch them. Don't go near them."

Josh nodded.

"Be sure to tell your sister."

He turned and got back in the truck. Ryan made his way around and gestured for them to climb in the back. A look of relief followed.

"Thank you," the father said. "By the way my name is Stephen, and this is Madeline, and our daughter Francine."

Ryan nodded. He looked off into the distance, as heat waves shimmered across the road. There were still around three hundred miles left to go, a good five and a half hours remaining until they'd reach the Florida coast. With all that had happened so far, he accepted it would take longer with at least one or more stops to get gas and sleep. If everything went to plan, and they didn't get a flat tire, they would arrive with at least two days to spare.

Ryan coughed hard, pulling a rag from his pocket. He took out his pills and tossed a couple back. Ren studied him.

He ignored her and climbed in.

"You okay, Dad?" Lily asked.

"As long as you two are safe, I am, kiddo."

He stuck the gear stick in drive and peeled away, leaving behind a cloud of dust and the horrors of a snake-handling church that were using the event for their own strange purpose.

From that point forward they didn't stop for anyone though they saw people along the highways thumbing a ride. Infected? Immune? Survivors? Who knew. It was a gamble he wasn't willing to take again. He glanced in his rearview mirror at the family and considered what might be different in them that would allow them to resist the pathogen, and if it could be used to create a permanent cure for the infected.

A few hours later, after refueling with the gasoline canister they had, and collecting more water, they rolled into Alabama and pulled off Interstate 10 following a sign for a service station.

"Bucky!" Lily said, pointing to the bright yellow sign with a beaver on it. Buc-ee's was a chain of travel centers offering convenience stores and gas across Texas, Alabama, Georgia, and Florida. Josh opened the rear windshield window and told them they were going to stop there for the night as they veered onto Baldwin Beach Express. One last pit stop before the final stretch of the journey the next day. The huge parking lot was practically empty with only five vehicles dotted throughout. A couple had their windows smashed, and doors open as if someone had fished through them.

Ryan pulled up close to the entrance and scrutinized the building. He wanted to be sure that it was safe to venture in before killing the engine. Heavy dark clouds drifted overhead as the sun dipped behind the horizon.

As Stephen and his family climbed out, they talked quietly among themselves, keeping their distance. Lily took hold of Ryan's hand as they cautiously approached the entrance. Off to the right was a line of gasoline pumps. It had to be the most pumps he'd seen at one gas station in his life. There had to be at least a hundred. Pump handles were dangling beside the machines. There was yellow tape blowing in the wind. It had been wrapped around some of the pumps to indicate that it was out of order.

If that wasn't clear enough, huge red and white signs had been posted high up to alert travelers that the station was out of gas.

Glass crunched beneath their boots as they stepped inside.

It was a mess. Buc-ee's was classed as one of the largest convenience stores in America. It sold snacks and drinks, clothes, hats, hot food, knives, barbecues, and almost anything else through to pet accessories. Unlike town grocery stores, this wasn't completely empty, probably due to how far away it was from the nearest town. It was out of the way, out of sight, and due to its size and the way the pathogen was spreading, it would have been one of the last places people would have entered. Survivors steered clear of crowds. Convenience didn't equate essentials and most of what was offered here was packaged junk food.

Sweatshirts lined the floors, covered in dirty footprints. Shelving blocked aisles, and snacks, trinkets, and gifts were everywhere. "Hello!" Stephen shouted.

"You want to keep it down?" Ryan said.

"Just wanted to check if anyone was here."

Each of them broke away exploring the inside, picking up items, opening snacks, and collecting bottled water. Much of it was gone but in a store this size, it would have taken a lot of people to empty it. Lily hurried over to the wall to try the drink machine. She pulled out a cup and filled it up at the automatic dispenser. It worked.

"It's good. Try it," she said, offering Ryan some.

The floor was sticky. Ryan waved her off as he ventured further in. She caught up with him and stayed close. He could tell she was afraid. They all were. Over the following hour, they perused shelves, ate, filled their bags with items.

The store wasn't entirely empty of people. There were others like them. He found them near the back. Two teenagers and a mother. There was a second of hesitation. He thought they might run toward him, but they didn't. They backed up and exited via a side door. Not everyone was infected but people were desperate. Hungry. Thirsty. Worried about the future.

As it darkened inside the store, they used lanterns and flashlights from the store to illuminate the aisles. Lily had found some books to read, and Josh was sitting cross-legged beside her, browsing a magazine. All he wanted for them was to relax.

Ryan stood a good distance away. He'd found a couple of cans of beer inside a refrigerator. He cracked one open and downed it fast.

Ren approached. "Is there one in there for me?"

"You're seventeen."

She chuckled. "You don't know much about teenagers, do you?" She reached in and collected a light beer and cracked it open.

"I know enough."

"Mind if I sit?" she asked.

"As long as you keep your distance."

She smiled, taking a swig and slipping down with the refrigerator behind her. "You don't believe me, do you?"

"Does it matter what I believe?"

She pulled a face and shrugged. "I guess not. Look, I appreciate what you did back there. I just wanted to say thank you."

"Don't thank me. Thank Josh."

She looked over at his kids, and he followed her gaze.

"Still. If you hadn't returned. I don't know what that group would have done to us."

"Well, you're safe now."

"Right." She nodded, looking back at Josh. "So your wife asked you to take them to Florida. What happened?"

"She died."

"I mean, why did you get divorced?"

She had no idea. He'd been asked that question many times over the last ten years and he'd always been elusive in his answer. There was too much pain associated with the way it ended and if he told the truth, it would have opened a Pandora's box of questions that he wasn't ready to answer. So instead, he would say that they fell out of love. It wasn't the truth. He never stopped loving Elizabeth.

"Oh, you know, we drifted apart," he replied.

"My parents nearly did. I'm surprised they stayed together so long. They always fought. It was over stupid things. Small things. They were always so self-centered. Even when this event unfolded. But not you."

"Ren, you don't know me."

"Maybe not but actions speak volumes."

Ryan began coughing, uncontrollably. He took out the rag from his pocket and coughed into it. Ren studied him. Although he cupped his hand around the rag, she caught sight of the specks of blood.

"How long you had it?"

He wiped his lips then pocketed the rag. "I'm not infected."

"I didn't say you were."

He didn't respond.

"Cancer, right? My uncle had it. One hell of a way to go."

He stared back then nodded.

"How far along?"

"Stage four. Lung cancer."

"How long you got?"

"Less than a year."

Ren eyed Josh and Lily across the room. His son had an arm around Lily. He must have told her a joke as she started to laugh. Josh glanced over and the smile faded.

"Do they know?"

He shook his head.

"Are you going to tell them?"

"When I'm ready."

Ren took another swig. She nodded as if she understood. "So, you think another day and we'll reach the coast. Do you know much about these boats? Are they staying out on the water?"

"Not sure exactly. There was mention of using some island as a safe zone."

"For someone intent on keeping his kids safe, you certainly are taking a gamble heading there. What if it doesn't work out? What then?"

"I'll figure that out if and when it happens. And Ren..."

"Yeah?"

"This conversation."

"I won't say anything."

He nodded. She walked off, leaving him to ponder how and when he would tell them. Eventually, he'd have to come clean but by then he hoped they would be with their grandparents. He'd been out of their life for so long that the impact wouldn't be as hard as it had been for him. His mind drifted back to the past, to when the symptoms first showed up. The cough that wouldn't go away, the chest infection that kept coming back, breathing difficulty, a lack of energy. He'd visited the doctor thinking it was minor, pneumonia perhaps.

It wasn't.

When the bomb dropped, his mind went blank.

No one prepared a person to hear that kind of news.

The doc had said it was the result of exposure to

second-hand smoke but he had to wonder if it wasn't the result of the stress he'd been under. "How long, Doc?"

"Five years if you're lucky."

He'd gone through chemotherapy and radiation therapy and for a while, he felt they were making progress when it went into remission.

That changed a year later when the pain returned and it had metastasized. It was then he was told he had one year and to get his affairs in order.

## CHAPTER TWENTY-EIGHT

July 9

The next morning, Ryan bolted upright. He gasped, his heart thrumming in his chest. Eyes wide open, he noticed Lily was tucked inside her sleeping bag in the same spot he'd left her but Josh wasn't beside her. "Josh," he said. "Josh!"

"I'm here."

He turned to find him standing a few feet away, getting a drink from one of the dispenser machines. Ryan hadn't slept a full night since leaving. No one except Lily had. It was too risky. Anyone could come across them at night. Instead, they'd taken turns getting a few hours in, at least four before the other one would take watch. Across the way, Madeline, Stephen's wife, was opening a packet of dried fruit for her daughter. Her brow pinched together, disturbed by the outburst.

"What time is it?"

"Just after nine," Josh answered.

He groaned, squeezing the bridge of his nose with a thumb and finger. "Why didn't you wake me sooner?"

"Because I figured you needed the extra sleep. You can't function well on a few hours, especially if you won't let me drive."

Josh handed him a bottle of water. "Thanks. You should wake your sister. We need to leave soon." As he crossed the room, Ryan downed the water, bringing his senses back to life. As he sat there taking in his surroundings, his gaze roamed the room.

"Josh, where's Stephen?"

"He went to the washroom."

Ryan twisted.

"But they're locked."

"The other one farther down."

He nodded and got up and stretched out his arms, releasing the tension gained from the hard ground. Ryan ran a hand around the back of his neck, snagged up a packet of peanuts off the ground, and made his way to the bathroom to splash some water and relieve himself. Rays of bright sunshine shone in through the skylight, spreading warmth throughout. He could tell it was going to be another hot one. Easily soaring into the high eighties.

The previous night, Stephen and his family had kept to themselves. He'd watched them come and go. Keen to know more about them and the lunatics they'd encountered, he'd thrown a few questions at them. Nothing invasive. Nothing that made it seem like he was grilling them. But he could tell Stephen didn't appreciate it. He'd exited the station, said he needed a smoke. While he wasn't a big talker, his wife was. She opened up to them. He soon learned they were longtime residents of Wiggins, Louisiana. They'd been a part of the snake-handling church and explained that to onlookers it was crazy but to them, it was just what they believed.

When the event kicked off, their pastor said it was a sign from God. A test of their faith. If God protected them from serpents and even swallowing poison, would he not do the same again? Apparently so. After being in contact with someone who had the pathogen, they'd felt that God had chosen them to handle the infected. That they were God's chosen ones, and he was like some kind of Noah. It was messed up and she lost Ryan at some point in the conversation as it went over his head.

Eventually, she stopped and said it was hard for people to understand.

She never argued with him and it was obvious why.

They didn't want to rock the boat or overstep the line.

Being stranded out here was better than the hell hole he'd pulled them out of, but still, with the hope of refuge before them, it was easier to stay in their lane than make life difficult.

Ryan sniffed hard as he made his way into the bathroom.

There was a ladies' room to the right, and the men's room was to the left. He pushed through the door to find Stephen pulling down his shirt in front of the mirror. He had multiple paper towels balled up in the sink.

"Morning," Ryan said, crossing to the urinal.

Stephen turned the faucet on and splashed water over his face. "Sleep okay?"

"Wasn't the Hilton, that's for sure."

Stephen chuckled. "Figured I'd have a wash. Haven't had one in days."

"I hear ya." Ryan zipped up his pants and went to the far sink to do the same. "Listen, I know we didn't get off on the right foot. It's just…"

"I understand. You can't be too careful."

"That's right."

Stephen tossed the paper towels into the garbage and ran his hands under the dryer. It let out a loud hum. "That's me. See you out there."

"We'll leave in ten."

"Got it."

With his hands and face wet, Ryan pulled several paper towels out of the dispenser. He ran them over his face and went to toss them into the trash below when he noticed something. He squinted and lifted the paper towel he'd put in and his eyes widened.

Ryan dashed for the door, swinging it open just in time to see Stephen strolling off.

He pulled his handgun from the back of his pants and held it with both hands lifted.

"Hold up." Stephen continued walking. "Stop!"

Stephen froze.

"Turn around."

They were far enough away that the others wouldn't have heard him. The second washrooms were on the west side, around a corner. Slowly Stephen turned. "Is there a problem?"

"You tell me," Ryan replied.

"I have no idea."

"Don't lie."

"I don't know what you're talking about."

"Inside the washroom. Those paper towels. There's blood on them."

"I cut myself, shaving."

"Bullshit. Lift your top."

"Why?"

"Don't make me ask again."

"This is ridiculous. I'm immune."

Ryan nudged the gun forward to make it clear he wasn't messing around.

Stephen clenched his eyes together as he lifted his shirt to reveal a large rash on the side of his stomach.

"Immune?" Ryan asked.

"I was going to tell you eventually."

"Yeah, when? In the middle of the night while I was sleeping? Huh?"

"It's not like that. I wouldn't ever do that."

"That's what everyone says until they get it."

"I didn't go anywhere near you."

"That's because my kid was awake watching you."

"Did you go near your family?"

"No. I stayed clear."

Ryan squinted, his brow furrowing. "Why wouldn't you if they were immune?"

He'd caught him in a lie. Stephen dropped his head.

"Do they know?"

He shook his head.

"You lied to me," Ryan said.

"No, I didn't." He put a hand out and moved forward.

"Don't come any closer. You told us you were immune."

"In the eyes of the church we are," Stephen replied.

"You're making no sense."

"Look, it happened last night. Okay?"

Ryan offered back a confused expression. His mind skirted back to the previous evening.

"I was outside. Having a smoke. I was taking a piss. My back was turned. I didn't see the guy. He came out of nowhere." He stared back. "I'm telling the truth. Look, Ryan, I can keep my distance from the others."

"I'm afraid you can't do that."

"Please."

Ryan shook his head. "What about your wife and child?"

"They think they're immune."

"Obviously," Ryan snapped back. He couldn't tell what was true anymore. "Why were you all in that room?" He waited for an answer.

"I told you."

"You lied to me. I want the truth or I leave your family here."

"I told you the truth."

"You lied!"

Stephen dropped his chin. He sighed and took a seat. Without looking at Ryan, he replied. "We were to be tested, a trial to see whose faith was strong. Douglas, our pastor, told us that God had told him that this event was a weeding out of the righteous from the wolves. Any not affected by a snake bite would be considered immune. We were to be tested."

"What a crock of crap."

"No, it's true. All of us were to be tested. If the snake bite didn't affect us, we'd be released."

"And if it did?"

"What do you think?"

Ryan ran a hand over his head.

"So your wife and child were bitten but you weren't."

"No."

"I'm not sure what to believe."

"I'm telling the truth."

"And yet you lied to me."

"Because I wanted to get my family to safety. The pastor had lost it. I didn't agree. Many of us didn't. I wanted to get away from that group. Is that hard to grasp? You're trying to do the same thing for yours." Stephen groaned. He knew he couldn't talk his way out of this. One lie marred any other answer he gave. "I know it's too late for me but don't leave my family behind, Ryan. Please. Take them with you."

"If they're infected they're not going."

"Check them. Do they look like they've aged? Are they showing any symptoms?"

"I haven't asked."

"Do it. If that's what determines whether they go or don't. Do it."

"You know what you're asking me to do."

"They will do it. If I tell them."

He pondered it for a moment or two before nudging him to walk toward the group. "If you're right, I'll take them but if they are showing any rash or any sign of aging, they're staying. And if you attempt to get near me or anyone I will put you down where you stand. You understand?"

He nodded. He walked a good twenty feet ahead of Ryan. As soon as they came into view, all eyes went on Ryan who was aiming his gun at the back of Stephen.

"Stephen? What's going on?" Madeline asked, moving toward him

"Stay right there, Madeline," Ryan said. "He's infected."

"That's impossible. We're immune."

"We're not, Madeline," Stephen said.

She wore a confused expression. "What?"

He lifted his top for her to see. It was one thing to explain, another to show the proof.

Madeline looked beside herself with worry and confusion. "But you told me. The pastor told us."

"He told us a lot of things. There is no immunity. It was a lie."

"But that means…"

Stephen nodded. "Yeah. I'm not going with you."

"Then I'm staying."

"No. You need to go with them."

"No. No. We're not leaving you here." She took a few steps toward him and Ryan bellowed.

"That's far enough."

"Don't you tell me what to do!" she snapped.

"Madeline. Madeline!" Stephen said. "Please. Don't make this harder than it is."

Josh approached. "What is happening…?" He stopped in mid-sentence as he saw the rash on Stephen. Stephen lowered his shirt.

"He needs to check you," Stephen said to Madeline.

"But…"

Ryan shrugged. "I'm sorry but if I'm taking you. I have to know."

"But that means, we have to…" The reality dawned on her that she would need to remove her clothes at least down to her underwear to let him see if there was any rash. It varied on people. It could be on their legs, their torso, or arms. It was often the first sign. The body's natural reaction. Like breaking out in hives. Her eyes darted to Stephen as if expecting him to do something but he agreed with Ryan. He wanted them gone. He wanted them to be safe. He didn't want them seeing his final days.

"You too, Ren. I'm sorry," Ryan said.

She wasn't opposed or shy in front of them as she stripped down. In light of what happened, Ren knew it made sense. How else could they know? Sure, they would remain in the back of the truck divided by the rear windshield but if one of them was infected, it could be transmitted. He couldn't allow that risk. He wouldn't transport someone who was a carrier of the pathogen.

One by one his wife and child removed their outer clothes.

Embarrassment spread, faces turned red as they turned around and Ryan scanned them.

They were clean.

No rashes.

No symptoms.

Stephen was the only one.

"I told you I was telling the truth," Stephen said.

"That's still up for debate."

"I understand."

Infection was a tragedy. Ryan couldn't help but feel for them.

His wife and child couldn't hug him. They had to resort to saying their goodbyes from a distance. Tears flowed. Anguish revealed itself in a mixture of angry words, most of which were directed at Ryan. Francine shook her head, she screamed as her mother held her back. Stephen got emotional. He told them that it was for the best. It was what he wanted. They would be safe. Once he was ready, he asked for a moment with his wife. He let them walk a short distance away. They were within eyesight but out of earshot. He couldn't tell what they were saying as they said their final words but it was clearly heartbreaking for Madeline. Then, as if unable to deal with the pain anymore, Stephen turned and walked off toward another area of the station.

Madeline came over and nodded. "We're ready to go."

As they collected their belongings, bags full of supplies, anything that might be useful for the road, Josh approached his father. "You did the right thing."

"Yeah? Then why don't I feel better for it?"

That morning as they pulled away, Stephen stood by the entrance watching them. There were no more tears. Just a simple wave goodbye. How many others around the country had to do the same thing to their loved ones? Had he accepted it or was he just glad to know that his family wouldn't have to witness his gruesome and painful death?

# CHAPTER TWENTY-NINE

*I*t seemed fitting that there would be no welcome sign as they entered Florida. All Ryan saw when they crossed the bridge was a "Florida State Line" sign. It was nestled in the trees at the edge of the highway almost out of sight, letting them know they were now in Escambia County. From the service station, it had taken no more than fifteen minutes to reach it.

He had figured it was clear sailing from here on out. Four hours tops and they would be in Franklin County.

Yeah, that was wishful thinking.

Ryan glanced at the fuel gauge. It was running low.

Less than a quarter of a tank.

The damn vehicle was even worse than his old clunker.

Add to that Josh using two of the gasoline canisters back at the lodge to create a distraction, and he knew they would be taking a big risk if they didn't stop and siphon at least one more vehicle. The last thing he wanted was to get stranded on some long stretch of highway. In Florida, there were areas where there was nothing but sawgrass marshes and wetlands for miles.

Again he caught the strong aroma of fuel but assumed Josh had spilled some of the gas when he was filling up the tank. He tapped the gauge, wondering if it was faulty.

"Josh. You did fill up as I asked?"

"This morning. Yeah. Why?"

He shook his head, confused. Ryan veered over to the edge of the road and got out. Going around the vehicle, he popped the hood, gave the engine a once-over then dropped down and looked. Although he couldn't see much, it didn't take long to guess what the problem could be.

"Damn it!" he said, getting up and kicking the pickup truck's bumper.

"Dare I ask?" Josh said, coming around.

"It might be a fuel leak coming from the line that comes off the fuel pump."

"So that's where the smell is coming from. How bad is it?" Josh asked.

"It's a moderate leak. Probably needs a new hose."

"So it's dangerous to drive."

"Well, you don't want that to catch fire but you do what you gotta do." He took a deep breath and patted the front of the engine. "I thought it was a gas guzzler. But it's newer than mine."

"Everything okay?" Ren asked from the rear.

He waved her off.

"So what's the plan?" Josh asked.

"To keep moving. Find another vehicle if possible. Get in."

Ryan took what little remaining gas they had left and

topped up the tank. It would give them three-quarters of a tank. Then he got back inside.

"But what if it catches on fire?"

"Then you use what God gave you." Ryan tapped his leg before shifting the gear stick into drive and continuing. They didn't make it far. They were just on the other side of Pensacola when the damn vehicle gave up the ghost.

Unfortunately, even Josh's hot-wiring skills wouldn't help. Lady luck wasn't shining on them. Without enough gas, they wouldn't get far.

So, on what should have been a quick pit stop in Freeport, the place where they obtained a new truck, they were back to searching for gas. As they'd left the service station late in the day, and spent hours searching for another vehicle and gas, it was early evening when they finally filled up.

"We have roughly another hundred and sixty miles. Maybe three hours if we don't stop or run into any other issues. Or we can bed down for the night and head out early in the morning."

"I'd prefer to sleep," Madeline said. "It's been a long day. I'm tired and hot." She ran a hand over Francine's head. The two of them still looked distraught. The child more than the mother.

"You know you can do that in the back of the truck while I drive," Ryan said.

"You might be able to but we can't."

"It is chilly in the back, and you get tossed around quite a bit," Ren said, supporting Madeline. "Maybe it would be good, you know..." She jerked her head toward Francine as if to suggest they do it for her.

Ryan looked at Josh. He shrugged. "What's a few hours, right? We still have a good day until the boats leave. We can get a few hours and then leave at first light."

Ryan looked off into the distance. They were so close. If it was just him, Josh, and Lily, he would have continued. He shrugged. "Okay. But we'll be leaving early."

They drove down near Freeport's harbor and parked at the end of a peninsula just off Beatrice Point Road. It was out of the way from the town and any heavily residential areas. There were a few homes dotted along the road on the way in, but they were spread a fair distance apart.

The road came to an end approximately thirty feet from the water's edge. He veered into a wooded area so they were out of view of anyone traversing the bayou. Across the water, they could see small fires where other travelers had opted to camp.

He walked down by the water's edge, listening to the gentle lapping of water against the rocks, trying to get a moment's peace. Lily and Josh followed him. Lily picked up a stone and skipped it across the water.

"I've never been on a boat," she said.

"Yes you have," Josh replied.

"I meant a big boat. One that has a lot of passengers."

"A cruise liner?"

"One of those. Yeah."

"I don't think that's what we're going on, are we?" he asked Ryan.

"Your guess is as good as mine."

There were boats out in the bayou. The water offered the best protection from the world that was steadily closing in on them. If it wasn't the infected hellbent on spreading suffering, they had lunatics like the religious group in Wiggins, or town lynch mobs to do it. At least out here, they could fish.

"Will we be on the boats long? What if I get seasick?" Lily asked.

"If you do, we'll throw you overboard," Josh said jokingly before giving her a nudge.

"I'll take you with me."

"Oh yeah?" Josh scooped her up and jogged over to the water's edge as if he was about to toss her in. She howled, a mixture of laughter and hollering for him not to do it. "Ryan!"

"Josh put your sister down," Ryan said.

Josh's laughter tapered off as he set her down. Lily punched him in the leg and then stomped off. "C'mon, Lily, I wasn't going to do it."

Ryan shook his head. "Don't go far, Lily."

"I won't."

She took a seat on some rocks nearby and continued to throw out stones.

It was odd witnessing the dynamics between the two of them. All those years he'd missed it. He was glad Lily had a brother, someone to take care of her. She was going to need him in the coming days. It gave him peace knowing that they wouldn't be alone.

Josh sidled up beside Ryan. "Look. I've been meaning to say this for a while. For what it's worth. I appreciate what you've done. You know, for Lily and myself."

"If I wasn't mistaken that sounded an awful lot like a compliment." A smile tugged at Ryan's face. "You ever going to call me dad?"

"That might be pushing it."

He snorted.

Josh looked back to the truck. "I can imagine what's going through that kid's head. Francine, I mean. One minute your father is there, the next gone." Ryan glanced at him as if wondering if there was some double meaning, a tip of the hat to the divorce. Josh must have picked up on what he'd said so he clarified. "I mean with mom and having to leave her after she got sick."

"Right." Ryan's thoughts went to his cancer. He would have to tell them soon. Eventually, he wouldn't be able to hide it. It just seemed like there was never a good time. The two of them had experienced so much loss already. The bond between their mother and them was strong. Would it even matter to them when he was gone?

"Hey, look, I'm going to see if I can't siphon some gas from a few vehicles in the area." He tossed Josh the keys to the truck. "I'll only be up the road. If you run into trouble. If anyone approaches. Get them out of here, you understand?"

"Got it."

"Can I go with you?" Lily asked.

"I don't know about that, butterfly."

"Take her. It'll give you some time to get to know her a little," Josh said.

"Sure. Okay. C'mon then."

Lily beamed as she hurried over. He collected a gasoline canister from the back of the truck and told the others they'd be back shortly.

"I'll give you a hand," Ren said.

"It's fine. I got Lily here."

"She can come," Lily said.

"All right but keep your distance."

The three of them walked up the road under the cover of darkness, Ren on one side, them on the other. At first, there wasn't much conversation. Ren eventually piped up. "You know I didn't lie to you back there. I just told you what he told me."

"I know."

"I just wanted that to be clear."

"Did anyone in that room touch you?"

"No."

"It was cramped."

"No one touched me."

"Maybe a cough then."

"People were wearing masks over their mouths."

"All of them?"

She shook her head. "Look, Ryan. I understand the caution. I do. If I thought for one second that I might be a carrier, I would have stayed in Wiggins. You wouldn't have even needed to have asked."

He nodded. "You know tomorrow…"

"Yes. You can check us again," she said.

"Just saying."

They approached the first house. It was empty. The garage was wide open. No vehicles inside. No gas canisters so they continued to the next farther down the road. Two more homes had nothing. The fourth was the trick. There was a 1960s gray Oldsmobile Cutlass outside. It had a flat tire. The lights in the two-story home were off. Cautiously, Ryan approached, scanning the windows. He dropped down beside the vehicle, opened the gas cap, stuck the tube in, and prepared to check. "Please have some gas."

"You know the truck has half a tank."

"Yeah, but we still have a few hours remaining tomorrow. We can't afford to have any more delays."

Fortunately, gas spurted out. He spat a wad of it and then watched as it began to fill the canister. All the while he kept his eyes on the house. A minute or two passed and a light came on inside. "Get behind the car," Ryan said. The two girls ducked down. His pulse sped up as the door opened and an old-timer stepped out with a shotgun in hand.

"I know you're out there. You come anywhere near this house, I'll…"

"Harold, close the door."

He squabbled with what must have been his wife for a moment or two before disappearing inside. Ren's eyes widened. She blew out her cheeks. A look of relief spreading. Once the canister was filled, Ryan screwed the top on and they hauled ass out of there, running at a crouch. As soon as they were clear of the house, Ren chuckled. "Seems some have decided to ride it out."

"Not everyone will leave. Most don't know where to go."

"Or who to trust," she added.

They'd only made it roughly halfway down the road when they were blinded by bright headlights. A vehicle tore toward them, engine roaring. Ryan raised his forearm to block the glare and stepped off to the edge of the road. As the vehicle got closer and his eyes adjusted, he recognized it as theirs. "Josh?" It swerved toward them, forcing them back into the ditch before correcting and accelerating.

"Josh!" he bellowed again, squinting, and then he saw her.

*Madeline.*

She caught his eye for a second.

Ryan dumped the gasoline canister on the ground and instinctively pulled his gun and fired off a few rounds, trying to hit the wheels, but it was too dark, and the truck was moving too fast. Hurrying back to where they were planning on camping for the night, he expected to find Josh unconscious or dead, but he wasn't there. Their bags had been dumped by the edge of the road, and on one of them was a note. Ryan snatched it up and shone his flashlight on it.

*I'm sorry but I won't let him die.*

"Sonofabitch!" He tossed the crumpled paper.

Madeline didn't need to say where she was heading, he knew.

"Where's Josh?" Lily said, looking frantically around, fear getting the better of her.

Not wasting a second, Ryan headed back to the home they'd siphoned gas from. The inherent danger Josh was in far outweighed theirs. He held on to Lily and told Ren to stay out of sight. The fewer people that showed up, the less freaked out they might be. He assumed that the garage had a vehicle inside. If it came down to it, he would hijack a car.

"Stay behind me, Lily."

Ryan knocked on the door. At first, there was no response. He knocked again and then a light came on. He heard shuffling down the hallway inside, then the man's voice. "You better get off my property."

"I don't want any trouble. We're not infected. Someone has taken my son. I need a set of wheels. Please. I will bring them back."

"I can't help you."

"Sir. My kid is sixteen. If I don't go now, he will die."

"That's not my problem. Get off my property."

It was to be expected. Tensions were running high. Trust was at an all-time low and with so many spreading the aging, what little humanity remained was weak. He knew if he pushed it any further, the guy was liable to shoot them through the door.

All he could think about was Josh.

Time was ticking.

If he didn't get on the road now, it might be too late.

He pulled out his wallet. There was less than sixty bucks in it. Money meant nothing now but it was worth a try. "Mister. Please. You don't even need to come out. Just let me use the vehicle. I'll bring it back. Look…"

Before the words left his mouth, Lily said it.

"We've got sixty bucks! Please. My mom is dead. My brother is the only person I have left." Lily looked at him. "Besides my dad."

On the other side of the door, there was whispering. A woman's voice. The man protested. There was some back and forth. Then a window opened. Their eyes shifted left as a set of keys were tossed out. "You can take the Cutlass. We don't have another vehicle. You'll need to fix the flat. There's a spare tire in the trunk. It has a full tank of gas."

"It did," Lily said quietly.

"Thank you," Ryan said, snatching up the keys and hurrying over to the vehicle. There under the glow of a flashlight, he hauled the jack and spare out of the back and began changing the tire. Twice, he hurt himself taking the wheel nuts off. He cursed loudly, most of his anger directed at Madeline. While he did that, Ren refilled the car with the gasoline they'd taken and Lily hopped in. Meanwhile, the two old-timers looked out of their window, observing them with curiosity. As soon as it was done, Ryan jumped in and tore out of there, exceeding every speed limit on the road.

# CHAPTER THIRTY

The wetlands blurred in his peripheral vision. Ryan drove like a maniac. His only saving grace was there were no cops on the road. Plus, the owner had stocked up on gas. When he was retrieving the spare he found two five-gallon canisters, which meant they wouldn't need to stop for the next two and a half hours.

That's how long it would take to get where they were going.

Madeline, on the other hand, hadn't been as fortunate.

They found the truck twenty miles outside of Freeport on I-10 just before Milton. Under the canopy of the night, he didn't see it. Ren did. "Go back. That's the truck," she said.

He slammed the brakes on and the back end fishtailed. He did a fast U-turn and came to a stop in front of it. Heart racing, Ryan hurried over. A spark of hope ignited, a moment that maybe she'd come to her senses and decided to dump the truck with Josh inside. The keys were still in the ignition.

Nope.

It was empty.

"Ryan. Over here."

Ren was at the back of the truck, her flashlight beam shining down on a body. "And here," she said, shining it on deep tire marks in the soil leading off onto the interstate. Ren went out into the middle of the road and noticed shards from a headlight on the ground along with brass. Multiple rounds had been fired. It was beginning to look like she'd hijacked someone. Possibly opened fire on a vehicle heading westbound.

They got back in the Cutlass, tires spinning out as he peeled off into the night.

No words were exchanged. What could be said? His mind turned to the worst possible outcome. It wasn't just being infected. It was Madeline turning the gun on Josh.

Every minute of the way he kept looking at the clock. Time couldn't move fast enough.

When he finally swerved into the parking lot outside Bucee's, the same vehicles were outside, along with a few others. Ryan brought the car to an abrupt stop, killed the engine, and took the keys with him. He dashed inside, handgun at the ready. "Josh! Josh! You go that way. I'll go over there," he said to Ren. He kept a firm grip on Lily's hand, guiding her through the aisles.

Their voices echoed as they called his name.

It was Ren who found him, on the east side in the same bathroom that Stephen had used.

"Ryan!"

He bolted toward her, looking at the expression on her face.

Was he dead?

As he flew past her, he only caught a little of what she said before entering the bathroom.

Josh was on the ground, back to the wall, legs tucked up against his chest. Bloody paper towels were surrounding him. His one hand was on the back of his head as if he was stemming the bleeding. His eyes were swollen red from crying. He wiped the tears away, his cheeks flushing red. "Don't come any closer!"

Lily tried to pull away to go to him but Ryan held her back.

"Josh, you're bleeding," she said.

"Get her out of here, Ryan."

"But Josh—"

"Get out!"

Ryan bent down. "Lily, will you wait outside?"

"Why can't I stay here?" Lily looked distraught. Ten years old, she wasn't stupid. She'd seen enough to know where this was heading. "No. I want to be here."

"I don't want you here. You hear me! Go! Get out!" Josh shouted. She burst into tears and left the room. Ren said she would keep an eye on her. Ryan made a gesture for her not to go near her. He still wasn't convinced that she was safe even though he hadn't seen any of the symptoms.

He turned to his son as the door slowly closed.

Josh wasn't trying to be nasty. He might have only known him a short time but he'd seen enough to know he adored his sister.

He'd said what he did because he didn't want her to get close.

"Where are they?" Ryan asked.

"Long gone. It doesn't matter. It's too late." He shook his head, staring at the tiled floor. "Just go. Take Lily and get her on that boat."

Ryan took a few steps toward him.

"Are you hard of hearing?! Go! Get out of here," Josh bellowed, struggling to hold in his emotions.

"Listen to me. I'm not going anywhere." Ryan crouched. "I'm here for you."

Josh managed to push a laugh through the pain. "Man, you've never been here for me."

"Josh."

"Don't."

He was still too young to understand the complexity of marriage, what had happened, the court system, the stress that had driven Ryan to drink, or any of the things that factored into the separation or the reason he couldn't see them. Maybe one day he would.

Josh stood up, sliding further away from him, into the corner of the room like a wounded animal. He eyed the exit as if he was considering making a run for it.

Ryan nodded. "You're right. I wasn't there for you. I haven't been there for you. But I can be here for you now." With that said, he reached for Josh.

Josh's eyes widened. "No!"

He tried to get around Ryan but he was too fast. He grabbed his son and held him, pulling him in close. Holding him tight, Josh coughed hard. "Do you know what you've just done?"

"Yeah. I made sure Lily has you around."

"You just signed your death sentence."

"I already had one."

"What?" he replied.

Ryan stepped back, still holding his arms. "Stage four, kid. I'm dying, Josh."

A look of astonishment spread on Josh's face. "What?"

"Cancer."

"When were you planning to tell us?"

"Sorry, kid. For everything."

"No. No, you don't get to do this."

"It's already done."

Even he couldn't argue with that. It wasn't like he could take it back. With that said, Ryan turned and walked out of the washroom, his thoughts a blur.

# CHAPTER THIRTY-ONE

July 10

*T*here would be no welcome wagon or cheering crowd to greet them. Elizabeth's parents wouldn't be at the window peeking out, waiting on their arrival and then swinging wide their front door and embracing them tightly as they had so many times in the past.

This final leg of the journey was a somber one.

They felt like the only people left on the planet but he knew that wasn't true. Millions were still out there, hunkered down in homes, hiding, traversing the back streets searching for food and supplies. All of them finding safety elsewhere or creating it where they lived.

Sharing the news with Ren didn't go over as he imagined.

He thought shock would be the response but it was far

from it. It was acceptance. She nodded then offered back a warm smile. She knew about his diagnosis, she'd seen what had happened with her uncle, and witnessed so much in a short time with her own family that it didn't have the same impact as it did for Lily.

Lily had been informed and told to keep her distance.

Her response was much different. Tears. A full meltdown. She'd had to use her inhaler just to catch a breath.

While videos put out by those who had passed on the aging to others had said their symptoms stopped, it would still take a few days to verify that. The decision to have him go with them was made by Ryan. There was no specific plan. He would keep his distance. He wanted to be there to make sure they got on that boat. After that, he would consider riding out the end stage of the pathogen or finding a quiet spot and putting a bullet in his head. He would ride the remaining journey in the back.

Ryan was slumped in the truck bed not far from Josh who was at the far end pressed in the corner near the tailgate. Ren drove and Lily rode shotgun inside the cab. The wind whipped at Ryan's clothes as he watched the landscape change and the night turned to morning.

A few times Lily knocked on the rear windshield and he would turn to see that smile of hers.

He would miss that.

He would miss them.

He would miss all of this.

Even though he'd only been with them for days, it felt like a lifetime and one he relished beyond all the years before that. In the face of death few things mattered. Work, differences, goals, it all fell by the wayside. They all felt like the CliffsNotes of a book only understood when read in their entirety. And for all his achievements in life, they paled in comparison to his kids. Those two were the best part of his life, and this time had made him see that in a way that he might have never seen had he watched them grow.

For that he was grateful. Grateful to Elizabeth. Grateful to God who had as he believed given him a chance to experience that before he passed on.

That morning as the sun rose above the horizon, and the truck rumbled over the four-mile bridge that spanned Apalachicola Bay from Eastpoint to St. George Island, Ryan's thoughts circled back to those early days of marriage and the years after Josh's birth.

The overwhelming joy he felt to have a son.

It wasn't about having someone to carry on his legacy but someone to dote on and share all the good things about life. And for the first six years, he did exactly that.

"Did your mother ever bring you here?"

"A few times, but it's been a long while," Josh replied as the wind whipped at his dark hair. Ryan stared at him, seeing Elizabeth in his face. She was there, a faint glimmer, a reminder that he would soon see her again.

"You probably don't remember our trips when you were tiny. It was one of the first places you learned to fish. You would collect shells on the beach and rush back to us to show them." He smiled, thinking about it like it was yesterday.

The water sparkled as they crossed over to one of the most picturesque unspoiled barrier islands in Florida. The 28 miles of sand and pristine marshes had drawn her parents, Ben and Gigi, away from Texas. It had been a vacation home they'd visit every year. When they eventually retired they opted to reside there permanently. There were no high-rises or big chain stores, it was a peaceful area where vacationers could rent a cottage or one of the many multi-story beach homes and bask in the tranquility.

"I always loved this place," Ryan said.

"You and mom came here?"

"Often." He squinted as he soaked in the landscape of palm trees, sand dunes, picnic pavilions, and tall grass. Ryan could almost hear Elizabeth's voice. Her laughter. He could almost feel her hand in his as they took walks along the beach. So many good memories and at the center of it all was Josh.

The memories faded at the sight of an unmanned military checkpoint. There were concrete barriers on the far side of the bridge. SLOW and STOP signs dotted on either side, along with bright yellow flyers flapping in the breeze that indicated infectious areas and who to contact.

The truck weaved around the barriers.

Ryan knocked on the window and hollered, "Hang a right up here."

They began heading west on Gulf Beach Drive. He could hear the swell of the ocean as the tide rolled in and out. In the distance, he could see the white St. George Island Lighthouse. He remembered the panoramic ocean views, and gifts they bought from the shop. Continuing, they drove past white and blue clapboard homes, a donut shop that had been a favorite of his, and a collection of gift stores. The road soon merged with Leisure Lane. The beach home was nestled at the end of Seaside Drive on a high, dry lot with a protective dune structure. It wasn't huge. Roughly 1,800 feet with two bedrooms and two baths.

"That one over there," Ryan said, guiding Ren into the gravel driveway. It was surrounded by palm trees and thick brush. Ryan hopped out, coughing a few times into his mask. The others kept their distance. Still nervous. Lily was the first to approach the house. She went up and knocked on the door. There was no answer. Ryan encouraged her to go around, and see if one of the doors was open. If her grandparents were in the back.

A minute or two later she re-emerged shrugging. "They're not there. But there's a pool."

Ren looked to him for an answer. He couldn't give one.

They'd got there on time. By the date, Elizabeth had given. They should have been there. "Perhaps they've stepped out." Ryan and Josh climbed the steps up to the open-air pool.

"Anything about this picture looks odd to you?" Josh asked

Ryan took out his binoculars and looked. There were boats out there but they were far away. Certainly none in close vicinity.

"Give me a minute," he said, making his way up to the rear doors. Above the door, etched into a piece of weathered driftwood, were the words "A Gift from the Ocean." The doors were closed but unlocked. He pushed inside and was greeted by the familiar smell of the home. It was warm and inviting inside with a vaulted living room that had tongue and groove wood, hardwood flooring, and ocean décor. There were two fans above him, and cream-colored furniture in the middle of the room, adorned with blue and white pillows.

Josh followed him. "What a view," he said.

It offered a stunning ocean backdrop from the kitchen which was bright and modern, with a center island that he remembered gathering around in the mornings for breakfast. "Ben? Gigi?"

No answer.

He entered the spacious master bedroom with an ensuite bathroom. It was empty. The beds were made. He checked the other bedroom that had a double bed. No one.

"Ryan."

He stepped out of the bedroom to find Josh holding up a note. "Seems they changed the date of collection to a day earlier. We just missed them." He set the note down and Ryan took a look. It was a message from Gigi telling them they were sorry but there was nothing they could do. It was out of their hands. There had been a wave of infected trying to reach the boats. They had to leave. It listed several Caribbean islands that were being used as safe havens, infected-free zones with the closest being Dry Tortugas National Park.

"They won't be back for another month." Josh slumped down in one of the chairs in the living room. "All that. All that we went through was for nothing."

Ryan stared. "It wasn't for nothing."

"Of course it was. Mom's dead. You're infected. And we're here alone. You should have just left me. Why did you have to go and take it?" Tears welled up in his eyes and for the first time since he'd met his son, he saw real emotion. "Huh? Why? I've just got you back in my life and now…"

"Son." Ryan took a seat across from him. "It's going to be okay."

"No, it's not. It never will be."

He allowed him to vent. He had every right to. Not only was he dealing with the outbreak, the loss of his mother, and news that his father would now die, he was grappling with the future, and the immense responsibility that no sixteen-year-old should bear.

"We'll check dock slips. There has to be a boat you can take. You, Lily, and Ren could probably find your grandparents out on the water or one of the islands."

"And we could probably die out there too."

"There is that. But right now you at least have one thing going for you."

"Yeah? And what's that?"

"Hope."

Josh gave him an incredulous look. "How can you think like that? Aren't you angry?"

He scoffed. "Josh. I've had plenty of time to be angry. Trust me. I've been there. But you can't be angry forever. I wouldn't be surprised if that's what gave me cancer. It eats you up from the inside. Blaming others for what's fair and what's not. No. Eventually, you have to accept what is and move beyond the past, forgive others but most importantly, forgive yourself."

Josh shook his head, looking despondently out the window at Lily and Ren standing by the pool. Lily was crouched beside it, dipping her hand into the blue shimmering water. Ren was holding on to the railing, looking out across the water.

"You have them to think about now."

"And you?"

"You know I can't go."

A tear trickled down Josh's cheek. Ryan so badly wanted to reach out and hug his son again, one last time, but they still didn't know much about how reinfection worked. There were mixed rumors online that someone who had it could be reinfected within two weeks, others said a month. He wasn't going to take the risk.

"Come on, let's go see if we can find a boat."

CHAPTER THIRTY-TWO

Three weeks later

*a*s fate would have it, in the days after arrival they did find several fishing boats stored in a charter repair warehouse along the northern side of the island. Unfortunately, most were unusable, missing parts, in a state of disrepair, or the engines wouldn't start. Whereas again Josh saw hurdles, life kicking sand in his face, his father's outlook was different.

He'd said it was Elizabeth's final gift to him.

Josh never understood it at the time but now he did.

"This one," Ryan said, standing back from the bow with a glint in his eye.

The twenty-foot white motorboat propped up on stands required extensive repairs to the hull. They would use the equipment and supplies in the storage area and what little knowledge his father had to work on the boat and get it seaworthy. It meant weeks of work. Days of sweat. Endless hours of frustration. For some, it might have seemed pointless to even try but his father was undeterred.

Until his final breaths, he was optimistic. Josh had never witnessed such resilience in the face of death. It was like his father saw something in those final days that he didn't.

Time.

The most valuable commodity.

It couldn't be bought.

It couldn't be sold.

Once lost, it couldn't be replenished.

But here it was before him, in the form of a boat.

And he put it to use, learning more about his kids.

Ryan gave directions from afar on what to do while Lily, Ren, and Josh worked together over the next week.

In the first week after arriving in Florida, he saw his father age approximately fourteen years.

After that, they watched the steady decline of his health like a flower withering in the sun. Instead of hiding away in a room as his mother had done, Ryan chose to be outside, soaking in the sunshine, feeling the breeze against his skin, and seeing them.

That's all he wanted, to see and talk to them.

Nothing else mattered. Josh could see that now. He learned more about his father in those final days than he imagined he ever could have had they lived together. There was an urgency to the conversation, trying to cram years into a matter of days.

He wanted to know everything. Even the smallest details of their lives.

At some point, his father became weaker as the pathogen ravaged his body.

"Dad," Josh said, waking him from his seat across the warehouse.

"What?" It took him a second to get his bearings. "For a moment there I thought I heard you call me dad."

Josh smiled. "That's because I did." He smiled again as he stepped out of the way so his father could see. "It's done."

The boat was patched up and ready for the water.

Ryan nodded, a tired smile tugging at his lips. He struggled to rise to his feet, and instinctively Josh wanted to help but he couldn't. Three weeks on and he hadn't seen any symptoms in himself. Confident that whatever had been in his body was gone, he couldn't risk being reinfected. His father had told him if he fell, not to help him up. Supporting himself using a walking cane, Ryan took a look at their handiwork. It wasn't professional but it would keep out the water and ensure they got to wherever it was they were heading.

"Well, what are you standing there for? Let's get in the water. Let's see if this beauty can float," his father said.

It wasn't an easy task but everything they needed was in the warehouse and a trailer could be found down at the dock. After a lot of fiddling around using boat jacks and a long trailer, they managed to get it loaded. Using the truck, they hauled it down to the boat ramp and backed it into the water.

There were a few tense moments when they thought it

might sink. That everything would go wrong, as it had throughout their journey.

But, that wasn't to be.

Lily fist-pumped the air. "We did it! We did it!"

"Yeah, you did, butterfly," Ryan replied, leaning against one of the wooden dock posts.

They spent one final night together, a supper that Josh wouldn't forget. His father was adamant that there were to be no tears, no sadness or pity for him. That wasn't the way he wanted to remember them. As hard as it was to keep it together, they did it for him. They drank, ate, laughed, and listened to some of their father's bad jokes as he tried to brighten the mood and keep their minds distracted. He was good at that. Making light of the worst situation.

As the night wore on, and final words were shared, Lily passed out from tiredness and Josh carried her into the bedroom to sleep.

When he came out, Ren gestured that his father was on the porch drinking iced tea.

The door creaked as he opened it and joined him. Ryan rocked back and forth, looking out into the darkness, watching the waves crash on the shore.

"It really is beautiful out here."

Josh nodded. "I remember."

"What?"

"You said I was probably too young to remember when you brought me here." He glanced at his father. "I remember."

"Fishing?"

"No. A playground. A merry-go-round. Spinning wildly. Faster and faster. Feeling scared as I saw some kids fly off it. I remember holding on for dear life. I remember you telling me to let go. That you would catch me."

"And then?"

"I let go and you caught me."

His father smiled at him.

"I love you, son," he said with weary eyes.

"I love you too, Dad."

Josh saw his father in a whole new light. The pain he'd once held no longer stung. Strangely, in many ways, it was a gift. Without it, he wasn't sure he would have felt as strongly as he did, and without it, he wouldn't have had something to heal.

"You think you could get me another glass, son?" his father asked.

"Sure."

"Thank you."

He went back inside. Ren was in the kitchen, looking over a map they'd found. She'd circled some of the islands the boats were going to and was plotting out a path. "I think they went here!" she said pointing to the closest island.

"Right." Josh was distracted, looking out at his father.

"You know, Josh, we can stay longer if you like. Until he passes."

He nodded. "I know but I'm not sure that's what he wants."

"Well, the option is there."

"Thank you."

Josh filled up a fresh glass with more iced tea and headed back out. His father's eyes were closed as he set it down on the table near him. Josh took a seat on the porch rocker, looked out, and then at his father. "Dad?"

There was no response.

Josh breathed in deeply, steadying his heart as tears welled in his eyes.

He'd never asked his father how he'd chosen to go. It wasn't his place, as it wasn't for his mother. It was their life. Instead, his father had told him when it was time he'd know and not to worry.

Josh couldn't help but wonder if his father had waited until he'd fulfilled what he had to do before he let go. And that life was like that merry-go-round of his youth — a collection of people spinning fast through time, rotating through a limited number of days filled with fear and hope — a short-lived event that made the world seem blurry and the outcome frightening. And as riders watched people fall off seemingly before their time, others held on for dear life, fighting for one more day, scared of what might happen, only to discover when they let go, someone was there all along, ready to catch them.

# EPILOGUE

A day later

*a*s the motorboat glided through the sparkling waters of the Gulf Coast, Josh looked back at the beach cottage. A pang of sorrow made his heart ache, and yet at the same time, there was gratitude. The boat bounced, sending a spray of water up into his face as Josh said a silent goodbye. He squinted through the morning light at the collection of rocks stacked around a cross embedded in the earth. Following his father's death, they'd covered him with multiple sheets and thick boat tarps and were able to tie the ends and drag him to a nearby grave.

It seemed fitting to give him a proper burial when so many hadn't received one.

Lily was spared the end.

She awoke to a mound with wildflowers on it.

Josh told her that Ryan had gone to be with mom to

keep her company. There was no way of knowing for sure but he liked to believe that she was there to greet him.

Standing there that morning, as a bright sun shone down, Lily held tightly to Josh and cried. He tried to not think about how she would remember the loss, only the time spent with him while alive.

It was at that moment he realized what his mother had told him. That it wasn't the number of days they were given with a person, but how a person chose to spend them.

∾

Hours later, they saw the first signs of the island, a dark blip on the horizon.

Dry Tortugas National Park was a small group of seven islands in the Gulf of Mexico about 67 miles west of Key West. All they could see was one island with a giant stone fort and lighthouse on it.

It was a sight to behold.

Octagon-shaped in appearance, Fort Jefferson was a massive unfinished coastal fortress that spread across sixteen acres on the 100-square mile island. The island was only accessible by seaplane or boat, making it a perfect haven for survivors.

A red and white blur burst into view, followed by the roar of an engine. They hadn't got within two miles of the national park when a Coastal Guard boat approached them at one hell of a clip. Onboard were armed National Guards. Ren powered down at the command of a booming voice over a megaphone.

They were told in no uncertain terms if they continued they would be shot.

Holding his hands high, Josh told them that they weren't infected.

A grizzled soldier held his gun low while two others kept theirs aimed at them.

"Where are you from?"

"Franklin County. Our grandparents are meant to be on the island."

Josh gave the names and one of them got on the radio.

A few tense minutes later, they were given instructions to follow them around to the Fort Jefferson Boat Pier. Josh's grandparents weren't there to greet them. The island inhabitants weren't taking any chances. After the boat was moored, they were hustled into a quarantine zone. They would spend the next seventy-two hours under observation before being released to their grandparents' care on the fourth day.

When they came out, Ren didn't join them.

It was discovered after a battery of tests that she was asymptomatic. She was the first of her kind. She'd told them she'd gotten the aging from her brother but her body wasn't showing any symptoms. The health experts on the island had felt that she could be the key to creating a vaccine.

It made sense now in hindsight. Her purposely choosing to keep her distance from everyone. Her incessant need to sanitize her hands. It wasn't OCD, it was the fear that someone might catch it.

They planned to keep her separated while they studied her.

Josh and Lily soon came to discover the aging had spread across the world, and efforts were being made to reach a solution so they could avoid genocide.

Somehow, it still felt unfair.

They'd made it. They were safe. But many weren't.

Here, on the island, people lived in isolation cut off from the world. Would that ever change? Only time could tell. And right now, thanks to his father, he had more of that to spare.

"Josh. Oh, sweetheart," Gigi said, hugging him tightly.

From behind him, footfalls fell fast and heavy.

"Lily!" Gigi scooped her up.

"Hey, kiddo." Ben approached Josh and placed a hand on his shoulder. "Your father?"

Josh drew in a long breath, trying to keep his emotions in check as he shook his head.

It was hard. He was exhausted not by the journey but by the weight of worry he'd carried.

After they reunited with their grandparents, he couldn't bring himself to speak of the details of those final hours. Those last minutes with his father felt private and he knew that he would keep them to himself for a long time. Being there for the passing of both parents had taught him a lot about life and death, and the mistakes made between. Both were flawed individuals and yet despite it all, they loved them and cared deeply enough to see them survive.

As for how they died.

Well, each of them let go in their own way.

And the way he saw things, no one was guaranteed anything in this life. There was no control over the outcome. Life was a precious gift. A beautifully tragic gift that could be embraced or wasted.

He planned to embrace it for as many days as he was given until it was his time to let go.

For that's what his parents had shown him. It wasn't the number of days allotted to a person but what a person chose to do with them while they were alive.

~

THANK YOU FOR READING

If you enjoyed that be sure to check out The Lookout, Rules of Survival, and All That Remains. Please take a second to leave a review, it's really appreciated. Thanks kindly, Jack.

# A PLEA

Thank you for reading The Aging. If you enjoyed the book, I would really appreciate it if you would consider leaving a review. Without reviews, an author's books are virtually invisible on the retail sites. It also lets me know what you liked. It also motivates me to write more books. You can leave a review by visiting the book's page. I would greatly appreciate it. It only takes a couple of seconds.

Thank you — **Jack Hunt**

## READERS TEAM

Thank you for buying The Aging, published by Direct Response Publishing.

Go to the link below to receive special offers, bonus content, and news about new Jack Hunt's books. Sign up for the newsletter. http://www.jackhuntbooks.com/signup

# ABOUT THE AUTHOR

Jack Hunt is the International Bestselling Author of over forty novels. Jack lives on the East coast of North America. If you haven't joined **_Jack Hunt's Private Facebook Group_** just do a search on facebook to find it. This gives readers a way to chat with Jack, see cover reveals, enter contests and receive giveaways, and stay updated on upcoming releases. There is also his main facebook page below if you want to browse. facebook.com/jackhuntauthor

www.jackhuntbooks.com
jhuntauthor@gmail.com

11218571R00194